SOME ENCHANTED EVENING

I had lousy taste in men. If I did have a therapist, she would have told me that I was purposely punishing myself and that chaperoning was a self-destructive means of barring romantic possibility from my life by fostering cynical detachment and intellectual superiority. I figured it was karma: Suitors turned to swine in my arms. My first crush had pelted me with mud balls during our second recess together. My most recent prince, Mr. McGuffin, hadn't even lasted until midnight before devolving into his toady self.

The bartender slid the glass into my hand. "Who's your friend?"

I twisted in the stool to see my private bloodhound hovering at the patio entrance.

"That's my secret admirer." He recoiled when I waved at him.

"Not so secret. So why's he trailing you?"

"Haven't you heard? The chief thinks I'm a killer."

The bartender's hand hesitated. "Chief Cosway?" The whites above her pupils widened. "That man is bad news. Don't get on the wrong side of him." She shook her head slowly, in sync with the rag and tumbler in her hand. "Your body will be bobbing in those breakers next."

CHRIS GAVALER

Pretend I'm Not Here

HarperTorch
An Imprint of HarperCollins*Publishers*

This is a work of fiction. Names, characters, places, and incidents are products of the author's imagination or are used fictitiously and are not to be construed as real. Any resemblance to actual events, locales, organizations, or persons, living or dead, is entirely coincidental.

HARPERTORCH
An Imprint of HarperCollins*Publishers*
10 East 53rd Street
New York, New York 10022-5299

ISBN: 0-06-000253-0

First HarperTorch paperback printing: July 2002

HarperCollins ®, HarperTorch™, and ™ are trademarks of HarperCollins Publishers Inc.

Printed in the United States of America

Visit HarperTorch on the World Wide Web at www.harpercollins.com

10 9 8 7 6 5 4 3 2 1

To Lesley

Pretend I'm Not Here

1

Do You Believe in Love at First Sight?

This week's bachelorette wobbled more than usual, as if thrown off balance by that crown of blonde curls. The host supported her arm in the classic father-of-the-bride pose, his grip noticeably tight. The drumroll thundered, the cameras zoomed, and the curtain snapped back like a magician's scarf. There he stood, the anonymous Bachelor #2 transformed into blood and suntanned flesh: *Randy!*

This was the one moment I still enjoyed, that instant of truth after all the jokes and posturing. Melissa smiled—she had been told to smile—but her gaze was unfocused. I doubted she could differentiate her beau-to-be from the smear of lights. But she faked it well, her eyes settling on him like a well-practiced blind girl's. The prompters stoked the audience into a touchdown roar, but I knew this couple was doomed.

I sat back in my love seat, the drone and surges of Manhattan traffic filtering through my 6th Avenue window, as I previewed an advance edit of *Who Wants To Be A Blind Date: Episode #71*. This was the best perk of my job, better than the monotony of identical weekends in the Caribbean. I preferred private evenings in my pajamas, body collapsed into the cushions after a long work-out, hair wet on my neck from the bathtub. I settled my wineglass—its unused mate collected dust in the cabinet above my sink—on a stack of contestant applications lying on my coffee table. The empty video box rested beside it with a sticky note from Donna, the other chaperone, curling from its front:

Ashley, enjoy your weekend off.

Yours,
D

She would be whisking this lucky couple off in the morning, her motherly presence a constant reminder that they were the escorted guests of a large and legally-minded corporation and not a pair of college delinquents cavorting on spring break. I poured a second glass of Viognier, curled my bare feet on the cushion beside me, and studied the tape, thankful to be alone.

Melissa broke her gaze first. The woman always did. It's part of the sexual contract, almost a legal obligation for the show. While she looked off, Randy slid his eyes down her front. The camera usually missed that, but it didn't matter. She had already given everything away. If he had known to watch the tilt of her smile, the direction her eyes swerved, how her fingers curled, he would have seen what he was walking into.

Men are easier to read. Even with the mute on, I

could tell whether a Bachelor left the toilet seat up, what sexual positions he thought he liked, and how often he called his mother. Randy strutted across the soundstage, stiff and cocky. He brandished the standard smirk, unable to disguise his pleasure at the sight of his prize. Melissa wore her body with the casual confidence of a small child or professional model. The third button of her blouse bobbed unfastened.

I sighed as the host drew them into an obligatory hug. Melissa was one of my casting picks, so I felt a maternal pang of guilt. Sort of like God looking down at the mayhem he'd wrought on Eden. I had finagled a choice guy into the Bachelor #3 seat, but of course she'd sided with Randy, the face my college intern had swooned over when she'd fished him from the sea of headshots in the bin on my desk.

My professional and personal esthetics rarely crossed. I had a soft spot for misfits: crooked teeth, crescent noses, connected eyebrows, any break from the monotony of billboard beauty. After my first week reading applications and forwarding quirky candidates to the producer's desk, my altruism was rewarded with unveiled threats: it was either them or me. I rose to the task, wielding my letter opener through the necks of the undesirable. The secretary taped over the "Ashley Farrell" on my mail slot with "Attila the Nun," a nickname I secretly cherished.

I maintained the lowest running average for predicting winning bachelors in the office, so I felt no shock at Melissa's treason. I guessed fewer than one winner in six, impressively below random odds. Donna always waited to see my pick before dropping her dollar into the betting cup in the conference room.

I had chosen Melissa not because I liked her face—

those pouty lips made me wince—but because of the modicum of wit displayed on her application. She was beautiful enough, the one *Who Wants To Be A Blind Date* criterion chiseled in stone. The homely I shuffled into a tray on the secretary's desk to receive our standard "Thank you for applying" letter, the producer's splotchy signature photocopied on the bottom of the page. But after that first cut, the application questionnaire ordained their fates.

Most of our candidates were as verbal as toddlers, their handwriting little better. I skimmed the same answers lunch hour after lunch hour:

"Why do you want to appear on *Who Wants To Be A Blind Date?*"

"So I can meet the man of my dreams."

The question, "What special qualifications do you possess?" usually produced a laundry list of bra and waist sizes, so Melissa's non sequitur had leaped from the page:

"Because I'm Zelda Shilling's #1 fan!"

I had assumed she was being funny or—as my college roommates once called me—spunky. Anyone who skimmed the front page of *USA Today* in the past month knew Zelda Shilling was the Mafia's answer to Jackie O. Though well-preserved for a middle-aged woman—if you didn't mind the taut cheeks and jawline that multiple face-lifts produced—she was not the look *Who Wants To Be A Blind Date* coveted. Worse, her years of scaling the underworld ladder of vice and avarice had filed her tongue to profane sharpness. Any sound bite on the evening news usually included two prominent bleeps.

I'd reread Melissa's answer, wondering if it could be a veiled threat. The thought was titillating. If we didn't choose her for the show, was she going to phone up Zelda and have the building firebombed? The notion half appealed to me. Certainly Mrs. Shilling had been accused of worse. Some people said she surpassed her ex-husband, the unauditable Richard Shilling. She had even threatened to gun him down during a press conference after their divorce hearing. Their separation had monopolized tabloids all year. No stand-up comic could leave a talk show without a reference to the First Lady of the Mob. Mr. Shilling seemed lawful in comparison, his guise as the legitimate businessman almost quaint.

So in a moment of optimism, I'd green-flagged Melissa's folder and sent my intern trotting upstairs with it under her arm, unwisely overlooking the fact that Melissa had drawn a smiley face in the circle dotting her "i."

I was punished a week later when the first draft of Melissa's bachelorette questions materialized on my desk. Errors aside—she thought "a lot" as one word—the list was a jumble of clichés and clumsy innuendoes half-plagiarized from previous episodes.

According to our press brochure, our contestants invented their own questions. This was a more blatant lie than most of our braggart bachelors could muster. My duties included rewriting the weekly drivel. With men, it meant substituting overt sexual references with fractionally less overt sexual metaphors. These elicited the rising giggle from audiences that the producer liked so much. *Who Wants To Be A Blind Date* skimmed the surface of smut, splashing its feet but never plunging in. Bachelorettes posed the greater challenge—line after sentimental line of romantic profundities gleaned from Young Adult novellas.

That's why I never met face-to-face with contestants. I was never very good with unmediated intervention. I dispensed the personal work to angels, those rotating interns hellbent on clawing past me on the network ladder. Assistant to the Producer—one of my shifting job titles—was usually a stepping-stone to higher fates, a stop on the way to the penthouse. But I had no desire to meet the Chairman of the Board, and I tried to ignore ongoing sagas of corporate takeovers and sell-offs. *Who Wants To Be A Blind Date* traded like a dubious rookie card. Rumors had it, Richard Shilling was our latest buyer. The Devil could be lounging on the top floor as far as I cared. I preferred working behind the scenes, shuffling fate in the privacy of my own living room, pairing headshots as I savored long sips of a dry white wine.

I never looked at the big questions.

2

Do You Like Surprises?

The phone woke me an hour early. I was dozing, half-expecting the interruption. My mother would call it premonition. I pressed the receiver to my ear in the dark, knowing I would be hopping a plane from LaGuardia instead of shouldering my way through my subway commute.

"Hello?" I exaggerated the groan.

"They need Donna at a board meeting Saturday. You're going to St. Thomas." I pictured the secretary's snide grin. He thrived on other's last-minute inconveniences.

I pawed my way to the edge of the mattress, grunting as he dictated the departure numbers. "This is the last time . . ." I struggled to think of his name but couldn't. The producer had fired three secretaries this year, all their names starting with the letter *P*.

"Whatever." His voice was a sarcastic singsong. I

would have muttered my resignation in his ear, but I knew he coveted my job.

"Call when you're checked in." He was trying to imitate the producer's gruff monotone, but his voice arced too high. The phone died before I could muster a retort.

After a short shower and a shorter breakfast—the last stale bagel from the half dozen I'd picked up Monday from the corner bakery—I was ready for Paradise. Packing was an art I had long mastered, just the necessities rolled methodically to prevent wrinkling, my fist-sized makeup pouch tucked in the center. I tossed the carry-on by the door and dropped my coffee mug in the sink with yesterday's dishes. The limo would appear at the curb in ten minutes. I watched out the window with the cell phone in my hand, dialing Ridgewood, New Jersey, my last chore.

I was relieved when I got the machine. "Hi, Mom and Dad, it's Ashley. Sorry, but I have to cancel dinner tomorrow. Something's come—"

The phone clattered in my ear. "Hello, dear, I was just out early in the garden. What did you say about Saturday?" I could hear the excitement in her voice. She thought I had a hot date. She didn't understand how her only daughter could make it past thirty without having a long-term relationship.

"I'm leaving for the Islands in a few minutes. The other chaperone had to cancel."

She sighed her disappointment. "Okay." She'd been lobbying me to quit for months, insisting that chaperoning was no job for a young single woman, that it fostered an unhealthy attitude toward romance. I think she was worried about my egg count, her dwindling brood of potential grandchildren.

"So let's make it next Saturday then?"

"You know they're not paying you enough. It's just too risky."

"Risky? Mom, I'm more likely to get in a wreck on a highway than for my plane—"

She gasped. "No, no—I mean that, too—but the . . . the—" Her voice dropped. *"The mobsters."* I thought she was searching her kitchen for hidden microphones.

"Mom, I really have to go."

"Didn't you read that article in *Playboy*? They've taken over the Caribbean. It's a shooting gallery down there."

"Playboy?" I hadn't known my father still subscribed. I shuddered with visions of my parents in foreplay. "My ride's here. I'll call when I get back." I dropped the phone in my purse and stared out the window at a delivery truck blaring its horn at a pair of jaywalking joggers.

Thirty minutes later, the network's limo was idling at Melissa's sidewalk as I punched the doorbell to her Hoboken apartment. Commuters streamed over the sidewalks, burdened by leather briefcases and briefcase-sized handbags as they staggered toward the railway, balancing convenience store coffee cups to their lips. I prided myself on efficiency, my tidy life arranged inside the brown floral purse tucked under my ribs. I needed only the essentials.

Melissa appeared in the doorway, giddy and blinking, her face slightly overpainted. She had spent the early morning trying to re-create her *Who Wants To Be A Blind Date* makeover. I shook her French manicured hand and said something flattering as she evaluated me.

I never fussed over my hair on these mornings, its brown darkened a shade by residual dampness. My tan troubled her, but she thought the olive blouse ruined the effect. The yellow skirt ensemble she had worn on *Episode #71* had morphed into yellow pants and midriff, a blouse thrown "casually" on top. She was trying to balance competing climates. I didn't know if she'd changed the navel ring or not.

I threw my arms apart and boomed in my best cheerleading voice, "You ready for the weekend of your life?"

She laughed and met my eyes with a smile. Though ostensibly friendly, in the language of sexual carnivores the behavior translated: *I do not fear you.* The laugh was a gasp of relief, even thanks. We chattered like old pals as we crossed her miniature lawn.

I phoned the secretary from the limo and learned, in code, that Randy had been procured and delivered ahead of schedule, so there would be no awkward waiting at the ticket counter, no fear of a jilted bachelorette. *Who Wants To Be A Blind Date* had started taxiing winners after a rash of airport no-shows. Not all winners had the mettle for a weekend in Eden. St. Thomas was an atypical choice for dating shows, except that the network owned the resort. Plus it allowed the host to leer at the camera and say "*Virgin* Islands" once a week.

Randy's driver waved from the rendezvous point, patted him on the back and vanished. I hadn't seen Randy since he'd swaggered off the set pawing Melissa's arm. I preferred him on video, or better, as a mute headshot. He was less deft with a bottle of mousse than our makeup people, but the arrogant expression never varied. I remembered the way he'd stomped across the swath of red carpet toward Melissa, his arms slightly forward, ready to snatch her out of the host's grip. They were crossed now, his foot planted firmly on his canvas suitcase.

We had met when my intern had called in sick the afternoon of the shoot. I'd edited his intended responses to Melissa's questions, drenching the paper in red ink. He'd had a knack for graphic metaphor, phallic imagery pulsing. He hadn't looked at me when I'd handed him the sheet, the on-air taboos marked out, my alternative phrases scribbled in the margins. If I'd left him to his fate, Melissa would never have chosen him.

"Randy," I called, knowing he would never remember me. "Hi. I'm Ashley Farrell." I knew better than to offer my hand, his eyes passing through me. "And of course you already know Melissa."

The winners beamed at each other, Melissa giggling at nothing and brushing an electrically curled lock over her shoulder. Randy said something loud, his cologne radiating like sonar.

They had not glimpsed each other since they'd parted in the stage wings a week ago and so were surprised to find each other undiminished. They expected a catch in the deal, a hidden clause in the contract, a last-minute substitution imposed by the show. It was the wariness of label-smart consumers, the need to exercise suspicion in order to feel savvy. But there was no trick. We only chose beautiful people.

Later on the island, after saying goodnight to her date on the patio, the bachelorette always turned to me with girlish camaraderie and confessed: *He really is handsome.*

When Randy condescended to look at me, it was with a dismissive, subtly hostile smile. I was not so much a woman as a rival, inferior but provoking. He offered a variation on the required joke: "I thought you'd be dressed like a nun."

Melissa laughed uproariously as her hands smoothed wrinkles over her hips.

I laughed, too. It was part of the job. I was supposed to be the homely older sister. The network didn't hire chaperones to compete with winning bachelorettes. This was not to say that I was unsightly, but I would have gone unnoticed among the horde of suntanned, chisel-cheeked applicants whose photographs inundated my slot in the *Who Wants To Be A Blind Date* mailroom. My eyes, like my hair, were brown—not honey, amber, or chestnut. Despite my daily health club regime, I fluctuated ten pounds above the unacknowledged starvation weight mandated by our producer. No professional photographer, no matter how skilled, could convincingly augment my bra size.

Weekdays, while shuffling between meetings with one of my interns in tow, my hair was curled in a chic bob and my face was—as my fashion-conscious colleagues would say—natural. Which meant I spent a scant two to three minutes applying makeup, squinting blurry-eyed at my cramped bathroom mirror every morning. At the moment I was wearing none. There was no blow-dryer in my bag. If Melissa was anything like her dozen predecessors, she would be scandalized by this discovery tomorrow morning. If her weekend went well, she would probably offer me helpful hints about my appearance, what shade of lipstick I needed, what color I should dye my hair.

Fate usually spared me the beauty tips. After their

forty-eight hours, Randy and Melissa, like most of the seventy star-crossed couples before them, would probably never meet again. Their blue-eyed überchildren would not populate the earth. *Who Wants To Be A Blind Date* never publicized the statistics, but everyone in the office knew that no lasting relationship had ever sprung from our matchmaking. Though if Melissa and Randy had met in a singles bar—a bleak but more promising site for romance—I would still have bet against them.

But they weren't the worst pairing. Some winners went white in front of the cameras, eyes wandering dizzily above their twitching smiles. Or worse, they fawned and hugged, overcompensating for their horror. Real romance was never a possibility. The producer seemed unaware of the concept. Cupid had no seat on the board of directors. The hearts and arrows adorning the TV logo were a marketing invention. The host had the unctuous charm of a pedophile, that lecherous uncle disturbingly popular with our demographic. We traded in spectacle and titillation. Melissa and Randy had not mailed their 8 × 10s in acts of desperation. They were not lonely; they were bored.

Randy grabbed Melissa's carry-on with the suavity of a purse thief. His triceps bulged under his cropped sleeves, but she was too thick in the haze of her own self-presentation to notice. When he eyed my bag, I pulled it under my breasts and led my supplicants to the pearly gates.

A jaded viewer might have said I was liability insurance against date rape, but even God learned not to let strangers frolic unsupervised in the Garden. I preferred to look at my role in psychological terms. Contestants shared one quality. They secreted it like musk.

Their bodies shouted: *Look at me.* The real thrill was the camera eye. Without me, they would have been anonymous. I was the audience, their only prophylactic against intimacy.

We passed a mother, an out-of-towner, with an improbably large infant strapped to her back and a three-year-old literally clawing at her hip. A heap of suitcases towered against her other leg as the frazzled woman dug at her purse in front of the last airport luggage cart locked inside the pay dispenser. She looked near tears.

I considered prodding Randy—what better moment to impress Melissa with his manly sensitivity?—but they had trailed ahead of me, leaving clouds of pheromones in their wake. I pulled my wallet out and started fingering change when I noticed someone else stopping to help her. The man dropped his bag and newspaper and wrestled quarters from the jacket under his arm while the mother stared up at him, a stream of thanks spilling out of her. I wanted to catch a glimpse of the knight errant's face—all I could see were a tousle of curls and the wrinkles on the back of his white linen shirt—but my wards were waiting anxiously in front of the metal detectors, a pair of camouflaged guardsmen ready to yank them from the line.

After reasserting his virility by stowing all of our bags in the overhead, Randy offered Melissa the window seat. The gesture seemed insincerely chivalrous, even comical, but it was matched by Melissa's overflattered gratitude.

I squeezed past him as he grimaced and forfeited the first battle. He sat with his legs spread, one foot in the aisle, oblivious of flight attendants and my crossed knees. I functioned as a kind of social operator, maintaining the lines of small talk between them. They had material enough for a one-night stand: an evening and a short breakfast. They knew they needed me to milk it. On the flights back—assuming the weekend didn't end in overt tragedy—I suggested that my couples sit together, though they almost never did.

I hadn't given up. I thought of *Who Wants To Be A Blind Date* as a testament of infinite hope. Love flourished despite arranged marriages, how-to sexual manuals, AIDS, and Dear Abby. Surely it could overcome me.

I gazed through the window at the baggage carts retreating from the plane. Soon the overhead lights would darken, and the stewardesses would vanish to their belted cubbies like stagehands. A world of possibility awaited. When the plane began to moan and vibrate, its impossible weight sweeping from its wheels, Randy and Melissa stole glances at each other, searching for omens of ecstasy.

If You Were the Pilot of My Plane, How Would You Cure My Fear of Flying?

When the seat belt lights stopped glowing, I pulled a paperback from my purse and tucked it in the mesh magazine holder under my food tray. My wards studied my movements peripherally, their relief almost audible. They'd feared this was going to be a flight-long conversation. They were used to smoky shadows, the clatter of music and beer bottles, their throats raw from sporadic shouting.

They knew enough to accept headphones when a flight attendant paused at our aisle. I chose the moment to make an escape. It was best to do this early and unannounced, like a pop quiz; couples got lazy and dependent otherwise.

Randy fumbled, uncertain whether to pull his knees out of my way or to stand. He opted for the latter, allowing himself an extra moment to muster his resources. As much as he thought he resented my presence, I was the closest he had to a life preserver. There was nothing but ocean and sky outside those windows.

I winked at Melissa before squeezing around the cart. She was balancing her head on her neck as if performing a juggling trick, the look of the attentive female: eyes wide, shoulders turned, a knee jutting into my empty seat. I mumbled a prayer for Randy and headed for the toilets.

My friends claimed to envy my job. Mondays off, every other weekend in the Caribbean during the TV season. Donna, the other chaperone, insisted I had the best tan in the building—for a white girl. She grew up somewhere on the Islands, and her skin maintained that same deep brown year-round. The people in makeup claimed they could distinguish mine from the tanning-booth complexions that start up in December. I didn't believe them.

Others asked me how I did it. They posed the question as a compliment, confessing how they never could. They thought they were commending a virtue, but they would speak of high school teachers and garbage collectors in the same tone.

My parents had teased me when I started working at the network. They'd thought designing the *Who Wants To Be A Blind Date* webpage, the reason I was originally hired, would transform me into a man-intoxicating vixen. They had had the same hopes for high school and college, my father worrying that all that softball he'd played with me as a kid had somehow fouled my feminine instincts. Once I'd passed thirty, the cutoff age for contestants, my mother stopped giving me the new Judith Krantz novel for Christmas.

I dated plenty. A transfer from marketing had asked

me out twice the month before. Once had been enough, but I'd accepted the second as armor against the world's disappointment. I rarely got past three, always attuned to other prospects. Once I asked out a man from my Laundromat after watching his CK briefs spin dry for twenty minutes.

But it did seem futile sometimes. Smile and chatter all I liked, there was still another me glowering over my shoulder, scrutinizing my potential mate with the charity of a customs inspector. The Laundromat guy blinked every time I used a big word. I was playing him like a video game before the salads were cleared. Which was not to say I didn't enjoy my first time on a water bed.

All of this was on my mind as I rounded the corner.

Freud, the inventor of twentieth-century sexuality, claimed that accidents are intentional. When I stubbed my toe on my coffee table, I was punishing myself for not splurging on a pair of Cole Haan heels I had coveted while window shopping on my lunch break. When I pressed the wrong number on my speed dial, it was because I would rather speak to an emergency operator than my mother.

And, by this logic, when I walked blindly into a perfect stranger, it was because I wanted to flatten my left breast and any shards of dignity that might have survived the impact.

I knew my cruising speed was fast, but I had never considered it perilous. I reeled backward, twirling my arms like a panicked trapeze artist. The image of myself sprawled across the aisle, knees up, panties exposed, balanced me. I grasped a storage shelf as though bracing for impact and raised my eyes, blurting an apology to my victim. I couldn't see him at first, just his arm reaching to help me.

"Are you all right?" There was both humor and concern in his voice, but I flinched from his touch.

"Yes, yes, fine."

The plane trembled as I looked up, my knees quivering with the turbulence. I tightened my grip on the shelf, hoping I hadn't seized the door lever by mistake. Our eyes met—his so light they were the color of sand. I blinked, startled by his face, its asymmetry enticing rather than disturbing, framed by an expensive hair cut lost in uncombed curls. His hand remained extended as though hoping to touch me.

A bachelorette crooned in my head: *He really is handsome.*

If I'd seen him as a headshot from my mail slot first, I might have shuffled him to the "Dear applicant" bin rather than chancing the producer's wrath. According to the show, women could only be attracted to a half dozen cookie-cutter archetypes. My professional obligations had so obscured my own tastes, I'd forgotten there was more out there.

"Are you sure you're okay?" He grinned as he cupped his chin in his hand—which explained the ache in my forehead where it had hit me. I felt my face warming.

"Positive." I forgot my urge to urinate and turned in retreat, but my body lurched, lopsided, my foot naked on the carpet. I looked down, but he was already bending to retrieve my missing shoe.

"I believe this is yours?" His smile widened, but I wasn't sure if he was charmed or only amused by clumsiness.

I willed my hair to curl, my lashes to lengthen, wanting to shout, *Really, I'm much cuter than this.* I accepted the brown mesh flat, conscious of how little it resembled a glass slipper. "Thank you."

He held my eyes a moment, his gaze flirtatious without seeming aggressive.

I was usually good at these moments, but I gawked, tongue-tied. I couldn't tell if the plane was teetering or not.

"Do I know you?"

I was too startled—and flattered—by the corniness of the line to register the sincerity of his creased brow. Then it clicked.

"At the airport," I blurted, "you helped that mother with her luggage."

"Oh," he said, "right." He seemed genuinely embarrassed, preferring his acts of kindness to go unrecorded. "I saw you getting out of that giant limo in front."

I nodded, the same self-conscious wave passing through me. It never occurred to me that someone might notice me in the shadow of a bachelorette.

"So," I said, glancing toward the safety hatch window. The walls fluttered like the cardboard backdrop of the *Who Wants To Be A Blind Date* set. We could have been in free fall. "Where in the Caribbean are you headed?"

The brightness in his stare flickered. "It's business," he mumbled. Some sudden compunction bent his smile away with his gaze. His legs juggled his weight back and forth a moment before pulling him unwillingly back.

"Were you waiting to—?" He pointed at the rest room door.

I registered the Unoccupied sign and shook my head no.

"Then you'll please pardon me?"

It required inhuman discipline not to stare as he slipped inside. When I noticed the shoe in my hand, I put it on.

Randy didn't stand the second time, so I had to squeeze past, his knees grazing my buttocks. My body plopped gracelessly into the seat, my head swimming.

"Do you believe this lady? I mean it's one thing to divorce a guy, but to sink his company, that's just nuts." Randy spoke around me, pointing at the soundless TV image projected onto the front of the cabin. "What right does she have to mess with his business?"

Melissa pulled the other half of her headphones off. "But isn't it her company, too? They're only separated."

She was ignoring me, and I was startled to realize that conversation had flourished in my absence. My returns were usually welcomed as timely reprieves, the silence broken by a barrage of questions I had already covered in the airport. Had I been paying attention, I would have hovered out of sight instead of planting myself between them like a tennis net, my bladder reminding me why I had gotten up in the first place.

"No, no, he's buying her out, top dollar. It was part of the settlement." Randy huffed contemptuously. "And so then what does she do? She goes to his competitor and blabs everything she knows. Every company secret out the window." He nearly struck a passing stewardess as he gestured.

"They don't know she did that."

Melissa, to my surprise, had sloughed the wilting

flower routine. Bachelorettes—if not women in general—agreed to almost any opinion on a first date, but her mouth was firm. The wrinkle at the corner suggested even a hint of contempt. I usually only saw that on return flights. How long had I been gone?

"You mean they can't prove it. Everybody knows she did it. Why do you think the stock nosedived?"

Randy swatted his hand toward the front of the cabin, and I finally registered the face on the projected TV screen. Zelda Shilling's crimson lips sneered in front of a phalanx of microphones. I couldn't tell what she was saying, but it looked grim, probably a new assault against her ex-husband. No press conference ended without her vow of revenge, her lawyers scrambling to cover her libel. According to her rants, the man regulated every criminal in the country, from pickpockets to cyber terrorists. But when it came to yielding evidence, the woman just muttered and sneered.

"If that were true, he could sue her." Melissa held her fingers up as though teaching a child to count. "The settlement stipulated that she would not directly or indirectly aid a new or existing firm for five years. She's not allowed to talk."

Randy looked stupefied. His lips were parted, but no sound came out. A fundamental law had been violated: Under no circumstances was a woman possessing superior knowledge or intelligence to reveal that superiority to her date. When one of my Melissas realized that her Randy was an idiot—a frequent discovery—she confessed the fact to my sympathetic female ear and persevered good-naturedly for the remainder of the weekend.

Randy's volume spiked. "Well, that's just stupid."

Passengers in the adjacent row looked over. I was never sure whether men employed this strategy consciously. The insult was irrelevant—for some reason a man was allowed that—but the loud voice, the imposition on strangers, that would cow almost any woman, preserver of the social fabric.

Melissa said nothing.

Randy, tentatively satisfied, continued in a softer tone. "No piece of paper can stop somebody from doing what they want. Like I said, there's no proof. Plus Richard Shilling is like some kind of big mob boss or something. She probably knows enough to put him away for life."

One glib, placating remark from me would have defused the moment. I should have been pulling the situation back under my control, but I turned to Melissa instead, tensed for the next volley. My breast, fresh from my collision, throbbed faintly.

"So he just lets her go do anything she wants? Destroy all of his businesses one by one? That makes a lot of sense." Her cheeks flushed as her head shuffled left and right, but I sensed excitement rather than anger.

"Well, he can't just have her whacked, can he? That would be like signing his own confession." Randy had the same look. My parents used to argue across the dinner table the same way. Then their bedroom door would click shut while I did the dishes.

I heard my voice before I realized I was speaking: "Maybe he still loves her."

They appeared startled, noticing for the first time that I had sat down. Melissa pressed the front of her blouse and sat back vaguely embarrassed, caught in a compromising act. Randy smirked as she glanced at him and then away again.

I had ruined the moment, their rhythm lost, but the damage wasn't terminal. Melissa's eyes avoided mine as she contemplated something intangible under those fluttering lashes.

I drew my paperback from the magazine holder and noticed my foot thrusting in and out of my shoe. I pressed it down and imagined the feel of smooth glass on my sole.

4

Is There a Soul Mate Meant for You, or Do You Make Your Own Destiny?

I knew who my handsome stranger reminded me of. We used to pass on the commons every Tuesday after my psych lecture. He'd strolled a little too self-importantly, interrupting his thoughtful gait to say hi and beam at me, but I knew he'd planned our paths to cross. Another guy with the same glint in his smile had lived down the hall in my last apartment building before my raise. He'd been a little shorter than my newest prince but had hesitated the same way whenever we'd passed on the stairs. It could have been just a matter of the right accident: a letter in the wrong mailbox, a minor fender-bender as we backed out of our parking spots. But the stars denied us. I sobbed like Juliet when I saw his U-Haul outside my bathroom window.

According to my mother, love struck only the tender-minded, like her. If I would only shed my cynical exoskeleton, I too would know the piercing joy of

Cupid's arrow. As far as I could tell, the gods designated me for target practice, my heart leaping with every blank round. I lay awake nights, sirens circling my apartment as I fantasized about strangers who smiled at me in elevators or noticed me from passing cars. She thought *Who Wants To Be A Blind Date* ruined me, but it only polished my shell. My underbelly was as tender as a jellyfish.

I stood up before the seat belt signs stopped glowing, my eyes working up and down the rows. I should have watched the toilets long enough to see which direction my perfect stranger had gone to sit. His poise suggested first class, but the rumpled collar threw me. If he was seated near the rampway, I knew I'd never glimpse him again. I rushed my wards into the aisle, and they followed obediently, mimicking my rudeness.

A dozen white shirts churned in front of me, but none possessed the right shoulder span, the locks of sun-lightened hair tickling the base of the neck. I watched them evaporate into the waves of heat rising from the San Juan runway as we descended the steps, and I knew it was hopeless. Our layover in Puerto Rico was less than an hour, hardly enough time to hunt down and woo an unsuspecting suitor.

Melissa squinted at me, her face a caricature of discomfort. It was less the glare than the Chardonnay she had had with the freezer-burnt ravioli—a bad move, but I couldn't lecture them about everything. Randy looked better for having dozed during the movie. He didn't know that the fairy tale princess turns out to be a green ogre, too.

Melissa appeared horrified by the sight of the thirty-seat Eagle about to shuttle us between islands, while Randy feigned interest in the engines dangling from the stunted wings. He had listed "flying" under hobbies on his application, though I suspected he was alluding to one of *Who Wants To Be A Blind Date*'s favorite sexual metaphors. I preferred a 747 because it was the size of a bowling alley and operated by magic, but at least I knew what to expect.

Melissa flinched when she spied the back of the pilot's head as she took her seat in the Eagle, the propeller blades scant feet from her window. Thirty seats meant fourteen couples, me and one other lone gunman. I eyed each pair of boarding passengers like Noah taking a head count. I tried not to expect the implausible, my lavatory Romeo jogging up the stepladder at the last moment. I hadn't registered it at the time, but even his scent had stayed with me, a cologne I assumed, though I had never smelled it before. It lingered elusively.

A woman eventually entered, an ex-blonde, mid-forties, the soccer mom type. She appeared almost as out of place as I did. She trudged toward me, nodded, and sat next to Randy, who was sulking because I had stolen the aisle seat beside Melissa. He was missing an opportunity to display his consoling side, Melissa wide-eyed as a cartoon mouse as we clambered into the air. She perched white-knuckled as I contemplated the crests of waves beyond her shoulder, thankful that conversation was impossible through the engine blare.

I replayed the conversation outside the toilets a dozen times, perfecting my lines as though carving up a bachelorette's questions with my red editing pen. Granted, it wasn't the most romantic setting, but it beat the *Who Wants To Be A Blind Date* set, that fake living room of retro '70s furniture. There was even a door like the one drawn on the curtain that the winning bachelor waited behind during the drumroll—only my contestant was headed in the opposite direction, away from me.

I ran through a hundred questions, searching for the line that would have pulled him back, but Melissa's soul mate clichés clogged my head. Did she really believe someone was lurking at the periphery, manipulating our steps until we literally collided with our perfect match? What God micromanaged flirtations? And if mating were left to the whims of the angels, it was even scarier, bored love gods eyeing mortals through their gun scopes. I preferred my own chances over the aim of an invisible deity poised at my shoulder.

The plane landed like a child's toy dragged on the end of a string. The other passengers, led by the steely soccer mom across the aisle from me, climbed off while Randy and I waited for Melissa to finish hyperventilating.

Her horror increased when we reached the St. Thomas airport lobby, Randy now gaping beside her. Birds swooped under the sloped ceiling, whole walls missing. Melissa mumbled something inaudible, uncertain whether she was staring at the impossibly tidy remains of a ruined building or an intentional structure, doors and windows made superfluous by its vast open sides. The latter seemed more disturbing.

The architecture had confused me the first time I'd landed in the Virgin Islands, too. Basic principles no longer applied. Doors meant privacy, cleanly boxed divisions, Man and Nature. But the elements weren't worth dividing here. It only rained in five-minute bursts and never dipped below seventy-two, at least not during the TV season. Hurricanes blew through during our summer hiatus, but the damage always seemed minimal. Buildings without walls attracted little wrath.

Melissa and Randy sighed gratefully when I deposited them in the Lovelund Resort waiting room, the carpet and wallpaper glowing in mismatched shades of pink. Newlyweds occupied the other wicker love seats, the women staring idly at their perfect manicures, the effect still novel. Randy was the only man not fingering a new wedding band. They all looked the same age, like a graduating class loitering before a group portrait. After commanding months of exclusive attention, they were slowly realizing what droves shared their anniversary.

A promotional video played in the corner, barely audible over the roar of the air conditioner. I hummed the jingle under my breath as the receptionist checked the shuttle schedule. An Islands newspaper rested open on her side of the counter, away from the impressionable guests. I read the upside-down headline: "Police Chief Vows Crackdown," then in smaller print underneath it, "First Probes To Uproot Corruption Underway." The receptionist dragged it out of sight as she handed me our verification slips.

The back of the open-air bus was arranged in pews, and, as usual, I threw the count off, an extra body crammed into the last row. We bounced as the motor whined up volcanic hills overlooking the grungy shopping plazas of Charlotte Amalie. We coughed in unison as a passing jalopy plumed exhaust under our canopy. Randy and Melissa clenched their jaws. At last, they thought they'd discovered the trick; they'd been suckered into a Caribbean version of Newark, New Jersey, a vacation in Purgatory.

I enjoyed their discomfort, knowing it would last only fifteen minutes. When the bus rattled through the Lovelund Resort gates, Melissa's face bloomed. Even Randy gave that toddler-in-Disneyland gaze, as a Caribbean Epcot shone before him. Though water was a precious commodity on the Islands, the lawns sprawled as wide and emerald as a golf course. The coconut trees obeyed the same architectural geometry as the bricked paths and pastel buildings. Employees in white pressed uniforms greeted us in the open lobby, while our luggage was whisked onto chrome-plated carts. The ones who knew me nodded conspiratorially. Melissa and Randy seemed cured of their aversion to missing walls.

Melissa's giggly breath returned as she and Randy marched down the row of bungalows, the porter and I trudging in the rear. Randy eyed the key card I handed him, apparently surprised that he and Melissa had separate rooms. If I decided network policy, they wouldn't. I despised sharing rooms with my bachelorettes. An office memo had rationalized the policy as a cost-cutter, but the real reason was even more pragmatic: No sex. No one was to sneak in or out without my knowing it, my ears primed to detect the faintest mattress creak or padded footfall. There was no connecting door between the matching rooms.

The porter opened both as I plucked a five from my purse. He stole a glimpse of Melissa fumbling with her bra strap through her blouse and retreated at a sprint as she stepped out of her pants. I wasn't a prude, but I had always been thankful for the partitions in health club showers. Melissa stripped, indifferent to the open curtains.

The Cupid routine worked for people like her. She batted her petal lashes, wagged her doe-tail, and the arrows went flying. How was I supposed to compete with that? I could never look that naked. I wasn't armored; I was calloused, my heart bruised thick. A couple of seasons in Paradise could do that to a girl. Sunblock was for tourists.

I had suggested a quick change then rendezvous for dinner. Randy paced on our patio among the wind-strewn flowers. His hair reeked of fresh mousse, and there was a red patch on his jaw from his electric razor. Otherwise he was identical except for the different-colored polo shirt. Men thought if they tucked their shirttails into their shorts it counted as evening wear.

Melissa had noticed the resort pamphlets positioned conveniently on her bureau. She asked if we could dine at Ciao Chow, a "transcultural eatery" contrived to lure tourists consecutive nights. Most of the restaurants scattered beyond the resort walls were better, but I agreed, knowing to shun the "Asian" half of the menu.

A piano wafted Broadway tunes over the upstairs balconies as I listened to Randy's fork scrape his teeth. He monopolized the conversation by describing how he got his pilot license again. Melissa cocked her head and blinked at appropriate intervals, while he mimed an imaginary cockpit, gripping the steering wheel above his soup bowl. He planned to circumnavigate the globe as soon as he accumulated enough vacation time.

My attention wandered to other tables. Besides the standard sunburnt newlyweds, there was an odd, burly-looking pair ignoring their dinners. They sat back from their table, a knee free on each side for fast escapes. If this were anywhere else, I would have wagered that a mutual friend had set them up on a date. Or maybe their health club had held a his-and-hers weight-lifting competition, St. Thomas tickets for the winners.

Near them, on the far edge of the veranda, there was something I'd never seen in Lovelund before: a woman eating alone. She hadn't even bothered bringing a book, like I would have, nose buried to fend off stares. I kept waiting for a husband to appear, but she moved on to dessert without once glancing toward the entrance or bathrooms. The waiter passed our table with a single serving of crème brûlée with blackberry garnish, the best item on the menu. I couldn't see her face from this distance, just her diamond earrings reflecting the sunset like police strobes. At least she was compensated for her loneliness.

A dozen heads perked up when a cell phone twittered. I knew it was hers before she bent for her purse. She murmured a hello, then erupted, "God damn it, stop calling me. I don't want to talk to the little shit. Why the fuck do you think I'm divorcing him?"

She could have been yelling at someone across the restaurant. Every conversation died, waiters turning midstride. Even the pianist paused, fingers tripping over an eighth-note run from "Annie, Get Your Gun." Melissa and Randy twisted in their seats as she continued, her voice unmodulated, "It's my vacation, I'll go where I want!"

She glared at the empty chair across from her as she

listened. Her pauses seemed louder than her shouts, the room tensed in anticipation as her invisible companion spoke in her ear.

"So he's paranoid. That's his problem. Who the hell does he think I'm going to talk to in this pit?" She gestured with a slash of her hand, the whole island included in her contempt, but her silences lengthened. I marveled that the person on the line had the mettle to speak at all.

"Fine. Fine. That's just fucking fine. You want to negotiate, talk to Wakefield. Leave me out of it." She smacked the off switch and tossed the phone away. Only the bodybuilding couple had the nerve to look at her directly. Everyone else sat, transfixed by their plates. The woman shoveled a spoonful of crème brûlée into her mouth, oblivious to us all.

At least the interruption distracted Randy from his monologue. I stabbed a forkful of iceberg lettuce and asked Melissa about *her* job. I had reread her bio sheet while sorting paperwork the day before and wanted to see Randy's face when he realized she made more money.

When he ducked his head to retrieve a dropped spoon, my heart pricked: I glimpsed something behind him. I tilted forward, studying a figure beyond the veranda. He stood outside on the brick path, loitering beside a grove of palm trees. It might have been anyone at that distance, but the ache in my breast pulsed again. I knew it couldn't be my stranger from the plane, but the longer I studied him, the more he looked like himself: the shoulders, the tangle of hair, a face more distinctive in profile. His white shirt had gone pink in the sunset.

My breath stopped as he raised his face to peer into

the restaurant. I was certain it was him, his gaze breezing past me. I traced his angle of vision, annoyed to find him staring intently at the potty-mouthed divorcée. Her diamonds sparkled as the spoon in my fist tapped against the table.

A dozen possibilities flashed in my head. They were secret lovers, plotting a tryst out of sight of the jealous ex-husband. She was eating alone because he'd missed the flight from San Juan—or maybe she was throwing the ex off their scent. In a moment we would witness their passionate reunion, more vulgar than the woman's cell phone tirade.

I noticed that Melissa's voice had trailed off, while Randy angled in his chair to see what had hypnotized me. "Sorry." I swallowed through my tightened throat. "I thought I recognized somebody."

They wouldn't resume talking until certain my attention was secure. They reminded me of small children unwilling to amuse themselves without an adult audience. I struggled not to blurt inappropriate questions: How many condoms did you pack, Randy? Did you know Melissa has her period this weekend?

When I looked back at the lone diner, she appeared unchanged, her back still bowed over her dessert. She wasn't checking her watch or preening in anticipation. She gazed over the veranda bushes once, casually, no trace of recognition flashing across her face. Her bored gaze settled on a pair of palm trees as her theoretical lover continued up the path. My heart beat faster as he rounded a building edge: *She didn't know him.*

Normally I would have smiled at my silent victory and coaxed my team through their second course. But something felt different, a tension coiling in my bones.

I tried to concentrate, but Randy's voice grated, Melissa's blonde curls bobbing in the humidity. The urge to escape bloomed in my gut. Randy halted mid-sentence as my napkin parachuted off my leg.

"I have to check something."

The lack of walls was convenient. I aimed for a quick exit between the bushes. The square-shouldered couple seated near the divorcée rose from their chairs as I shuffled past. For a moment I thought the woman was going to body-check me. Was I that much of a spectacle? I wondered what Randy and Melissa were mumbling.

Mulch scattered over the grass as I steered a short-cut down the sloping hillside. I considered stopping to get his name and room number at the registration desk—I kept on a first-name basis with most of the staff—but I couldn't slow my trot. My mother's voice pleaded in my head: *Ashley, what are you doing? You don't behave this way.*

I circled half the resort, expecting him to appear around the next pastel-brick corner, but he was nowhere. Round granite walking steps dotted the green expanse. Had I hallucinated him? Was my brain that desperate to avoid chaperoning? I swerved into a row of adjoining bungalows, surveying the identical tiled patios. He could have vanished behind any door. A reasonable person—like me—would have walked back to the restaurant now. The resort wasn't that big; the island was smaller than Manhattan, and a fraction as populated. Chances were I would bump into him again tomorrow. But I noticed that my legs weren't slowing.

I strode to the first sliding glass door and peered in: untucked pillows, open suitcase on the bed. I veered to the next window, peeking into the same darkened bathroom. I started vaulting the cement partitions, navigating around patio furniture. The sun had slipped behind the hills, so I wagered the occupants would see themselves rather than me through the glass. One couple was dressing in the flicker of their TV, matching rolls of flab illuminated in blue.

The last room appeared dark, but I checked anyway, my nose touching the glass. Some of my friends called me dauntless—I once asked out a busboy and a waiter during the same meal—but this exceeded even my record. This was a complete stranger I was stalking. My mother always said that true love struck with a gavel's authority, but even she had needed a second date before declaring my father Mr. Right.

I stepped away from the window, conscious of a movement behind me, tiny arrows pricking the back of my neck.

"Are you looking for *me?*"

I gasped and clutched my chest as if shot. The voice was too high to be my mystery bachelor's. At first I thought the divorcée had followed me, enraged with jealousy, a switchblade gripped inside her purse, but a different woman studied me from the edge of the path. I stammered something moronic, mortified by how long she might have been watching, her arms crossed in silent judgment. Who would believe I had misread a dozen room numbers in a row?

"I know what this must look like." What did it look like? A voyeur out for a jog? "But I hope you don't think—"

"I remember you from the plane."

I knew her, too, worn sandals, denim skirt, brown hair tied back, the soccer mom who had sat across the aisle from me. Only now her jaw was held more tightly, the corner of her mouth wrinkled with a frown. We hadn't acknowledged each other the whole flight, but now I felt I was being eyed through a rifle scope.

"Not often you see three people traveling *here* together."

The thought that I wasn't the only one on the island taking notes disturbed me. I always considered myself invisible among the navel-gazing honeymooners. I almost snapped back an insult, but then it clicked. What were the odds of both her and my mystery lover traveling to the resort on lone adventures? He wasn't rendezvousing with the divorcée; he was meeting this woman, maybe for an anniversary, a second marriage probably. He looked a little young for her, but the divorcée could have been his mother.

I cleared the stammer from my voice. "I'm so sorry, ma'am." But I'm infatuated with that hunk of a husband of yours. "But I'm supposed to meet a friend this weekend and thought her room was around here."

Her eyes widened. What did I say wrong? Then her face turned stony again. "Rude not to give you the number."

"Last-minute plans."

She squinted, debating whether to pat me on the back or gun me down. "I thought you looked like an odd one."

I felt my face flush while I fumbled for an explanation: this was really not like me. I wasn't this desperate. The mass of my life had been quiet infatuation. It was the heat, the airplane food, the piano music.

She was gone before I opened my mouth.

5

Are Aggressive Women a Turn-on?

Melissa amazed me when she agreed to Randy's after-dinner swim. Hadn't their parents lectured them about digestion? Plus, with all that makeup and hair spray, she might sink like a stone.

I had no intention of getting wet, but she insisted that I change, too. This was for contrast, because she sensed there was a one-piece in my suitcase—navy blue. I undressed in the bathroom, inspecting my tan lines and stray freckles. I didn't look bad in a bathing suit—my stomach was tauter than most women's—but I resented the exposure, the hint of cellulite on my upper thighs visible to the world's scrutiny.

It took Melissa fifteen minutes to change into a bikini. The tan mesh and French cut hid nothing, but I preferred them over the sheer cover she draped on top, her body wafting in and out of a teasing mist. Randy stared, half paralyzed. His pair of fluorescent trunks grazed his knees as he strutted beside her, a pink resort towel hanging over one shoulder. He was hairier than I had wanted to imagine, but at least he wasn't in a Speedo.

They moored me in the middle of three lounge chairs and waded for the wet bar, a garish waterfall peninsula built into the pool. The bartenders hated it. Speakers blared from the grove of artificial coconut trees. The band was decent, despite the synthetic drum machine and the fact that the resort insisted they play only Marley and Buffett covers all evening.

I had brought my book in case Randy anchored Melissa in the shallow end. He knew to stay within visual range, but every inch out of earshot represented a personal victory. I ordered an Amstel Light from a roving waitress, the same one I had flagged two weeks ago from the same chair. There were better bars three minutes away, and the beers didn't cost four dollars, but I sipped mine, content that *Who Wants To Be A Blind Date* was footing the tab.

I had a paranoid streak wider than my mother's. I avoided chatrooms and deleted e-mails for fear of corporate spies. If I heard a click on my phone line, I assumed the FBI was tapping my calls. So when I noticed someone stealing glances at me from across the pool, I figured it was my imagination. Or at least hoped it was. The guy eyeing me could have doubled as a professional wrestler, his neck as thick as my thigh, but he looked too somber to be flirting. He was the only person in slacks on the patio. He wore the same red polo shirt Randy had worn, only it fit like a gym uniform, the buttons straining against his chest.

When I noticed the woman sitting across from him, I remembered them from the restaurant, the grimmest, brawniest newlyweds I'd ever seen. I pictured them meeting in a bodybuilding class, falling in love on the bench press. Except they seemed too indifferent, their eyes roaming over everyone but each other. If they were looking for swingers, they'd come to the wrong island.

I spied another familiar face behind them. The divorcée lounged in a corner chair, breeze-blown palm leaves fanning her as she conducted another heated conversation with her cell phone, though this time the profanity was syncopated with a reggae beat. The sun had dropped an hour ago, but she wore a wide straw hat and sunglasses with lenses the size of grapefruits.

If this was designed to deflect attention, it had the opposite effect. Half the pool was whispering about her, the guitarist chopping harder upstrokes to drown out her voice. She could have been dead silent, and they would still have ogled her. It was the way she gestured with her cigarette, oblivious to the rings weighing each finger. Everybody assumed she was somebody.

I preferred to skim the crowd's faces, catching giggly expressions and husbands' fingers groping along bikini strings. The audience always made the better show. If I were ever promoted to producer, I'd point the cameras in the other direction.

I was panning left when my stranger came into focus: sandy hair, fingers propping his cheek. His face blazed orange from the candle on his bar table. Until that moment, I half believed I'd hallucinated him, a mirage in my love-parched heart.

My bottle went clammy in my hand when I realized he was alone. I told myself to forget it; he must be married. But I sloped half out of my chair, unable to detect the glint of a wedding band. My eyes lingered up his legs stretched across the adjacent chair. Was he saving it for someone? The soccer mom was nowhere in sight. Was I wrong about them? Why had they arrived separately if they were married? The chances of the Lovelund Resort simultaneously hosting four unrelated singles were remote, but I had played worse odds before.

He sipped a cocktail, something with an umbrella. My lips quivered every time his touched the glass. Though too distant to meet his eyes, I remembered them precisely, the way his attention coalesced, his stare confident but warm. If he looked over here, I might have burst into song. But there was little danger of that, given the way his attention was locked on the other side of the pool. Like the rest of the crowd, he was scoping out the resident celebrity, only more intensely, staring over the top of his newspaper as though to make eye contact through her grapefruit sunglasses. His legs pointed at her like compass needles. If he found her so intriguing, why didn't he just walk over and introduce himself?

I swigged my beer and asked the same question of myself. It wasn't shyness; I regularly asked strangers to dance in bars. Once I'd spent a lunch break making cold-calls from the Personals. But the rules were different in Paradise. On the other hand, I'd never seen so many single women here before: three bachelorettes vying for the lone Adam.

I lowered my empty bottle onto the cement and buttoned the olive blouse over my bathing suit. The unknown was always more alluring. The band broke into "I Shot the Sheriff" as I rounded the deep end—an auspicious omen.

He sat with his back to the bar, so I detoured for another fortifying beer before reconsidering my strategy. The bartender mirrored my nod hello. I was one of his only two regular customers. He slumped forward so I could talk to his ear. "What's he drinking, Uche?"

His eyes flashed up, then he grinned. I assumed he was laughing at me—the crazy *Who Wants To Be A Blind Date* lady was on the make—but he shook his head with contempt. "Virgin."

I peeked back at the table. The glass in his hand was mostly empty. Bits of daiquiri mix clung to the rim. "No rum?"

"Not a drop."

I shrugged and ordered two. So my weekend mate was on the wagon. There were worse flaws: I passed on the right and undertipped waitresses. We could work this out.

"Hi." I set one of the matching glasses by his elbow. "Is this seat taken? I'm tired of sitting by myself." He snatched his legs out of the way but stared, bewildered, his copy of *The New York Review of Books* lowering to his lap. I sat anyway. "My name's Ashley. We met on the plane."

When his face registered me, he looked even more shocked. His limbs retracted into his seat, hands tightening in his lap. This couldn't be a good sign. He mustered a winded "Hello" and dropped his stare to the rim-filled glasses. I picked up mine.

"Don't worry, it's not poisoned."

He hesitated, then laughed, wide-eyed, as though he had just heard the most audacious joke of his life. "Thanks." I wasn't sure what was wrong, but at least the color was coming back to his cheeks.

"I hope I'm not interrupting anything."

His eyes flashed over my shoulder. The divorcée

was still back there, her voice as constant as the ocean. Then he gave that dismayed shake of his head again. Had a woman never approached him before?

"It just seemed dumb for the only single people on the island not to introduce themselves."

This was both a lie and a hint, but he didn't take it. He mumbled as though admitting a professional failure. "I must look pretty conspicuous." He fidgeted like the Wizard after Dorothy tore the curtain back, his fingers combing back his bangs.

"No more than me." I sipped my drink and looked coyly across the pool. "I'm a chaperone for the show *Who Wants To Be A Blind Date*. What's your story?"

His laughs were windy, like punches to the gut, and I wondered if I were missing the jokes. "That's good, I like that." He lifted his new glass and sipped it without sniffing. "I'll give you credit. You're direct. I didn't think you'd just give yourself away."

Was that an insult or a compliment? I forced up a smile as I wiped daiquiri from my lip. "What do you mean?"

"The way you walked into me on the plane. I thought that was an accident. Didn't give it a second thought. You had me pegged from the start."

Great. He thought I was a stalker. I buried my face in my drink, mumbling over the rim. "Looks can tell you a lot about a man." Dumb line, dumb line, dumb line.

He seemed to weigh its verity. "What about him?"

I looked up, surprised to find him pointing at Randy. He and Melissa were perched on the pool steps, swishing their ankles in the turquoise waves. I felt vaguely pleased they hadn't drowned. Had he seen us enter the pool area together?

"He leaves the toilet seat up, prefers the missionary position, and phones his mother once a week."

His chuckle was loud but sincere. He seemed to be easing into a new role, liking me despite himself. "And me?"

"You don't know your mother's number."

"Who does?" It was true. Speed dial had eradicated half my long-term memory. "What else?"

"You pee sitting down to maximize efficiency." I rubbed my glass, realizing that I had just revealed how I brushed my teeth in the morning.

"It's the main benefit of an electric razor."

I pictured him naked on a toilet, cross-hatched with sheet marks. "I know."

He was pondering me now, though I couldn't tell what the shock and admiration were giving way to. This wasn't flirtation. Men competing for my raises feigned more warmth. He swallowed a mouthful of daiquiri, eyed the glass, and skidded it across the table. "So where do we go from here?"

My spine stiffened. Was this his idea of a come-on? I'd heard more romantic shouts from car windows. The man needed better coaching before going in front of the cameras. But my heart was thumping anyway. I pictured his bare stomach flickering in blue TV light.

"Don't ask me." I was stalling. A one-nighter in Paradise would be fun, but even Eve knew Adam's name first.

He rapped his fingers on the tablecloth like an impatient businessman. "Well, you approached me, didn't you? I figured you wanted to negotiate."

I felt my face blanch as I gaped back at him. I could hardly believe it. Did he think I was a prostitute? It seemed insane, but I had no other explanation. My daiquiri would have been cascading down his face, but I was too shocked to breathe. My chair toppled as I stammered. "Of all the . . . the . . . the—" The band chopped a final chord as my voice burst through the speaker hum. "You think you can just—?!" He jolted up as if expecting me to draw a gun or karate chop him in the throat. I couldn't even complete a sentence.

"Fine." The candle rocked as he shoved his chair under the table, his newspaper unfolding on the patio blocks. "We can do this the hard way. But I'm not leaving this island till I get what I want." He leveled a final glare at me and spun away, vanishing between the hedge and amplifier stack.

I stood, heaving enraged breaths through my nostrils, my skin prickling from the crowd's stares. Even the bassist was looking. I righted my chair slowly, glaring back at the turning faces. Only Melissa and Randy met my eyes. They watched from their perch in the shallow end, their expressions confused, like children walking in on their parents in bed. I smiled curtly and eased back down.

Melissa didn't seem to notice Randy's arm snaking around her waist. Chlorinated waves lapped their knees as his fingers grappled her hip. At least someone was getting somewhere.

Would You Kill for Love, and If So, Whom?

"Was that one of your chaperone friends or something?"

Randy was worse when he was trying not to insult me. I ducked inside and left them to their goodnights. The bar by the dock always blared dance music until two, but their hormones were ebbing. Even Randy didn't expect to get lucky the first night.

The glass doors remained parted, but I turned my back to the open curtains to give them an iota of privacy. As far as romance goes, this was the apex of the weekend: the chaste patio kiss. The second kiss would be weighed with too much anxiety. The panic to feel that they were having enough fun, that their contracted relationship was progressing on a timely schedule, would cripple most of tomorrow.

I was hovering at the bureau when my paranoia flared again. I usually left the zipper of my carry-on bag hanging to the left of the handle, not underneath it. I had mastered these espionage tricks in high school, when my parents had taken turns searching my room for drugs. I flipped through the contents: clothes balled into a neat bundle, underwear and toiletries nested inside. An emergency pair of shell earrings rattled in the top compartment with a lost eyeliner pencil I'd since replaced. There was a lone condom at the bottom of a pocket I had forgotten was there.

Melissa slid the patio door closed behind her. Her gaze was unfocused, but she maintained her perky stride. I braced for the obligatory interim evaluation: she loved those hunky pecs, despite the pelt of fur. Bachelor #2's crass chivalry was paying off. His sports metaphors and probing sexual jokes probably wouldn't start to annoy until Saturday night. I sat on the bed with my toiletry bag in my lap, trying to look neither too occupied nor too attentive.

Melissa wheeled at me. "Isn't that amazing about Zelda Shilling?"

My eyebrows rose, and I dragged them back down, trying to maintain a friendly expression. This blonde was flightier than I thought. The name hadn't come up since morning small talk on the plane.

"What about her?"

Melissa kicked her sandals at the foot of the bureau. "I mean, I know they own real estate all over the Islands, but still!" Her palms turned up, fingers spread. Then it hit me: the strobe-light diamonds, the softball-sized sunglasses.

"That was . . . ?"

Melissa looked at me. "You didn't know?" She sniggered superciliously. "Don't you watch TV?" It was the expression I had once used on high school teachers—

men in leisure suits who had never heard of U2. Melissa paced around the bed, unable to keep her feet still. "I bet she's hiding from her husband. Lying low till all the publicity settles? Imagine having to live in a spotlight like that. All those reporters."

She shook her head, gaze distant again. She didn't seem to be commiserating so much as contemplating a career move. When she whisked her bikini top off, I escaped into the bathroom and brushed daiquiri pulp off my teeth.

I hated sharing rooms with a stranger. I never brought a man home and never dozed off on someone else's pillow. Showering in a man's bath was more intimate than sex. They never picked their hairs out of the soap.

Even as a kid I had avoided sleep-overs, those feet and food smells worn into rec room carpets, the giggling and snoring keeping me awake until dawn. Melissa claimed the bed nearer the bathroom, ignoring the wristwatch and paperback I had lain on the nightstand nearest it.

I hadn't turned two pages before the talking started, explosive monosyllables followed by garbled strings of half-words. She flung her arms, slapping at the mattress, her subconscious trying to lecture me about my inadequate makeup supplies.

When I thought she'd quieted down, the snores erupted. They caught in her throat at uneven intervals, jerking her body as they burst. Reading was impossible. I considered flopping her onto her face, or dialing our room number on my cell phone, but there was no point. My focus was sharp, fingers drumming "Margaritaville" on the mattress. Sleep was hours away.

I knocked her mattress as I passed. Melissa grunted and kicked hard under the sheet. I traded silk pj's for jeans and a T-shirt and headed for the patio. *Who Wants To Be A Blind Date* would never splurge for a beachfront bungalow, but I could still glimpse a corner of moon-rippled water between the building edge and palm leaves. I kicked my feet up on the wicker table with an insomniac's resignation.

I'd gotten a lot of reading done this way—shopping bags full of my mother's Harlequin Romances in eighth grade, Foucault in college. I preferred Austen now, despite the DeMille on the nightstand. It wasn't nice to frighten the bachelorettes with erudite authors.

If I were home, I would have picked something racy and run a bath. I hadn't forgotten about him. Whenever the noise in my head receded, I could hear his voice, a distant sexy rumble playing behind my thoughts. Though still bewildered by our conversation—he couldn't have taken me for a prostitute—I thought my mystery man was worth a second shot. If the gods had managed to get us on the same tropical island on the same weekend, I could at least restring my bow.

The breeze carried a low dance-floor buzz, but nothing loud enough to disturb the less gregarious newlyweds dozing through their refractory periods. A familiar voice drifted nearer, too, and I craned my neck to watch two approaching silhouettes. Though distant, the woman's words reverberated down the canyon of glass doors:

"What do you mean you don't know where he is? Isn't that your fucking job?"

Her outline lacked the sunhat now, but I knew it was Zelda Shilling. The second figure towered beside her, echoing her profanity but without the conviction.

"What am I now, his fucking mother?"

Zelda wheeled at her, a finger in her face. "Don't talk to me like that, girly. You hear me?"

I recognized her as she froze, the ludicrous span of her shoulders, thighs like palm trunks. Though twice Shilling's size, the bodybuilding bride said nothing, cowed by a painted fingernail in her face. I started concocting stories, one of my favorite pastimes. Was the thuggish groom by the pool Shilling Junior? Had this Amazon married into the nation's premier crime family?

"Find him." The mother-in-law from Hell continued on, her heels loud on the walking stones. "He's probably out trying to poke one of those bimbo waitresses."

The Amazon defended her groom in a softer tone, "He wouldn't do that."

"Oh, he wouldn't, huh? He has a dick, doesn't he? You know how many times I caught my husband—"

She halted at my patio with a piercing glare, my T-shirt aglow in the shadows. I yanked my feet off the table, ready to dive under it. The Amazon reached for something behind her back as I cleared my throat and mumbled a weak "Good evening."

Zelda huffed disparagingly and started off again, her voice low until they reached the end of the bungalows, and a profane shout echoed into the stars. I remained perched on my seat edge, heart rapping like a hummingbird's. Would I ever get to sleep?

Too fidgety even to sit, I started in the opposite direction, hoping to walk off some of my restlessness.

The opposite happened: I glanced between the palms and spied a ripple of movement. I couldn't see the boat dock, only the tangle of waves at its edge. Someone had just passed on the boardwalk. I wanted to laugh at myself: *Yes, yes, it was a white shirt.*

The chorus to "The Electric Slide" swelled as I rounded the darkened duty-free shop, grass cuttings clinging to my toes. I skidded at the base of the hill and scanned: beach, walkways, bar pavilion glowing like a circus tent. The dance floor lurched in unison, the synchronized movements looking oddly militaristic. I hoped the object of my desire hadn't wandered into there. I never so much as two-stepped with a crowd of strangers.

The rows of beach chairs stood empty. I could see the water rippling through their plastic slats. No lovers were enjoying that disco ball of a moon. A clique of drinkers had spilled onto the boat dock. Their laughter was hoarse and thoughtless. The sound tugged the muscles in my neck. I stood at the perimeter where the grass has gone gritty with sand, a no-man's-land. The waves crashed soundlessly in the moonlight, reaching scant inches up the sloped beach.

I needed to go home, not back to the room, but to New York or further. What sort of dead-end life had I dug myself into? I was chasing fantasy men. Even my parents' house, that castellated tower of New Jersey suburbia, was better than this. A few ragged concert posters and my dad's study would have passed for my high school bedroom again. Bono and Bowie were no more tangible than my nameless Prince.

I hiked past the gazebo instead. A path began where the beach ended, all rocky and overgrown, the way the whole resort would go without the annual barge of polished sand. The white shirt I'd glimpsed had been headed in this direction. He, I expected, would have had the sense to wear shoes. My arms flapped with each sharp pebble.

I knew the path's whole length, the way it meandered to the tip of the horseshoe bay. I had interrupted a couple in the bushes there once. They'd yanked at their bathing suits in panic, the trees rattling as they'd skittered away.

My shoulders tightened as I registered the sound again: a branch clattering on the slope above me. I watched but caught no motion, no flicker of white. What bride would rest her bare cheeks on those brambles? It was probably a mongoose. I'd seen them scuttling in the manicured bushes by the pool, knocking over beer bottles beside startled guests.

The water was only a few feet below, but the thorns didn't tempt me. I perched on my favorite rock instead and inspected my soles. It would only have taken a couple more minutes to reach the end, but I'd seen enough dead ends for one night. Of course he wasn't here. He never was. I had a lousy habit of finding the most romantic corners of the earth on my own. This wasn't my first sleepless stroll through Eden.

I listened to the waves and watched the anchored boats roll. My bungalow had receded into the lower hills. Only the pavilion burned a silent orange behind the dock. On Monday I would scroll up my old résumé on the computer in my cubicle and ask the producer for a letter of recommendation. He called me Donna half the time, but at least he remembered how I had defanged the Love Bug virus before it crashed our system.

I resigned myself to a night of Melissa's nocturnal bleating and stood. Lucky for her she was beautiful; most men wouldn't suffer a second night otherwise. I took a farewell glance at the water and lover's perch, the bay shimmering as if lit for a skinny dipping-scene—something else I've only done alone. I pictured his lean, bare legs, the way the water would stream over his ribs and pool in his navel.

I turned to leave but pitched back suddenly, startled by a shape in the water. Someone was down there. I crouched instinctively. If Dick and Jane had hung their thongs in the trees, I preferred to exit unnoticed.

But curiosity craned my neck. I fought to distinguish shapes from the wrinkles of moon in the water, a hip, a burly shoulder, a head. Then my breath lodged in my throat. Trousers clung to the swimmer's tree-thick legs. Tiny waves lapped over his face, his mouth open.

Two bounds and I was waist-deep. A third and I had a soaked sleeve in my fist. I expected him to be light, hollow like driftwood, but he resisted my tug, his skin as cool as the bay.

I yanked as I stepped back to the rocks, telling myself that I could revive him. The thought kept me from screaming. I pictured diagrams from my high school health class: tilt the neck, pinch the nose, cup the mouth. Only I couldn't catch my own breath.

Water drained from his mouth as I rolled him to the bank. He seemed impossibly large, a sponge expanded in water. I recognized the shirt as it tore in my fists: red polo shirt, form-fitting. I was holding the bodybuilding honeymooner from the restaurant and pool. The Amazon bride had been right; he wasn't holed up in some bungalow with a waitress after all.

I couldn't bear to look at his face again, so I freed a hand and waved at the boat dock.

"Hey! I need help! I need help here!"

I could see them leaning against the railings, skin glowing in the floodlight. I glared, furious that they couldn't hear over the music. One woman bent forward in a laugh, her arm counterbalancing a glass.

"This man needs help!"

No one turned. Their world extended no further than their shadows.

"He-ee-ey!"

I screamed until my throat throbbed, then rolled the dead groom into the weeds.

7

Is Chivalry Dead?

Co-workers always said I was good in a crisis: a flat tire, a stolen purse. They considered me calm, a pillar of decisiveness, but they'd never been inside my head.

The path was twice as long on the return trip. I couldn't feel my feet slapping the rocks. They looked like someone else's lumbering beneath me. I flinched and slapped every time a drop of water dribbled down my arm because I imagined it was blood—thick, congealing, polo shirt red blood.

I slogged through the sand toward the pavilion lights, wet denim tight around my legs. I had no idea why I was running. I half believed he could still be saved. I'd heard stories about drowning victims revived after hours under water. I was willing to think a Caribbean bay could flash-freeze a body.

I wove between a drunken couple cradling Coronas into the lawn. They shot me the same startled look, a shared hallucination. Uche was flipping chairs onto tables as his head tilted up. I dripped on a bar stool and gasped, busboys gathering from the corners of the room to stare at me.

"There's—there's—" I was trying to point, arm weak as though swatting a very slow fly. "A body out there." I expected a shocked silence, maybe a chuckle, a few amused nudges between the older boys. Crazy drunk lady fell in the water. My finger pointed out to sea.

Uche touched my elbow. "Where?"

He tried to trot at my side, but branches kept knocking him back. He followed at my heels, asking repeatedly if I was okay. The busboys rattled a few yards behind us. They had looked both excited and horrified when Uche had recruited them—but not surprised. No one seemed surprised.

Uche stepped on my foot when I stopped. I felt shaky and nauseated, but adrenaline stiffened my legs. Uche looked around, at the weeds, at the water, at the absence of a body. "Was this the spot?" I ignored the hint of incredulity.

We kept passing the same tree, the same row of rocks, my breath fluttering as I slashed at weeds. Maybe he was okay—a gasp of fresh air and he'd been on his way. I found myself checking the waves, imagining the arc of his arm in the moonlight as he breaststroked out to sea. Uche studied the sailboats, their masts swaying like inverted clock pendulums.

"Over here!"

We darted back. The busboys were already groping in the weeds, trying to brace the body from below. The drowned man kept growing, taking on weight. He nearly crested on the rock edge before tumbling over Uche's foot, the water rippling as he hit.

They eventually heaved him to the path. He was even huskier than I'd thought. Uche took a knee in each arm, crotch to his belly, each busboy claiming a shoulder. I followed like a flower girl, watching how the dead man's neck wobbled as they marched. I expected him to mumble something drunken, twist over to vomit. Sometimes his eyes flashed at mine as his head bounced up and down, up and down.

A Lovelund manager paced on the beach as we emerged. He was a new one; Lovelund juggled lower management more than *Who Wants To Be A Blind Date* shuffled directors. He scowled, his tie crooked, the side of his hair dented from sleep. "Take it to the boathouse."

Two cops met us on the path steps. I wondered who'd called them, how they'd gotten there so fast. I'd never seen a uniform inside the resort walls before, the polyester blue clashing with the pastels. They waited beside a palm tree, their shadows long in the security floodlight, content to let the corpse come to them.

The manager hurried us all inside. Someone hit a switch, and the door closed after me as the fluorescent tubes blinked on, flickering like strobes. I didn't realize why they were avoiding looking at me until Uche draped a towel over my shoulders. I hadn't noticed how far I had waded into the water, my T-shirt translucent where it matted against my stomach and breasts. They eventually sat me on a folding chair and handed me a Coke from the dispenser in the hall.

The dead man got a plastic tarp and the picnic table to himself. No one suggested trying to revive him. I read somewhere that investigators assumed every corpse was a murder victim until proven otherwise. These two didn't look too worried. They probably figured that between the bay, me, and Uche's wrestling team, there wasn't much evidence to be had.

The cops looked like nice guys. I swore one had doughnut crumbs in his razor stubble. I studied his wedding band as he took my statement, the sides of the can growing warm in my fingers. I gripped it with both hands, because my arms kept shaking from adrenaline withdrawal. All I wanted was to go to bed. Melissa could slink next door to Randy's and fornicate the morning away while I slept till noon. I'd scribble my resignation on the back of a cocktail napkin and ask her to fax it: *No more show biz.*

Uche and his busboys vanished within minutes. There was a bar to be closed and the lure of overtime pay. Only the manager remained, pacing, apparently anticipating some worse fate, a surprise visit from the Lovelund CEO perhaps. He adjusted the tarp twice, walking a wide circle around me. I couldn't decide whether his frowns were frightened or resentful, but he held me responsible as sure as I had drowned one of his guests myself.

The cops stationed themselves in the adjoining room. I overheard voices and an occasional door thumping closed, the manager bending to it all. They were talking to someone new, maybe a drunk witness from the bar. I couldn't make out the words, just her husky murmur.

When the door opened wider, I saw Zelda Shilling frowning behind an officer's shoulder. The hat and sunglasses were gone, but the diamonds still stretched her earlobes, their glitter dull under the fluorescent tubes. She looked pale, her eyes dissecting the water stains on the floor. All the profanity and bluster had drained out of her.

I couldn't see the other woman, just the width of her shadow on the concrete. Her tone was low and firm, more a grunt, as the cop gestured her toward the door. The frame was barely wide enough, her shoulders brushing both edges. She shoved past the cop, her size-twelve Nikes clumping to the picnic table. She flung back the tarp herself as he scurried to her side. I couldn't see the corpse, just her resigned grimace. The dark plastic rattled in her fist as she sighed, "Yeah. That's him."

I fidgeted when she glanced my way. I wanted to apologize for being there—the cops had told me to wait—so I tightened my lips and tried to look earnest. I was never very good with sympathetic expressions. My cousin's toddlers fled at the sight of me.

I expected either anger or thanks, but the glare she flashed was defiant. I said nothing and examined the mouth of my can as she turned on her sneakered heel and brushed past the cop again. He looked confused and shrugged when I looked up: *Widows—go figure.* I wanted to slap them both.

Zelda Shilling was slumped in a folding chair like mine, her forehead pressing into her hand. She looked like she needed a cigarette, a double vodka and a box of Kleenex. The Amazon towered over her, her paw patting her shoulder. It was an awkward gesture, clearly outside of her job description. I knew now that I wasn't the only paid professional visiting this island.

I glanced at the tarp, crooked where the cop had skirted it back, and finally accepted that the corpse didn't belong to anyone's newly married son. I should have figured it out before: the three-hundred-pound thug was one of Zelda Shilling's bodyguards. A woman like that didn't go anywhere unprotected. I was surprised by how genuinely shaken she appeared by his death, all the contempt just an act. My boss wouldn't give me a half thought until unopened applications spilled out of my cubicle.

Zelda stood as the surviving half of her private army guided her toward the outer door. Her face was expressionless, the flattened wrinkles slacker in the stark light. She stared into the outer blackness as though mounting a pirate's plank, eyes as deep as an insomniac's.

I watched as she trudged out of view, expensive heels scraping across the cement, then stood to leave myself. There was no place to put the full Coke can, the picnic table being occupied, so I leaned over and tucked it against the chair leg. I'd left a puddle on the seat, another under it where my pant legs had dripped, and I suppressed an urge to mop up, aware of what bad health club etiquette it was to leave a nautilus seat sweaty.

There was a new face glaring at me when I straightened.

"Hello, Miss Farrell."

The stripes on his sleeve glowed like roadside reflectors, a silver badge and sundry decorations drooping his shirt front. I decided I was looking at St. Thomas's chief of police. He was darker than his officers and probably twice their age. His chest and stomach protruded, but our eyes met at the same height.

"Hello."

I wasn't sure what he was doing here. It was a small island, but not that small. The manager was standing very still in a corner, quiet as the dead man. When the chief motioned for him to leave, he broke into a sprint, the door slamming behind him. The chief started pacing beside the picnic table, indifferent to the hulking mound.

"I understand that you found the deceased."

It wasn't quite a question, but I nodded. I was expecting an introduction, maybe a word of condolence for my trauma, insincere or not. That was what a *Who Wants To Be A Blind Date* man would do.

"How did you know him?" His tone teetered toward rudeness, not the laid-back native mode the tourbooks liked to brag about.

"I didn't."

"You said you recognized him."

I was surprised he had bothered to read my statement. I'd thought this was a formality. The error woke me. "From today. I saw him around the resort." I pointed through the cinder blocks, which he didn't turn to look at. The wrinkles around his mouth formed a permanent frown.

"Did he talk to you about anything?"

"No."

"Just the weather, that sort of thing?"

"We never spoke." Exhaustion made my voice harsher than I intended. It was usually harsher than I intended. Weren't there any drug dealers jailed in Charlotte Amalie for him to interrogate? "I just recognized him from dinner."

His single eyebrow rose. "You ate together?"

This was an intentional mistake, the note of surprise flat. I didn't like this game. "He was across the room." My first producer, the one who got promoted, used the same ploy.

He crossed his arms and feigned admiration. "You must have quite a memory for faces. Lots of people in Ciao Chow on a Friday evening."

I'd never said anything about the restaurant to the other officers. Apparently, the chief had done some quick legwork of his own. "Yes, I do."

"What did you say when you went to his table?"

I was trying very hard not to dislike him. The God of a small Eden was a terrible thing. "I never actually—"

"Do you always leap over hedges when exiting a restaurant?" He watched my jaw work up and down. "Where were you going in such a rush?"

The back of my calf was touching the folding chair, but I resisted the temptation to sit. My arms mirrored his. "Are you accusing me of something?"

He ignored the question and stepped to the picnic table. The tarp slid to the floor in a deafening flutter. He scrutinized the body, frowning as though disappointed with him, too. "And he was gone when you returned?"

I could see the dead man in the corner of my eye, his open eyes gazing at the ceiling. His pants bulged, with an erection maybe. The thought wrenched bile into my throat.

"And you didn't see him again till he washed up at your feet?"

The chief stepped to the other side of the table, knowing I would have to look at the corpse to look at him. I clenched my jaw and turned, always a sucker for a dare. "He was at the pool tonight."

"So you saw him again?" His refrain of surprise.

I faked eye contact, keeping my gaze on the spot on

his forehead where his brows met. "It's not that big a place."

He wrinkled his mouth and continued orbiting the corpse. "True." The word stretched over two syllables. "But most tourists don't know about that seaside path you were on. Lucky for us you decided to take a stroll when you did. The currents could have dragged the body out to sea or grounded it on a remote beach."

I held my jaw still so he wouldn't hear my teeth grinding. "You're welcome."

His sleeve brushed the towel on my shoulder, and I could smell either his aftershave or his deodorant. "You're not leaving today, are you?"

"Sunday."

"You visit St. Thomas a lot, don't you?"

It was an easy fact, but I didn't like that he knew it. I adjusted the towel, suddenly conscious of the T-shirt clinging to my chest. "I'm a chaperone for—"

"I know what you are." The threat under his voice flared. "You register here twice a month."

The statement sounded like an accusation. I heard his two-syllable "True" in my head, but fought to keep my tongue still.

"I hope your *employers* don't suffer any negative publicity because of this incident." He pointed at the corpse as if I might have forgotten it. "They own Lovelund Resort, don't they?"

My leg jerked as I felt my face change temperature. If he knew about the show, then why the hell was he drilling me? I wanted to bark my outrage but nodded instead.

"Under the circumstances, I'm sure they would understand if you and your party chose to return early?" The statement ended with a feminine rise, but his jaw was clenched. He would have just as soon seen me on the picnic table. "The first plane for Puerto Rico leaves in . . ." He pulled his sleeve back, and a gold watch sparkled under the ceiling fixture. "Seven hours." He met my eyes and grimaced. "Goodnight, Miss Farrell."

It took me a moment to realize that I was being dismissed. I wanted to quip something vicious and brilliant, but I could barely speak. My leg tensed as I shifted weight; I wasn't too angry to fantasize punt-kicking his crotch. I peeled off the towel and draped it over the chair back as I faced him. He looked startled, his eyes swerving to the picnic table, less threatened by a dead man's bulge.

The married cop called goodnight to my back as I marched through the connecting room. Somebody had already folded Shilling's chair back against the wall. The night air wasn't cold, but I shivered as I walked up the grass. My feet set the rhythm for the mantra in my head: *good in a crisis, good in a crisis.*

The chief of police wanted me off his island, probably hoping to scuttle the bad press. The only thing worse than a dead body was a witness blabbing about it. If the local paper got wind that Zelda Shilling's personal bodyguard had drowned at Lovelund, the tabloids would spread it nationally the next day, and the Virgin Islands tourist trade would suffer. *Who Wants To Be A Blind Date* had adopted the same policy when a felony record surfaced after the week's Bachelor #3 had already won his weekend prize. The bachelorette never knew that her date was a two-time ex-con, because the producer swore the staff to secrecy. They didn't tell me until I got back.

Melissa's snores greeted me as our door slid back. I locked it this time. My eyes adjusted as I changed in the darkness, my wet jeans peeling off my legs like banana skins. Melissa sprawled across the bed in an *X*, her mouth an *O*. The noise was stunning. I considered sleeping with both pillows over my head, but then wedged my hands under her hip and shoulder and heaved. She was a lot lighter than a dead bodyguard.

"Wha? What?" Her voice was panicky.

I faced the wall and curled around myself. "You were snoring."

8

What's the Worst Piece of Gossip You Ever Heard about Yourself?

The ringer chimed, distant and muffled. I was dreaming something about shipwrecks when I surfaced from sleep, bodies bobbing around me. I slapped at the clock on the nightstand, but the phone kept bleating.

"Hello?" A dial tone blared in my ear. Wrong phone.

I spied my purse on the table and hobbled around Melissa's bed. The cell phone skittered at the bottom, avoiding my fingers—they felt numb and bloated like a drowned man's.

"Hello?"

"So what's your excuse this time?"

I winced and shifted the phone away from my ear, the speaker volume set preternaturally loud. "Excuse me?"

"You didn't call in last night." It took me a second to place the secretary's voice. I pictured him at his desk, hair in perfectly moussed waves as though he were posing for a headshot. "You're always supposed to call after checking in. You know that." Here was a lover of straight columns and check marks. He'd been hired only three months ago, but the producer adored him because he worked weekends.

I rubbed my knuckles against my eye and mumbled, "Yeah, sorry, I forgot." I considered mentioning how the man of my dreams had distracted me, but I'd met his shrew of a girlfriend in the office once; they were not people who would understand pursuing a romantic impulse.

"You know, Ashley, this is the third time this has happened. We do have rules. You're not just on vacation down there."

I glanced over at Melissa's bed, her body facedown and motionless. I couldn't believe this wasn't waking her. "Thanks for the clarification." I glanced again, and something held my gaze this time. I expected a faint snore, a twitch, but the wrinkles in her white nightie looked chiseled in granite. My voice dropped to a slow mumble. "I'll keep that in mind."

I crept closer, straining to see by the sunlight at the curtain's edges. Melissa's pose was wrong; the arm appeared bent, palm up as though twisted on impact. A leg jutted from the sheet at an impossible angle. She looked as if she'd been dropped from a great height, a stewardess sucked through a plane hatch.

"Is there a problem?" The phone started slipping down my ear. I stared at the sheet, willing it to rise with her breath. I remembered the sound of the tarp rattling off the dead man's stomach.

"No. Everything's fine." I was whispering now, as

my hand reached toward Melissa's bare foot. But I couldn't touch it, my arm shuddering with the memory of cool, slick flesh.

"Well, it had better be. I'm expecting your call tonight, first thing after dinner. I've got a press release to type up and I need interesting details. You know, something about how the couple is . . ."

I let the phone slump as he chattered insect-like against my shoulder. I tried to speak, but no sound came now. I coughed and swallowed.

"Melissa?"

The corpse remained still. I tried again, with my mother's voice this time: *"Melissa."*

She gasped and yanked her head up, a string of drool dangling from her cheek. I watched a tuft of hair waver vertically, then collapse in a stiff heap. She squinted but didn't seem to see me.

"Good-bye, Paul." His name wasn't Paul, but it was close. I snapped the phone off before I remembered my intention to resign. It was probably better to wait in case the producer got peeved and revoked my return ticket. I worked my face into a smile and waved at Melissa, imitating my mother's rise-and-shine fervor.

"Good morning, Sunshine!"

I had been on chatting terms with Luis the porter for the last few weeks. He teased me about my identical breakfast order—strawberry crepes, hazelnut coffee, cranberry-walnut muffin—once he got over his initial embarrassment. New staffers never knew what to think when they found a man and two women lounging in bathrobes together on the patio—an eyebrow-raiser for the other guests, too.

But this morning he was awkward again, the covered dishes rattling onto the table without his meeting my eye. Word was out about last night. He was worse than the manager, stepping around the radius of my shadow, my karma liable to rub off on him.

I didn't care. I'd decided to treat it like a dream, one more dead body in a lifetime of nightmares. My subconscious had never been subtle with metaphors: vampires, mutant fetuses, human organs in my mother's pot roast. I was the only woman I knew my age who had never seen a therapist.

I watched Randy dismantle an omelet slightly smaller than his head. He smacked the bottom of the ketchup bottle as Melissa sipped her tea, one anorexic leg draped over the other. She didn't do breakfast.

This was inevitably the worst meal of the weekend. The buffet had better food, but a room service menu was too decadent, too tempting to a winning couple. It created the illusion that they'd had sex. My father used to make my mother breakfast in bed every Saturday while I watched cartoons in the den with the door closed, a third wheel all my life.

Melissa crossed and uncrossed her knees so the hem of her nightgown tumbled in and out of view. She pretended not to notice Randy's stares. She'd spent twenty minutes adjusting her hair and makeup, striving for that natural, fresh-out-of-bed look. Randy employed a more literal approach. His stubble looked almost simian.

Melissa did not take her beauty casually; it was a discipline. I'd spotted an eyelash curler on the bathroom counter as I'd peed. I didn't even know what one looked like until my sophomore year in college. The only makeup in my house growing up was in a travel bag my mother stored in the back of the guest closet. Even now in her fifties my mother's beauty remained thoughtless, almost impudent. Melissa wouldn't have survived one of her boyish haircuts any better than I had.

She kept throttling her teacup and smiling at the side of Randy's head. The silence was getting to her, so I relented and prodded Randy from his eggs with a question.

No, he'd never snorkeled before, but he was interested in experimenting with water sports. He leered at Melissa as though practicing to be the next *Who Wants To Be A Blind Date* host. She giggled, satisfied with the attention.

No one noticed as I replaced the silver cover on my untouched plate. The strawberry glaze was polo-shirt red.

Melissa's second bathing suit was an elaborate *Sports Illustrated* concoction. She must have splurged for the occasion, because the tan lines on her hips dipped too low to match the cut. She lathered herself twice, while sitting on the bed, then waved the sunblock at me to do her back. I obeyed.

It never occurred to Randy to bring any. If Melissa offered hers, he would decline out of an obscure principle of masculine integrity. Unless, of course, she offered to rub it on for him, which I was betting against. All that hair—it would have been easier to apply lotion to a cat.

He was waiting on the walkway as we emerged. He'd added a pair of aviation glasses to his bathing ensemble—the lenses mirrored, so he could steal longer glimpses of Melissa's cleavage. I strapped my purse over my shoulder and started walking.

"Everybody ready?"

They positioned themselves automatically at my shoulders, Randy's flip-flops snapping as the day's schedule scrolled through my head: morning at the resort, lunch and early afternoon on St. John, dinner and shopping in Charlotte Amalie. Most couples would never have ventured beyond the resort walls, but I needed the variety.

The sand shimmered like splintered glass as our shadows led us across the narrow beach. Most of the honeymooners were still sleeping off their debauchery, so we had our choice of chaise longues. I opted for the left bank, furthest from my bayside path. When the breeze carried laughter over our heads, I glared at the empty dock.

"Oh, I want one of those." Melissa pointed at the water. Several figures bobbed on pink resort rafts, but her finger stretched toward the bicycle-paddle boat beyond them. The couple under its plastic awning reclined in a royal pose.

"Yeah, how do we get one?" Randy spied the two-seat arrangement, pleased at an opportunity to ditch me. The second boat was still tethered to the dock post.

"I'll go up and register." I peered up at the rental desk, where a couple in matching suits skimmed a waiver as the recreational manager stifled a yawn. A figure slanted in a doorway behind them. I wouldn't have noticed him but for the glint of his badge as he turned away.

The hairs on my neck rose and fell as my charges

waited expectantly. Randy prompted me, "The boat?"

I nodded, not listening, convinced the cop had been looking at me. He feigned interest in the brochure rack when I glanced a second time. It was hard to look casual in polyester. The fluorescent stripes on his pants glowed like landing arrows.

I looked down, feeling sweat rising under my bathing suit.

Randy and Melissa duplicated each other's impatient frown. "You're going to go register a paddle boat?" His tone sounded testy but careful, the way I used to speak to my senile grandmother.

The third time I looked, our eyes met, just for an instant. He wasn't either of the officers from last night, too lanky and young, like the bass player from the pool band. I tried to swallow my paranoia. Why would a cop be assigned to me? He could have been there for anything, a routine follow-up, safety inspections. Maybe he wanted to ask one of the managers out on a date. But I wanted to know for sure.

"Just go to that table and tell the manager—her name's Candice—tell her to put it on the *Who Wants To Be A Blind Date* account. I'll be back."

Melissa cocked her head, her lips mouthing my words as if learning new vocabulary: *Be back?*

Randy looked betrayed. Melissa alone was only marginally better than Melissa with me. It was the sport he wanted, not an open goalpost.

I trudged up the path. My pang of professional guilt vanished as I glimpsed the cop ducking into the boathouse. For an instant I imagined that the corpse was still inside, salt water dripping down the folds of the tarp. How many hours before flesh rotted? I winced when the scent of flowers wafted over the walkway.

I wanted answers.

After detouring to throw my sundress over my suit—I didn't perform investigative work half-naked—I peered through the sheer curtain of our bungalow. I wasn't crazy. My new friend waited near the corner bungalow, his eyes gazing squarely back through the gauze. He didn't have to read door numbers; he knew which one was mine.

The fact bolstered me. A man was chasing me for a change. I strolled onto the patio and angled a slow right in the opposite direction. When I turned the corner of the last bungalow, inches out of his view, I broke into a sprint and circled the row. In a half-minute, I skidded to his old post and peered around the corner to glimpse his back vanishing around the distant bricks, yards off my trail. I grinned a quiet victory, jogged around the next row of bungalows, and cut behind Ciao Chow to the staff parking lot.

A police cruiser sprawled between two illegal spots, maximizing the remains of the building's shadow. I pressed my palm against the hood, avoiding the peeling paint and rust spots. The metal was cool in the shade. The cop had been here a while, probably peeping at me while I'd poked my crepes. No wonder the porter had seemed antsy.

I considered waiting there to ambush him, but this was probably the last corner of Lovelund he'd think to look for me. Plus I doubted he'd be helpful. I recognized the rote movements of an obedient peon, uniformed or otherwise. I already knew he was shadowing me; the question was why. The police chief had bad press and a mobster's wife to contend with. Why was he squandering his resources on me?

Maybe it was none of my business, but then what had my job trained me to be but a wedge in strangers' private lives? Too curious to idle on the beach, I padded to the registration lobby with a new plan. Somewhere a pair of diamond earrings rested on a bungalow nightstand. I'd found her dead bodyguard for her, why shouldn't Zelda Shilling return the favor with an answer or two?

I was lucky, because Phoebe had the morning shift. She stood with her head bowed over the counter, but I recognized the wrist-thick ponytail resting against her neck. She had checked me in the first weekend I had chaperoned, smiling at me when my signature had left a nervous squiggle on the charge slip.

"Morning."

She finished logging something onto her screen and echoed my greeting, her accent more relaxed than with tourists.

"Phoebe, can I ask a quick favor?" I hated how melodic my voice grew when I needed something. "Can you tell me what room Zelda Shilling is staying in?" My head tilted as I smiled sheepishly. I felt like Melissa. "It's important."

The information was confidential, but Phoebe's nails started tapping, her eyes flashing between me and the screen. "About last night, huh?"

"You know too?"

She coughed a single high laugh: *Of course.*

My shoulders deflated. I didn't know how Melissa kept her back arched all the time. After a life of operating the spotlight, I wasn't used to center stage. "What did you hear?"

"The usual." She scouted for civilians before delivering the monotone headline: "Drunk tourist drinking by water. Falls in. Kerplop." She punctuated the tragedy with a stab at the enter key.

"He wasn't a tourist."

Phoebe perched her elbows on the counter, her voice dropping a half octave. "I know. That rich lady, she officially has a room to herself, next to the dead guy and his supposed wife, but that looked fishy from the start. We figured they were sharing him, you know, taking turns or something. But my cousin Tia, she's in room service. She says he always slept alone." One side of her mouth curled. "The wife bedded with the rich lady."

I imitated Phoebe's expression. She expected me to be appalled or titillated, probably both. They thought Zelda Shilling vacationed with a lesbian prostitute and her steroid-addicted pimp. It might have made a more convincing cover than a fake honeymoon between the bodyguards.

Phoebe read the room numbers off the screen. "Twenty-four and Twenty-five." Then she added with morbid indifference, "Though I suppose one of them is vacant now." You might have thought the boathouse doubled as a morgue most weekends.

I smiled my thanks and started away, then stopped again. "There's one more thing." I'd almost forgotten about my virgin daiquiri drinker. As long as I was there, what was one more invasion of privacy? Once I had stolen a college boyfriend's phone bill from the mail carrier before breaking up: thirty dollars of long-distance charges to his ex-girlfiiend. "Do you have any other single registrations?"

The keyboard taps drew me back. "Yeah. A, ah, Margaret Parker?"

I tried to match the name to the roguish cheekbones and five o'clock stubble. A camera guy named Lesley had asked me out once—but Margaret? Then I remembered the soccer mom from the plane. "No others?"

Her chin dropped again. "One more. Andrew McGuffin." I reached over the counter to steal a pen and Post-it note, pleased finally to have a name to match the handsome face. "Room Thirty-one." She paused, then added mischievously, "Nice guy."

"You know him?"

"He's been here a couple times this month."

"Why?"

The roll of her eyes expressed a general bewilderment with the tourist population. "He tips well, and he's not obnoxious about it. Mrs. Caldiera said he left her the signed copy of some book he was still reading after he found her looking at it. It was something rare she couldn't get around here."

"Thanks," I said, mentally tallying Phoebe's endorsement against the points he'd lost at the pool last night. He was ahead again. "If this works out, I'll send you our firstborn or something."

This time when I turned, the cop was hovering behind a row of azaleas. He looked down, feet backpedaling. If the police chief wanted to keep tabs on me, he could have gone a subtler route. I pointed at the hall behind the counter. "Is Ricky back there? I want to say hi."

Phoebe noted the cop and tugged open a folder of

Visa receipts, knowing that I was lying. "Yeah. You can't miss him. He's right by the *rear door*."

I followed the hallway back and hid in the one-stall rest room, the one room I knew he wouldn't look in. The overflowing wastebasket seemed an act of defiance against the resort's antiseptic facade. I fought the urge to pee, wishing I'd changed into underwear before throwing on the sundress. I listened at the door for boots on the linoleum before cutting through the administrative wing, wondering why he hadn't followed me back.

When I looped around the front bushes, I spied my polyester shadow chatting up Phoebe. At first I thought he was pumping her for information, but the pose was all wrong—gregarious slouch, elbow on the counter. He was hitting on her, snippets of their laughter carrying in the breeze. Was I the only person on this island not getting any action? I waved at Phoebe over his back. She grinned without moving her head.

Shilling's room was situated in the opposite corner of the resort. I jogged across the grass and nearly collided with a pair of newlyweds at the corner bungalow. The woman clung to her mate, anticipating a mugging. I apologized and started reading door plates for Shilling's numbers, finding hers tucked into a private corner at the end of the row, no view of the ocean at all.

I scraped my calf on the wicker table and rapped on the glass, unable to see through the slit in the curtains. The longer I waited, the less I knew what I was doing. How did you address one of the richest women in America? My second knock echoed more softly, my knuckles hesitating midair.

Maybe this wasn't such a good idea.

So an infamous celebrity took a pair of bodyguards on vacation with her. If my ex-husband were Richard Shilling, I would too. Even I knew the rumors connecting him to every headline death from Princess Di to Sonny Bono. Of course she was spooked. But that didn't mean anything. Her bodyguard had drowned; he hadn't been murdered. There weren't any bullet holes in his polo shirt, and no one could have pushed that brawny neck under the waves against his will.

I remembered how the Amazon had glared at me in the boat room. She must have thought I'd killed her partner, she and Shilling awash in the same paranoia. Zelda wasn't shattered with grief; those fingers had quaked with fear. She figured that Richard Shilling, the little shit she hadn't wanted to talk to over her creme brûlée, had found an alternate means of communication. The chief must have assigned the extra cop to me in order to placate her. What choice did he have? Heads rolled at her command. Putting my name on the top of an imaginary suspect list probably soothed her, even if her bodyguard was dead only because he couldn't handle a drink on his evening off. The guy had probably slipped on the wet leaves and knocked his head. Three hundred pounds of comatose muscles had done the rest.

I backed away from the door, hoping the Amazon wasn't poised on the other side of the curtain, a Magnum barrel centered on my silhouette. From the outside, the bungalow looked the same as mine, only with more shade trees and no foot traffic. Definitely not millionaire swank. That was the one detail that didn't add up. If the woman wanted privacy, she could have rented the whole island. Why was she at the resort at all? Hadn't Melissa said the Shillings owned a beach-front mansion near here?

"Nobody home, huh?"

I yelped and twirled, expecting St. Thomas's finest ready to cuff me. But then I saw the sun hitting those curls and recognized my Mr. McGuffin. I laughed and stated the obvious: "You startled me."

His frown held steady, but I approached anyway, embarrassed by how I had misread him before. We had already exchanged injuries and insults; this had to go better. "Sorry about yesterday. My name's Ashley." He stared at the hand I extended. "I think we were victims of a misunderstanding?"

He returned my shake without squeezing, as though unsure whether he wanted to be touching me at all. "And I suppose that cop following you is suffering from the same confusion?"

Mother chimed in my head: *Be charming, Ashley. Be charming.*

"No, no, that's something different." I laughed a string of high notes. "I had this—little adventure last night."

All of the intelligence and humor I had sensed before vanished under his rigid expression. "Is that what you call it?"

I dropped the smile. "Look. You got me wrong. I'm not a—" I couldn't even say it. *Whore*. Why was I wasting my time on a guy who would pay a stranger for sex? "Never mind. I was just trying to be friendly." I marched past him and spat his name. "*Andrew*." It sounded like an insult. *Asshole*.

He should have been startled that I knew it, but his voice betrayed no surprise. "So it's just a job to you? Nothing personal about it?" His call grew louder, angrier as I walked away. "*Your kind makes me sick.*"

I flipped him the finger over my shoulder. I never thought he was cute. *Who Wants To Be A Blind Date* had standards. I pictured his headshot sailing through the shredder behind the secretary's desk.

9

If You Were a Drink on My Bar Tab, What Would You Be?

I had lousy taste in men. If I did have a therapist, she would have told me that I was purposely punishing myself and that chaperoning was a self-destructive means of barring romantic possibility from my life by fostering cynical detachment and intellectual superiority. I figured it was karma; suitors turned to swine in my arms. My first crush had pelted me with mud balls during our second recess together. My prom date, an otherwise sane-looking A student from my A.P. European History class, had appeared at my door in a camouflage tuxedo with a safety orange cummerbund and tie. My latest prince, Mr. McGuffin, hadn't even lasted until midnight before devolving into his toady self.

I trudged down to the beach with my fists in my pockets. Randy's and Melissa's towels draped their chaise longues like drop cloths, but they were nowhere to be seen. I surveyed the water until I spotted the second bicycle boat, surprised they had mustered the gumption.

I read my watch as I plopped into a chair. Ten o'clock. I could hear the police chief's snarl in my head, knowing that a plane was leaving the island that very moment. I imagined the lift of its wings and wished I were on it. If I had left, I wondered how long it would have taken Melissa and Randy to discover my missing bag. The image of their panicked gapes cheered me. I crossed my legs and watched their boat turning barely a dozen feet from the dock. I thought Randy would have ventured deeper, out toward the rocks if he could, but then I noticed the black couple emerging from under the shadow of the awning. It wasn't them.

A wave of needle pricks climbed my back as I hopped to my feet and squinted up and down the edges of the bay. Though absurd, my panic gripped me with certainty. *They're dead.* Abandon my duties for fifteen minutes and this is my punishment. It was just a matter of spotting a swath of skin in a breaker, a limb wedged into the rocks. My eyes kept returning to the opening in the path where the busboys had trampled the weeds lugging out the dead bodyguard.

I tried to ignore the hysterical shouts in my head, but I was already convinced that they had been abducted, probably murdered. Zelda Shilling was taking her revenge on me—my two bimbos for her bodyguard. God knew what the crazed gun moll was capable of. If she thought I worked for her ex-husband, the deadliest gambler since Al Capone, then I was just a betting chip, Randy and Melissa the ante.

My sundress snapped like a flag as I ran for the telephone, debating who I should dial after the police chief—my mother or the secretary. I had a real "tidbit" for his press release for a change, though I wasn't sure whether a dead bachelor and bachelorette would tank the show or catapult it up the Nielsen chart.

That's when I spotted Melissa at the edge of the bar. Randy had wedged himself against her, his hand resting tentatively on her bare thigh. Though it was still morning, they both twirled celery stalks in their glasses. Bloody Marys, an alcoholic's health food. I slowed to a casual pace and tried to convince myself that I wasn't disappointed.

"Hi, guys."

Melissa bristled, as if caught on a basement room couch with a boyfriend. She smiled an exaggerated hello, while Randy scowled proudly, desperate for my disapproval. The bar had been his idea. I wanted to lean to his ear and whisper, *Why don't the two of you take a bottle up to the room and hump until lunch?*

I pointed at Randy's glass instead. "Whatcha drinking? I could use one of those."

A pudgy couple in matching bathing suits occupied the adjacent seats. I considered dragging a stool from the next table but dreaded the conversation. I steered for the other end of the bar, the bartender rising to meet me halfway.

"Just an O.J."

She grabbed a glass from the row. "Hard night, huh?" She spoke with Phoebe's knowing ring, but with the wrong accent. I didn't recognize her, her skin a shade lighter than most of the locals', an odd, almost Asian height to her cheekbones. But I could tell she knew my story as well as the rest of the staff.

She slid the glass into my hand. "Who's your friend?"

I assumed she meant Randy, but her head tilted in the opposite direction. I twisted in the stool to see my private bloodhound hovering at the patio entrance. He'd cut his reconnaissance distance in half, his arms crossed in pouty vigilance. I felt a little guilty for ditching him.

"That's my secret admirer." He recoiled when I waved at him.

"Not much of a secret."

The ice shifted in my glass as I raised it to my lips. It would have tasted better with a shot of Cruzan Rum, but my stomach felt hollow. My whole body felt hollow.

"So why's he trailing you?" The bartender stayed near, polishing a row of clean glasses suspended above her head.

"Haven't you heard? The police chief thinks I'm a killer." A dry chuckle echoed into my glass. "I took that beefy bodyguard on a midnight stroll last night—and whacked him."

Her hand hesitated. "Chief Cosway?" The whites above her pupils widened.

"I guess."

"That man is bad news. Don't get on the wrong side of him." She shook her head slowly, in sync with the rag and tumbler in her hands. "Your body will be bobbing in those breakers next."

She stepped away, and I glanced behind me, furtively this time. The cop had staked out a table on the other side of the pool, a stark blue isle in a sea of white wicker. I tried to picture him in an interrogation room, extorting his percentage from a dealer or smuggler, but he lacked that look of hardened corruption, his gaze too mild. If there had been music playing, I would have asked him to dance.

"Hey, you're the one who found the body, aren't you?"

The voice boomed over my other shoulder, my drink splashing as I turned. I recognized the soccer mom immediately this time, but couldn't remember the name Phoebe had given her. Parker, something Parker. She wore the most touristy-looking Virgin Islands T-shirt I'd ever seen, the decal angling up at me from her breasts.

I smiled blandly. "Afraid so." I hoped my nonchalance might defuse interest, but every conversation around the bar halted, Melissa and Randy staring with doe-like surprise.

Parker perched her sunglasses over her bangs and peered at me. "That must have been so awful. I don't know how you can bear to stay here after something like that." She overacted her sympathy; it was details she wanted.

"You found a body?" I hadn't thought Melissa's voice could drop that low. Randy released his grip on her thigh in order to face me.

"Who was it?"

Parker pounced on the question. "Some guy staying here on his honeymoon. Isn't that horrible? I heard his wife had to identify him. Can you imagine?"

Melissa could not imagine.

"Was it a swimming accident or something?" Randy assumed a professional air. His slouch vanished, but a shred of tomato clung to his lip.

She gave a half-snort. "That's the story they're telling."

The muscles at the base of my neck began to tighten. "You don't think it's true?"

She spread her knowing chuckle up and down the bar. "Well, St. Thomas has more than its fair share of drownings, if you know what I mean." It was the same smutty laugh the *Who Wants To Be A Blind Date* host used.

"No. What do you mean?" I couldn't stand innuendoes.

Randy made an elaborate show of rolling his eyes and cut off Parker. "Mob business. You don't know about that?" His expression was piteous contempt. "They own half the Caribbean. *Playboy* had a story about it this month. They send people down here that they don't want to come back."

Melissa's eyes turned to perfect cartoon circles. She tore herself away from Randy long enough to glare at me: *This is where you brought us?*

"You can't believe everything you—"

"I wouldn't be surprised if the resort was empty by noon." Parker was enjoying herself, a grin edging behind the grimace. "It's just not safe anymore."

"I'm sure the police have things under control." Without intending to, I shot a sideways glance at my personal constable. The row of eyes followed, while the cop writhed back in his chair. How could I tell them I was the hot lead? "Besides, I saw the body. I didn't see anything suspicious."

Parker's face warped through the bottom of my orange juice glass. "Did you look for bruises under the hairline? Or injection marks? Sometimes they insert the needle under a fingernail. Or he could have ingested something. Never know without cutting him open."

I choked on a piece of ice while the morning drinkers listened in silence. "You know a lot about this sort of thing."

"Part of my job." She held my gaze longer than most lovers would.

"What are you, a mortician?" Randy cackled at his own joke, the others joining in, desperate to laugh at something.

He shut up when she met his eyes. "Reporter for the *Washington Post*. I'm covering the Shilling story."

"There's a story?" Melissa shook Randy's arm free as Parker's grin finally broke through.

"Honey, there's always a story."

She turned on a sandaled heel and strolled between the wicker furniture, the cop half rising as she passed. I didn't want to like her, but I couldn't help myself. I imagined myself in her brazen gait. It took guts to book a single room in a couples' resort, story or no story. I wondered if I'd be as confident at forty, or as alone.

I slid my empty glass across the bar top. "C'mon, kids; we've got Paradise to conquer."

If Columbus Discovered You Naked on the Beach, What Would He Conclude about the New World?

I offered the cop a seat on our patio while Melissa browsed her suitcase, but he only gave me a Buckingham Palace guard's stare. His hair sparkled in the sun like new asphalt. Melissa was searching for the right combination to wear over her bikini. She wanted to go shirtless, but I warned her that the locals would frown. She emerged in short shorts and a sheer white blouse tied around her midriff. Not much better.

Our taxi, a two-bench truck with metal railings and awning, idled outside the Lovelund lobby. The cop watched us scramble in the rear but made no move to follow. I expected a squad car to emerge from the dust at each hilltop, but we arrived at the Red Hook pier unaccompanied. Apparently Chief Cosway's indulgence of anxious millionaires had its boundaries.

The boat ride to St. John, a standard on my weekend itinerary, was nauseating but short. I stood at the prow like a figurehead, keeping Cruz Bay in my line of vision and trying to ignore the waves buffeting the hull, but it didn't help my stomach. I glimpsed corpses in every crest.

Melissa tottered as she crossed the dock. Randy looked pale despite the start of a sunburn. They both blinked at the town, waiting for their vision to clear. Downtown Cruz Bay was a half dozen blocks hacked out of the forest leaning over it. Randy gazed wistfully at the closed Wendy's while I chattered about my favorite lunch spot, ignoring the fact that a tree was growing out of the ruined building in the next lot.

Despite the chalkboard list of fresh seacatch, Randy ordered a cheeseburger. Melissa went vegetarian. She couldn't seem to get over the fact that a chicken was pecking under the adjacent table. Randy appeared more disturbed by the absence of Anheuser-Busch products from the menu. He sipped his Red Stripe suspiciously.

I lobbed conversational gambits but kept my eyes roaming. I'd seized the chair opposite the railing so I could watch both roads. It wasn't the clean geometry of a Manhattan intersection, but at least I'd know if my cop had caught the next ferry.

Halfway through my grouper, I spotted a different Lovelund neighbor. Zelda Shilling emerged from the dock crowd, her ruby dress blazing, though presumably the hat and shades meant she was traveling incognito. The Amazon towered a full foot above her, head swiveling methodically while Shilling counted cracks in the pavement. Neither had come for the scenery.

They headed away from the row of cafes, toward the national park entrance, a roller-coaster hill at the end of the block. I reached for my wallet, my curiosity careening ahead of me.

"Oh goodness, look at the time." I didn't look at my watch, but no one noticed. Melissa swallowed a mouthful of cottage cheese as I tucked a pair of twenties under my glass. I lost sight of Shilling behind the rental lot, thankful that I'd booked our Jeep while Melissa was lazing in the shower.

"They'll only hold our Jeep till one." It was a blatant lie, but they believed everything. Randy chugged his second beer, then jogged to catch up, belching with each step.

Shilling's Jeep bumped out of the lot as we neared, the Amazon muscling the wheel like a sailor working a rusted water valve. The Virgin Islands hadn't discovered power steering yet. Shilling clung to the outside of the door, her other hand clutching her hat.

I broke into a full sprint now. Melissa held her own, but Randy dropped back, winded. "Christ—it's five till—can't we—?"

Shilling's Jeep was white, like all the other rentals on St. John, but I managed to catch the plate as they whirred around the bend. USVI-149. Melissa nearly collided into me when I stopped; Randy had bent over to wheeze over a pothole a few feet back. If the Amazon glanced at her rearview mirror, she would spot us—Richard Shilling's mod squad of crackerjack assassins. I listened to the engine roar vanish into the growth and rehearsed the numbers in my head.

National forest claimed nine of the island's fourteen square miles, with only two roads connecting the dozen beaches. I still had a chance of finding them—and maybe a reprieve from Cosway's suspect list if I could convince Mrs. Shilling of the misunderstanding. I didn't much care why or if the bodyguard had been murdered. Parker's theory sounded like the fantasy scoop of an overzealous reporter, like almost everything else I read in the papers. I just wanted to keep myself out of a police lineup when the story broke. That and I was curious. If Richard Shilling had his ex-wife running scared, why on earth had she cornered herself here? With no Romeo left to chase, I needed something to relieve the monotony.

I didn't know the guy working the rental counter, so I couldn't coax him along, the tune he hummed under his breath maddeningly slow. He copied the number on my network credit card with monkish diligence. I slashed my signature and ignored him fingering the carbons.

Randy's machismo flared when he saw me going for the driver's side door. "Sorry, cowboy. Insurance requirement." That one was actually true. He wouldn't have admitted it in front of Melissa, but his nod betrayed relief. He'd forgotten the roads were reversed, an obscure influence of the British Islands to the east. At least they didn't mount the steering wheels on the passenger sides, too.

Melissa clutched the dashboard when I took the first turn too fast, Randy bouncing in the rearview mirror. I knew the blind hairpins by heart. Breathtaking view after breathtaking view blurred by while Melissa yelled something over and over. It was impossible to hear with the windows down and the top rolled back, but I saw her pointing at her camera.

"The view's better on the way back!" I wasn't sure what that meant either, but it seemed to placate her.

I slowed at the first parking lot, craning my neck to see the rows of painted asphalt, empty but for a cluster of cars at the beach entrance. I glimpsed another white rental Jeep and wrenched to a stop in the middle of the road, only to squeal the tires when I read the wrong numbers on the license plate. Melissa yelped and groped for a handhold, her purse flinging out of her grip. She gawked at me as I continued to accelerate.

"Too crowded!"

I contrived an excuse about wind while we left the second parking lot. Randy had stopped trying to hold himself between our seats and was fastening his belt. They'd given up reasoning with me. I was worried that Shilling was headed to the other edge of the island. East End was less of a town than Cruz Bay, literally one stop sign, but I would never have found her between the private drives and dilapidated garages.

As I cruised the fourth parking lot, I noticed the Jeep tucked beside a safari bus. USVI-149. Randy and Melissa wondered but did not question why I ignored the empty slot next to it, motoring instead to the far end of the lot to park.

"Easier to get out."

Melissa tried to return my smile, but her lips were pale. Randy muttered profanities as he extricated himself from the back.

If Shilling was trying to stay low, she had chosen the wrong beach. Trunk Bay was the most gorgeous and so the most frequented beach on the island. Picnic tables, changing rooms and snack bars lined the path from the parking lot. Cruise-ship tags hung from half the tourists' shirts and halter straps. I stopped at the snorkel rental while perusing faces, mostly pale wrinkles and double chins.

Randy no longer felt obliged to offer his gentlemanly assistance. I threw the bag of flippers over one shoulder and the life preservers over the other. He and

Melissa were busy gaping at the beach: a hundred yards of pearly sand, water bright enough to be chlorinated, an island of palm trees decoratively centering the bay. Sky blue and ocean blue merged at the horizon. Little wonder they'd shot one of those God-awful 1492 movies here. I dropped the bags where Columbus had collapsed on the sand in prayer.

"Okay, let's gear up!" I tossed the scuba masks at them. I doubted Shilling had come to soak up the rays, but I scanned the beach behind Melissa's shoulder just in case. She had that betrayed expression on again. She saw only two sets of flippers in the bag.

"You're not—?"

"Naaah." I swatted the air, dismissing the invitation. "You'll have more fun on your own." My smile wavered briefly. I'd let a couple go out alone only once before. When I'd caught up with them, they were bobbing in their life preservers, fornicating.

Melissa lifted the equipment, reluctant to dress. She hadn't planned on mussing her hair that much. The orange vest made her arms hang funny. It was a fashion leveler. No one looked good snorkeling. Even Randy protested the flippers, but I insisted, watching them waddle penguin-like toward the waves.

"Just follow the underwater trail markers." I pointed at the reef. The flock of pelicans circling the water and dive-bombing fish looked for all the world like pterodactyls. "Good luck!"

I waved and jogged up the beach. A row of picnic tables extended past the rest room pavilion, but I could see the nearer ones stood empty. That was where the cannibals had watched Columbus' men through the trees. Shilling would have needed a better vantage point, so I steered toward the changing rooms, hoping not to interrupt a Mafia powwow. I spotted a girl inching on bikini straps in the corner, her sunburn the same shade as Zelda's dress.

A vision of high school flashed through my head, Mrs. Zaranko kneeling on the bathroom floor to peer under the stalls for smokers. An epiphany saved me from the humiliation: if Shilling was here, she wasn't looking for privacy.

I passed through a platoon of sallow-skinned tourists speaking something guttural on their way back out. The welcome center housed a cafeteria the size of a basketball court. The lunch rush was winding down, so only a few people waited in line, but half of the tables in the courtyard were still overflowing. I grabbed a hiking pamphlet for camouflage and peered over its edge for my prey.

A tower of poorly stacked food trays teetered above the garbage can, as half-wadded hamburger wrappers flapped at its base. Randy would have been in ecstasy, but I couldn't imagine Shilling being caught dead in the place.

Then I spotted the Amazon's head protruding behind the toupees. I shifted windows for a better view. Neither ate, but this time a cigarette quivered in Shilling's hand. It rolled off the table the second time she dropped it. The Amazon bent toward her, apparently mumbling something reassuring. She patted her arm as though petting the top of a dog's head, while Shilling frowned, unconvinced. She would have agreed to any of her ex's demands now, recanting all of her public accusations, pleading guilty to libel, suppressing a lifetime's worth of damning evidence, all in exchange for an unguarded night's sleep.

I wanted to get closer, but the only set of doors to

the patio stood in plain sight. If I worked my way around the building, I could have listened from the wall of bay-trees tilting behind them. I was debating whether I could crawl under the patio beams and scrutinize their soles when the Amazon saved me from my schemes. She gave a final, perfunctory glance at her watch and rose, while Shilling remained riveted. Their eyes met, then Shilling pawed for another cigarette, apparently anxious about being left alone. This was where a second bodyguard would have been handy.

I hid behind the pamphlet stand, watching the Amazon near the window. Her gait was long and businesslike without being hurried, the stride muggers avoided—not that anyone would have considered taking her on. Tourists parted from her path and pointed at her back. She was a walking steroid billboard.

I studied Shilling, who was drawing almost every breath through the cigarette. Her shoulders hunched as if from cold. I could have approached her now, asked her anything I wanted, charmed her with my warmth and innocence. She would have listened to anything I said, answered any question, agreed to the most whimsical of requests—then phoned Cosway from her cell phone to arrest me. I had no legitimate reason for following her, nothing I could explain into a police tape recorder. I should have been watching Randy and Melissa sucking in water through their breathing tubes.

Zelda examined her nails, back bent small, like a child's. She wasn't checking the entrance for anyone or studying her watch. She was just sitting, content to be out of the action. The familiarity of the pose struck me. That could have been me, bowed over a bowl of cereal at my counter, or lost in a pile of paperwork at my desk. How many hours of how many days had I passed that way? I shoved the pamphlet back, knowing that the real show had already headed out the door.

The Amazon made a right off the beach steps. I followed behind the trees, swerving between picnic tables. I tripped on a camper's backpack propped against a palm trunk, straining to keep her in view. My path narrowed first, but I could see the beach towels dwindling around her, her bulky sneakers stomping at the waves' edge. I had to scamper over boulder-sized roots, but I knew where she was headed. She checked over her back a last time before ducking into the bushes.

The wind blew more harshly at the periphery, the tree limbs maintaining a constant shudder above the wave-pelted rocks. Otherwise, I'd have no chance of following undetected. My clumsiest steps were swallowed in the woody hum.

The Amazon charged yards ahead as I improvised my own trail on a higher bank. Chief Cosway's voice murmured in my head: *Most tourists don't know about that seaside path.* This was another of my favorite getaways; Donna and I agreed that it was the only way to enjoy the best bay on the island without suffering the tourists. I'd brought a couple down here last year. I wouldn't have risked it if they hadn't small-talked hiking boot brand names on the plane. I had a hard time explaining the twisted ankle to my producer. Bachelorettes were such fragile creatures.

I scuffed skin from my toes trying to keep pace in my sandals. The sundress caught twice on the thorns. I was ready to turn back when I noticed the Amazon had stopped moving. Her yellow shirt—bodyguards apparently preferred primary colors—hovered near the rocks, blue waves lapping behind her. She braced her legs and crossed her arms, chin raised as though facing someone. If this was a rendezvous point, it was ideal for both its remoteness and its proximity to crowds.

I continued at a crawl, straining to catch their voices.

"Where is she?" The bushes obscured the speaker, but his voice wafted up the hill with the cries of low-flying gulls.

The Amazon had to yell to be heard. "She's had enough."

"Then what are you doing here?" The wind carried his next sentence seaward. I scampered a few feet nearer and stared over the clearing.

"To tell you she's given in." The Amazon slashed a slow sideways karate chop through the air. "It's over."

I could discern his legs now, but his face fluttered behind two tree limbs. "I'm surprised. I didn't think she'd cave that easily."

She shrugged contemptuously. "You were wrong. Now go home."

The sound of his laugh congealed my blood. It wasn't sinister, only familiar. I'd heard it the first time by the lavatory doors in the airplane, the second time with a virgin daiquiri in my hand beside the pool.

"If it's all the same to you, I think I'll stick around a while."

"Suit yourself." She pointed a barrel-sized finger at his face. "Just stay the hell away from Zelda."

She spun away, fists swaying. McGuffin stepped forward, mouth open, but yelled nothing. He rooted himself on her rock and glared at her back, his maroon shirt billowing.

I wanted to believe this was the look of a jilted lover. He had expected Shilling. He had a cooler of champagne and a downy blanket hidden around the next rock. Maybe Zelda was protecting him from her jealous ex-husband, the dead man a warning to curtail her sex life, not her press conferences.

But the frown looked all wrong, not the vulnerable quiver of love spurned. He rubbed his chin, tapped it with a knuckle. Romeo never looked so conniving. I was staring at Richard Shilling's hit man.

My feet shuffled backward automatically. He was lean but strong, the wind molding his shirt against his chest and arms, muscles toned to precision wiriness. He had drowned a three-hundred-pound bodyguard last night and had no casts or bruises to show for it. I imagined an arsenal of holsters strapped to his belt back, hidden under billows.

My dress caught against a branch, and I yanked as though fighting from his grip. I pictured his hands on me, the palms damp with my blood and calloused from gun handles. I remembered the ungiving crush of his body against mine in the airplane and scrambled faster, amazed that I had fallen for him, a new zenith in my saga of bad picks. That was never warmth and intelligence eyeing me but amused calculation. The man was a killer.

It was foolish to stand, rocks foundering under my feet, but I couldn't quell my panic. I needed to be on the other side of the hilltop, out of his range of vision—his range of fire. It was only a few yards away.

When the ground gave, I lurched forward, skinning

my palms and knees. The pain registered distantly, my frozen attention focused on a dislodged rock thundering through the bushes behind me. Everything else fell silent, the wind gripped inside my lungs. I couldn't bear to look, but my neck turned by itself. I saw him: face creased, eyes fixed on mine.

11

Should a Girl Play Hard to Get?

The slope tilted suddenly, rocks spraying in my wake. I grabbed at weeds, dirt, anything to pull myself up, branches breaking against my face. When my sandal caught, I shook it free, deaf to everything but my own gasping. How would a bullet feel as it punctured my skin? I pictured a string of blood spooling from the back of my dress, blood staining the cotton daisies, and then the slow clomp of his boots approaching as I gazed up, paralyzed.

I didn't turn around until I reached the hilltop. I imagined him feet behind me, fingers clawing my dress hem, but the path was empty behind me. Branches quivered where my body had slapped them. I ran further, hurdling downed trunks and ditches, but when I looked again, he was still missing. I wanted to think I was safe, that he'd never seen me, but I heard Parker's no-nonsense voice grumbling in my head: *Use your brain, girl.*

The clearing stood empty, too. He had to be somewhere. My muscles trembled, each a compressed spring straining to fling me forward, but I made myself breathe, made my body obey. It quaked but eased into a crouch. McGuffin couldn't have climbed the hill that fast. I'd stood yards above him, a violent slope between us. Only an imbecile would have tried to pursue me directly.

I probed the length of the path below, realizing that he could have covered twice the distance on flat terrain and no thorns clawing at his skirts. I searched for a flash of maroon between the yellow-browns and yellow-greens, grateful that my sundress blended. For once my hair color was a survival asset.

I inched between the bushes, eyes analyzing each new angle. It felt familiar, searching for a puzzle piece among the forest of jigsaw shapes. My father and I used to spend hours at our dining room table assembling denser landscapes. I scrutinized each square of the imaginary grid.

I had crawled a dozen feet before I spotted him, or at least a splotch of color that could have been him. I'd overlooked it twice because it was so close, barely yards ahead of me, halfway between the hilltop and the seaside path beneath it. A Manhattan jaywalker could have covered the distance in seconds. I held my breath and shivered, my dress soaked with sweat, my toes and fingers aching with my weight. I wanted to get it over with and shout: *I see you!*

Instead I waited, telling myself that I had the advantage. I wasn't the hunter; I didn't have to move. Then I pictured his shirt draped across a bush, the classic TV show gambit from every outdoor chase scene ever filmed. He could have been zeroing in from anywhere.

My fist tightened around a rock, wide and flat, perfect for slicing air. I hurled it in a high curve over the saplings. It crackled through branches, then shattered on a boulder near enough to my target, but the splotch of maroon didn't move. My throat constricted, fighting down panic as I twisted, searching the trees behind me. I felt blind, inundated in darkness. He could have been anywhere.

Then the maroon splotch stood, and I saw his face. He was glaring at the hillside, clueless where the rock had come from. He'd assumed I'd spotted him, so he'd abandoned his hiding spot. This should have worked to my advantage and gotten me points for flushing him out. Only now his movements grew bolder. He had nothing to lose as he thrashed up the rest of the hillside in a reckless climb.

If I were to bolt, I would pass the crest first, but then he would trail me by feet. The more branches I beat back, the faster he could catch me. So I wormed backward, watching him cut off my escape route back to the mainland. If I dropped to the lower path—the real path—I could make a dash for the beach. But if he glimpsed me, I was dead. How could I outrace him with one sandal? I was used to exercise bikes, legs pumping furiously to hold me in one place.

He paused at the top of the hill and bent to inspect something, a broken branch probably, evidence of the trail I'd blazed following the Amazon. He turned his back to me, bobbing his head to peer between trees. He was debating the possibility that I had escaped him, that I'd raced out of the woods and was already halfway across the parking lot to my Jeep. I stared, willing the thought into his head: *Yes, yes, go that way. She's getting away.*

His legs wavered, about to obey, but another thought held him. He was a professional, a pragmatist. If I'd made it past him, then there was no catching me, no point in trying. But if I hadn't, he still had a chance, regardless of the odds. Better to chase the hypothetical prey he had cornered. The good, sound reasoning of a hit man.

He began at a cautious pace, but I didn't wait, knowing I only had a few yards' head start. He startled when I sprung up, even stumbled back a step, as though he were the one risking his life.

I plunged over the first bank of bushes. The rocks hurt my foot, but I landed in a skid and leaped through a web of branches. Fear made me fearless. My feet struck at anything; balance meant nothing. I was falling, not running.

I pitched onto the open path and glimpsed blood somewhere—my arm, my leg? But I was already standing, lurching forward. I'd never felt so much adrenaline, my body desperately alive.

I started in a sprint toward the beach—then halted. He had nearly descended the hillside already. If he'd chased me, as I'd hoped, I might have had a chance, but he'd backtracked, taken his own path down to cut me off.

I turned in the opposite direction, my legs moving heavily now. Each stamp flushed energy from my body. This was futile. I knew where the path ended. I knew I was racing toward the edge of the peninsula.

The trees thinned, a turbulent blue looming between the stripes of bark. I arrived at the clearing sooner than I expected, sooner than I wanted to. The path slanted into ocean, the rocks propped in the waves like piled tombstones.

I considered jumping. An anchored yacht shimmered mirage-like, maybe a mile offshore. I was used to lazy laps in an Olympic-sized pool, but I might last a couple of minutes, assuming he didn't pick me off in his gun sights when I bobbed up, lungs bursting for air. I peered back at the beach, but the stripe of white looked no closer, the colored spots of towels as tiny as lint.

His footfalls rattled nearer, maroon jostling behind the leaves. Then he emerged, chest heaving as he slowed. He eyed me as his hand reached for a tree, back bending to catch his breath. I expected a gun in the other fist. Was that too easy? Shilling's bodyguard had outweighed him two to one, but he'd offed the guy without suffering so much as a skinned knee. I couldn't remember what Parker, the reporter, had said, something about injection marks and bruises. I was going to die at the hands of an artist.

He shook his head as he muscled his panting into words. "I knew it was you." I couldn't remember his face without that grimace of disgust. He looked me up and down and laughed, his finger gesturing tentatively. "You don't look so tough."

I clenched my jaw but couldn't stifle my own panting, each breath in sync with his. We might have just had sex. I frowned at my dress, the bloody backs of my hands, and imagined what my face looked like. The sea air stung in a dozen places. I swallowed and met his eyes again, surprised that he hadn't moved any closer. He was used to facing down Schwazeneggers, but something was making him hesitate.

He licked his lips. "You think you've got me beat, don't you?"

Beat? I was cornered, alone and defenseless, no witness within a scream. How did I have him beat? Then it clicked: I'd caught him off-guard at the bar last night, too. I made *him* nervous. He hadn't mistaken me for a prostitute but another of Zelda's people, a third bodyguard reinforcing the ones flanking her. He thought I was calling the shots from the sidelines, covering the Amazon's back when she retreated to the beach. When I had refused to "negotiate" at the bar, he had knocked off her partner like a piece from a chessboard. He thought I was a killer, too, Zelda Shilling's top employee. Why else would he hesitate about eliminating a witness, just some pesky tourist who had spied him meeting with the Amazon? His ignorance was the only thing keeping me alive.

My spine straightened. Tough. I could do tough. I crossed my arms and pictured myself staring down the secretary by the watercooler. "Do I?"

He started nodding. "You think you've seen the best of me." He stepped toward me, the motion of his chin cranking up his courage. "Don't you, Miss Farrell?"

I shouldn't have been startled that he knew my name, too. Phoebe must have been feeling gregarious this morning. She'd probably thought she was helping me out. The cute guy in Thirty-one.

I visualized myself in my best pants suit—pale blue Jones New York—and threw a hip as I sneered. "If this is your best, I don't need to see more."

It sounded like something yelled on a school playground, but his legs stopped. The ripple of insult on his face looked sincere. Did he chat this way with all his victims? I didn't know what kind of con I was pulling, but I didn't dare stop. The only way to walk off this peninsula was on the path behind him.

He'd stopped breathing hard, but his face was still flushed. "Oh, there's more, there's plenty more."

I rolled my eyes. "Let's cut the games." All I had to do was walk past him. There was a yard between his shoulder and the rocky drop. A thorn pushed into the heel of my bare foot as I made my leg bend. "When you're ready to get serious, you know where to find me."

I'd practiced this walk a thousand times in my head, the way I wanted to stride victoriously from my producer's office. The name on the door had changed, but not the fantasy. I radiated pure confidence, my resignation letter unfolding in his confused fingers.

McGuffin studied me, stunned by my approach. I held my head straight, as though alone on a busy sidewalk, but blind, a bachelorette strutting into her spotlight. Four steps, three steps. The wind drummed like applause as his shirtsleeve grazed my shoulder. A thousand heartbeats.

Then a tourniquet of hard flesh seized my wrist. "Not so fast."

I stumbled, his touch clammy but painful. The tips of his fingers dug into my arm. A scream boiled in my gut, and I glanced toward the water, praying for a stray pair of snorkelers, Melissa and Randy coming to rescue me.

I steadied myself instead and raised my chin. "Let go of me." I tried to drain my voice of emotion, but the last note wavered.

He pulled me nearer, almost close enough to kiss.

"What are you going to do? Take me for a swim?"

He twisted my wrist back. He wasn't quite as muscular as I had feared, but plenty more than my one-week self-defense course could handle. His biceps tightened under his sleeve. I felt brittle beside him, hollow as bird bones.

I reached to pry his pinky back, the weakest finger. Anyone could break it. But he was expecting that. He yanked me off balance so easily that I had to reach over his fist to support myself. I even whimpered in case he didn't realize that he had me completely, my whole body as limp and defenseless as a bent flower stalk.

Then I swung my elbow into his throat.

His jaw dropped, but no sound escaped. His fist opened on the same pulley, and I watched him stagger backward. It had never worked half as well on the aerobic mats with my instructor.

McGuffin clutched his neck with both hands, unable to breathe. I was startled by what I'd done. Part of me wanted to comfort him, cradle him to the ground. I reached for his arm, debating whether CPR would help, but he backed away from me, oblivious to the edge behind him. I opened my mouth to warn him, but then remembered the feel of the dead bodyguard's skin, the cool slickness against my fingers. I tasted it as though I had just kissed those fish-pale lips. When I inhaled, my sweat smelled like decay.

I roundhoused McGuffin in the stomach with my sandaled foot. He folded in half like a playing card and rolled down the rocks in slow motion. I watched him cling to the bank as though easing into a bathtub, the water pulling him in without a splash.

My head swiveled back every few yards, but the path remained empty behind me as I limped toward the beach. I would have run, but the thorn in my foot throbbed too much. I wasn't about to stop and look for the lost sandal.

12

Are You Turned on by Catfights?

I knew I was going to get some stares. One couple retracted their legs as I passed. I considered kicking sand at them but didn't want to sacrifice my look of self-absorption, my remaining shred of dignity.

I expected a pair of empty Lovelund Resort towels, but Melissa and Randy lounged side by side, toes and knees touching. They appeared alone in a postcoital chat. Melissa was saying something coy, tapping Randy's chest slowly with her fingernails. They might have stayed in the water five minutes. Her hair was almost dry.

Randy's expression froze as he noticed me behind her shoulder. When Melissa twisted to see me, I could see the bulge in his swimming suit.

"What happened?" Her exclamation conveyed more shock than concern.

I glanced at the shredded hem of my dress again. At least it covered my bleeding knees. "Fell down."

Her mouth quivered, the words *how* and *why* vying on her lips, but she said nothing more. I caught sight of the other end of the beach, thankful that no one was emerging from the path. No one had a gun barrel trained on my head.

"We should go."

Melissa jerked up. She wasn't obedient, only embarrassed by the interruption. "Already?"

"Shouldn't you—" Randy raised his finger but couldn't bring himself to point at me. "Clean up first?"

"Back at the resort." I didn't need a mirror to know how bad I looked. I could feel the bruises congealing. I wanted to inspect my sundress more closely—if the Lovelund sewing kits had the right color thread I might salvage it—but I feared revealing the abrasions underneath.

I pulled my keys out of my purse and rattled them to demonstrate that I was serious. They'd left the snorkel equipment strewn around their towels. I shoved the flippers into the net bag, spraying Randy's legs with sand as he leaped up.

The guy at the rental shack started when I plopped the gear down, a nervous mumble following me as I passed beside the line. I heard "Sharks?" whispered incredulously.

Randy startled when I chucked him the keys in the parking lot. "Your turn." It hurt to sit. I wanted to curl on the backseat and sleep, but I probed my cuts instead. Randy took his revenge on every turn.

A cop was interviewing the cashier at the Jeep rental as we pulled in. The conversation halted when he spotted us, so I guessed the topic. It was a different officer than the one at the resort, which explained why he hadn't tailed us when we left. How much of the Virgin Island police force had Cosway devoted to me? I left my unmatched sandal in the back of the Jeep, wondering if they would bag it as evidence.

As much as it hurt, I led my entourage in a limping jog to the pier. The ferry was loading, and I wasn't waiting around for McGuffin while the next one chugged back. I claimed an uncoveted, no-view row in the center and pretended that no one was staring. Melissa kept an arm's length between us, pretending she'd never seen me before. I couldn't hear the whispers over the boat roar and didn't want to.

My thoughts churned with the waves: *stupid in a crisis stupid in a crisis.* I inspected the floor, muttering obscene rejoinders to myself. I'd exhausted my share of adventure for a lifetime. I swore I would never leave my cubicle at work again, a spinster assistant ogling studs through her bifocals.

But when I looked up, my sweat chilled. Zelda Shilling and the Amazon were poised at the front of the boat, the shadow of the second-level awning dividing them. Shilling gripped her hat and sunglasses in her fists as she hissed something undoubtedly obscene. The Amazon held her arm, trying to reason, while anger scribbled over the bleached fear on Shilling's face.

I wondered if I could hide under the seat. The boat was crowded; maybe they wouldn't see me. Then I noticed Shilling stab her finger in my direction and the Amazon's eyes flash. They were arguing about me.

The Amazon tried to steer her away, but Shilling yanked her arm free, every glance at me tightening her scowl. I thought I understood now. Her anger and fear made sense. She thought I worked with McGuffin. We were partners, taking turns tailing them, knocking off her bodyguards whim by three-hundred-pound whim. What was Cosway's miniature police force against her husband?

I dropped my head, praying that the Amazon would win the argument, when Melissa's voice burst in my ear, "Oh my God, look, it's Zelda Shilling." She slid against me for a better view.

Randy poked over her shoulder. "Where?"

"Don't look, don't look. She'll think we're gawking." He obeyed, and they perched on the seat edge and stared at their laps for all of two seconds. Melissa peeked first. "I'm going over to talk to her."

The words knotted my chest. "I'm not sure if that's such a good—"

But she was already shoving past me to stand, almost giggling with excitement. "I mean we're just two people on the same boat, right? I won't even let on I know who she is. I'll just, you know, be real casual, start talking about the weather or something." Her knees knocked against my bruises as she escaped into the aisle.

I would have yanked her back by her bikini strap, but my hands were numb. "I really don't think—" Then I saw Shilling storming toward us, the Amazon's head bobbing behind hers. She struggled to cut in front, but the aisle was too thin, legs and bags protruding. She almost collided into Shilling's back when she stopped in front of Melissa.

Shilling's rage rose from an exhaustion set deep behind her eyes, the muscles at the base of her jaw pulsing. "You people are animals—*animals*." Melissa jolted as Shilling's glare ravaged the three of us. "What do I have to do to be left alone?"

Melissa's mouth dropped open, every perfect tooth

showing. Shilling must have thought I was running an assassin-in-training program, Randy and Melissa this month's junior graduates. Before I could stop myself, I was standing and inserting myself between them, afraid what an irate millionaire might do to my bachelorette.

"Look, I understand what you think. I'm sorry about what happened. But we had nothing to do with your friend's death."

She spat as she talked. "No, of course not. You were just doing your job." Her shrill voice rattled against the metal walls. I didn't bother to see who was staring.

"No, ma'am, it's true." Melissa elbowed back into place. "We're not reporters. I swear it. We would never want to bother you." She pleaded with utter conviction, an empathetic hand rising to her mouth. "It must be *so hard* living in the center of *all that attention* all the time."

I could only blink at her.

Shilling grimaced, her fury twisting into anguish. Melissa's sympathy must have sounded like ridicule, every blink of those innocent lashes a slash of contempt. Shilling's red fingernail stabbed toward Melissa's heart. "You're a filthy piece of shit." Her face clenched as she sputtered for words. "You—you—should be flushed out to sea!"

Shilling's spittle hit Melissa's cleavage, drops soaking into her knotted blouse. Melissa was dazed at first, her face paling, then flushing. Her mouth opened, hacking out the word, "H-Ho-How—" It stuck in her throat like a hair ball. "How—how dare you talk to me like that?" Melissa was so enraged she could barely breathe. This was the worst thing that had ever happened to her. "Who do you think you are?!"

She shoved her fingers into Shilling's collarbone. I hadn't seen the gesture since my middle school playground. The Amazon swooped in like a recess aide and wrenched Melissa by the wrist. Melissa was a string of bones beside her, but her screech deafened the cabin. "Don't you touch me!"

The Amazon shied back a step with the same wary look that McGuffin had showed me. Randy was scrambling to his feet now, though I wasn't sure if he wanted to protect Melissa or get a better view. The chivalry handbook was ambiguous about girl-on-girl skirmishes. Plus the Amazon could have decapitated him.

"You think you're so important?" Melissa bobbed in Shilling's face, her head working side to side. "You think you can treat anybody any way you like? You think you're so high and mighty?" The entire boat listened to her shrieks of indignation, every face in every row turned. At least there would be witnesses. "Well, you're nothing but a dried-up call girl trying to turn her last trick. I'm amazed Richard Shilling ever let a whore like you near him."

Melissa didn't see it coming. I flinched before Shilling's hand reached her face. The slap echoed like a balloon popping, and Melissa bounced against Randy's chest. He strained to right her, but she clung dizzily, red finger marks brightening her cheek.

Shilling shoved her face at mine. "You can only push me so far." I could smell her toothpaste. "You tell Richard that." Her lower teeth were crooked—not the perfect Hollywood bite I expected. For the first time I wondered whether Richard Shilling really knew what he was getting himself into.

She spun away. The Amazon shot me the same look

and followed. Melissa whimpered against Randy's chest. I could barely make out the words between the gasps: "This—is the worst vacation—of my entire life." She shook free and stormed toward the opposite deck, trembling with self-pity. Randy trotted at her heels, all eyes following but mine.

What's Your Biggest Fashion Turnoff?

The married cop from last night in the boat room was camped at the pier looking bored and overheated. He returned my wave as I climbed into the taxi. Melissa and Randy slumped at the other end of the bench, Melissa clinging to his arm, mindless of his sunburn and winces. She wouldn't look at me, but everyone else stole glimpses while I stared out the back, the gashes on my hand cracking as I clenched the handrail.

The taxi unloaded while I waited on the resort sidewalk, but Melissa steered Randy past me as if we were strangers. His expression was almost apologetic. I limped behind them, happy to give them a head start to the rooms.

My fall from grace was unprecedented. Bachelorettes usually befriended me to escape their weekend mates. But her chilliness wasn't unwelcome, since it relieved me of half my duties. Plus I could brag to

Donna that one of my couples had hit it off for once. She considered me an unwholesome influence, claiming I whispered anti-romance propaganda in my sleeping bachelorettes' ears. Maybe I'd get the room to myself, my last night on a company-paid bed.

My threats to quit were heard so often around the water cooler that no one took them seriously anymore, me included. Only Donna asked what I would do instead, surprised that I had ever imagined myself behind a producer's desk. I laughed it off, knowing *Who Wants To Be A Blind Date* was a barricaded door for that ambition. When I got home, maybe I would finally mail out my résumé to some other stations, maybe get outside of the New York market.

I rounded the patio, disappointed to find my door slid open. I'd hoped Melissa would vanish into Randy's room and be done with me. Air-conditioning wafted through the curtains when I parted them and found Melissa standing in the center of our room gaping. She swung her open jaw at me. "What happened?"

My eyes adjusted as I stepped around the overturned suitcase blocking the doorway. Clothes crisscrossed the carpet: my white blouse, Melissa's black bra, a leather pump pinning my olive shorts. I eased past her, surveying the bare bureau top where Melissa had arranged her lotions, perfumes and hair gels with cabalistic precision. The carpet stuck to my bare feet. I pictured a team of St. Thomas' finest ransacking the drawers, emptying every container for hidden evidence.

"*What happened?!*" Tears welled in Melissa's eyes; her breath heaved into enraged gasps. She looked like she might lunge at me, slapping and sobbing, convinced that everything was my fault—the room, the bruise on her cheek, her estrangement from her cherished Zelda Shilling.

"House cleaning."

She blinked. "What?"

"They've had to hire some new people." I swiped a pair of pink panties— Melissa's—from the chair so I could sit down. "It happens. But I'll lodge a complaint, don't worry."

Her face wrinkled and unwrinkled twice, then she snatched her pursestrap and stomped past me. "Unfucking-believable." The curtains tangled around her arms as she slashed her way outside. I watched them drift back into place before limping to the shower, grateful at least that the thorn had worked its way out of my foot.

I avoided my reflection and draped my dress over the shower rod, scowling at each tear and stain before inspecting the row of bruises winding up my legs. The one circling my knee looked like part of a banana I would slice off before eating, but the largest blackened my hip. I peeled my underwear back and peered over my shoulder at a palette of orange-browns and blues.

My face could have been worse. I didn't plan on kissing anyone soon, and the smaller cuts vanished when I backed a couple of feet away from the mirror. The longer, diagonal slashes down my jaw might have been the result of a drunken vampire attack. I supposed Melissa wouldn't notice if I borrowed some of her makeup, assuming I found some not ground into the carpet.

The shower proved more harrowing than I'd feared. Cuts blossomed under the stream, erupting from patches I thought untouched. Objects emerged from my hair, clumps of dirt, a leaf, tiny thorns clinging like Velcro. I lathered three times, discarding the complimentary shampoo bottles on the tub ledge.

The Islands usually suffered a water shortage this time of year, but I stayed until the steam wearied me and the drip marks on the mirror looked like fingernail scratches. I cracked the door and let an arctic gust raise goose bumps as I toweled dry. Something peculiar wafted in with the chill. I inhaled a dank, burning scent as I pulled the towel around me and creaked the door wider.

"Melissa?"

I expected to find the bed in flames, Shilling and the Amazon standing outside cackling with an empty gasoline canister. But the smoke was the gray, stringy kind that dissolved from the tip of a cigar.

Chief Cosway crossed his boots on the edge of my bedspread, his back sunk low in the chair. A glass dangled from his other hand. He sucked a long drag and exhaled the words in a cloud, "I believe I saw Melissa go next door."

I couldn't stop my fingers from pulling at the towel; it had shrunk to the size of a hand cloth. "What do you want?"

Cosway lifted his drink. "Oh, this is fine, thank you. But help yourself." He pointed at the refrigerator beside the TV, and it took me a moment to realize he'd looted my mini-bar. The fact somehow braced me.

I skimmed the floor for something to wear, lucky that some of my clothes had landed near the bathroom door. "Did you have fun fingering my underwear?" I plucked a pair of briefs from under a wood hanger, recalling life in my college dorms.

"I preferred your roommate's collection."

I couldn't argue. Melissa's panties glowed like exotic

fish against the beige rug. How many pairs had she brought? I wondered if one of Cosway's troops had smuggled out the teddy I'd glimpsed in her suitcase last night while she was unpacking.

"Maybe you should be talking to her." I ducked into the bathroom to dress.

"No need. Though I am impressed by your ingenuity." His voice rose when I moved out of sight. He sounded like an actor shouting his lines from offstage. "They have absolutely no idea, do they?"

I yanked the briefs up before flinging the towel over the bath ledge. "Idea of what?" I should have asked, "who?" Melissa and Randy? Zelda and the Amazon? McGuffin and his boss?

"It almost worked. When their backgrounds panned out, I almost stopped investigating. The chaperone scheme is inspired. Every week a new pair of dupes to cover your operations. You deserve every cent Mr. Shilling pays you."

"I don't work for Richard Shilling," I yelled through the ribbed top I wrestled my head through. It was wrinkled and smelled from yesterday's flight.

"Of course you do. That's the one detail you overlooked. It took me a while to work up the corporate totem pole, but I eventually found him." He paused for dramatic effect. I looked up as if to see Cosway through the bathroom wall. My scabs frowned back at me. "Mr. Shilling maintains fifty-five percent of *Who Wants To Be A Blind Date* stocks through two parent corporations. He can plant anyone anywhere in the company. Clearly, he has been priming you for this assignment for some time."

I wished Cosway could see my expression. "So you think Mafia hit men have seized control of network broadcasting?" I buttoned the shorts before stepping back into the room. "It would explain a lot." Like why our Nielsen ratings kept slipping.

"I don't expect a confession, Miss Farrell." Cosway's eyes wavered on my clothes for an instant, and I glanced at my clashing shorts. He thought I was a professional killer, and he still had the nerve to critique my outfit? This from a man wearing a clip-on tie. "But I do know syndicate interests have been expanding on my island for the last two years. The same two years that you've been a loyal patron of Lovelund Resort—another of Mr. Shilling's holdings."

He smiled, trying to convince me of his self-satisfaction. He had rooted me out, the snake in his garden. I could have blurted McGuffin's room number, described every step of the Amazon's rendezvous, but I just stood there with my jaw closed, nursing a nagging conviction. Cosway didn't believe this story either.

"And what evidence did you uncover during your illegal search?" I looked down, remembering the condom in my suitcase. It had absconded with the teddy.

Cosway chuckled, sounding less demonic than avuncular. "Evidence is a funny thing." He swirled his drink a last time before tilting it into his mouth, his Adam's apple bobbing. "It has a way of showing up when it's most needed." The empty glass banged against the tabletop.

"What do you want from me?"

"For now?" He cocked his head, pretending to think about it. "Go home." His boots slid off the bed, heels landing with hoof-like thuds.

"And never come back?"

The chair stood low, so he had to rock his stomach forward to stand. He carried his weight like armor plating. “We’ll see. New York state has an excellent extradition policy with the Virgin Islands.” His voice was so placid he might have been commenting on the weather.

Mine rose, suddenly shrill. “I didn’t murder that man.”

He shrugged as he inspected a print on the wall, a pastel sailboat on a pastel sea, the same signed copy in every bungalow. “Somebody did.” He turned his back and trod toward the patio, his body darkening. “It might as well have been you.”

My ears popped when the glass door slid back. He could have been opening an airplane lock at a thousand feet. The curtains stretched after him.

14

What's the Most Embarrassing Thing I Could Find in Your Bedroom?

I wanted to curl up in bed with the remote and a box of Peak Freans and hide in some Saturday afternoon rerun. Bette Davis, Katharine Hepburn, Godzilla—it didn't matter. Drop the blinds and switch off both phones; that's what Cosway wanted. If I obeyed, maybe he would leave me alone.

I started cleaning instead, scooping up armfuls of clothes and flattening them into empty drawers. It was my mother's fault. When under stress, I organized.

In five minutes, Melissa's ankle socks and underwear lay in color-sorted rows, and everything with a neck hole was swaying on a hanger. Her shoes resembled an arrangement in a display window. I'd folded the teddy—it had been under the bed—back in her bag, but never found the missing condom.

I changed clothes twice, picturing myself photographed in black and white, a convict number over my breasts. My parents would be so disappointed—

their only daughter, an incarcerated murderer with no non-lesbian dating prospects.

After washing Cosway's glass out twice in the sink and stacking the resort flyers on the TV, I was stranded again. How long would they wait to arrest me, hours, days, weeks? The bamboo stripes in the wallpaper hung with jail bar symmetry. I should have hunted down Parker and offered her the exclusive she craved, the confessions of the chaperone killer. Maybe I'd stop by McGuffin's first and ask for some pointers, mobster to mobster.

My pacing stalled as the thought rattled in my skull. McGuffin had traipsed into the resort the same day as Zelda Shilling, registered in a single room with no pretense of a cover, parked himself in front of her entourage all evening—and Cosway suspected nothing? I pictured the police chief last night in the boathouse, his mouth in a tight frown as he'd bent over the corpse. He hadn't asked questions so much as implied answers, plodding through the interrogation with an actor's flair. Why would he presume that the person who found the dead bodyguard was the same one who had knocked him off in the first place?

Of course Cosway knew I was innocent. He was setting me up. If Donna hadn't traded weekends with me, he would have been framing her instead.

I paced now, remembering the bartender's face when I'd mentioned Cosway's name. The whole island knew their police chief was crooked, his anticorruption campaign a publicity ruse. He probably took his paychecks directly from Richard Shilling. He hadn't assigned the polyester uniform to placate Zelda's fears but to stir them. If she and the Amazon kept a lookout for me, McGuffin the real killer, remained free to maneuver as he liked.

If Cosway had filled McGuffin in on the facts, I would have been dead, too, another drowning victim washed up in the weeds, but I suspected the chief kept his mouth shut out of general policy. According to his wife's accusations, Richard Shilling ran his business like a CIA bureaucracy, dispensing single puzzle pieces to each player. That's why she was such a threat and why I finally had an advantage.

I snatched my purse on the way out. My other pair of sandals—the new pair—chafed my ankles, but the limp was gone. I rounded the patio partition and grabbed Randy's closed door, the rollers squealing as it ground open.

Melissa and Randy scrambled up from the bed as I slapped the curtain aside. Her lips looked puffy, but she wasn't crying anymore, her bikini strings dangling under her top. Randy had progressed onto more involved methods of comfort. Melissa stood, her tan going crimson.

"We, we—"

My hand rose, and she shut up. They both inched backward as I neared. I felt like my own mother, except their gropings were the last thing on my mind.

"Take a taxi into Charlotte Amalie. Lots of shopping. I'll meet you for dinner. Six o'clock reservations at Bluebeard's Castle. It's on the tourist map."

One perched on top of the untouched stack of flyers on Randy's nightstand. A Lovelund Resort pen rested beside the lamp. I circled the restaurant and scribbled the time in enormous print, obliterating half the bay. He grabbed at the sheet as it fluttered toward his lap. I spun toward the patio before either could muster a syllable. If I'd executed my chaperone responsibilities as efficiently every weekend, I might have enjoyed working for *Who Wants To Be A Blind Date*.

I jogged onto the bungalow path and searched for my uniformed pal, betting Cosway would still have him shadowing me to keep Zelda's paranoia stoked. After trotting down the row of bungalows, I hung a sharp left and parked myself.

I waited a half minute, then peeked. Sure enough, my man in blue followed hot on my heels. He thumped down the center of the path, his head twisting left and right, his reflector stripes blazing. It would have taken more than a day of reconnaissance work to break this rookie in. The poor guy probably had no idea he was stooging for a crooked boss. I ducked back before he spotted me and scrambled up the side path.

The next row of bungalows blocked my route, but I noticed a couple munching a late room service lunch on the second patio, their door open behind them. I strolled up, erect and beaming.

"Hi!"

The man's fork halted before his open mouth.

"Don't want to bother you. Just have to check the mini-bar!" I wove between their knees as I reached for an imaginary clipboard in my purse. They blinked, heads following me, but neither protested.

I knelt in front of the refrigerator and studied the patio through the corner of my eye. The woman eased back in her seat after I rattled a couple of Perrier bottles. The man greeted the cop as he passed, and I closed the fridge, a grin stretching my face.

"Thanks, folks. Hope you're enjoying your meal."

The woman flagged me back as she elongated her frown. "The champagne we opened last night was flat. We would like another." I gave her my attentive expression, the one I used on the producer whenever he cornered me in my cubicle. "No charge, of course."

"Of course." After checking that the cop had worked himself out of sight, I followed the room numbers two rows back to McGuffin's bungalow.

His room commanded a better ocean view than mine. I approached his window at a right angle, hoping he was still balled over on the reef on St. John, ten miles and a ferry ride away. I crept behind a bush and peeked around the drawn curtain, expecting to find him cleaning his guns on the mattress, stacks of unmarked bills lining the bedspread. But the room was dark but for the thin column of sunlight splitting the drapes. I pressed my cheek against the glass, unable to see past the foot of the made bed. Except for the unzipped suitcase on the bureau, the room appeared unoccupied. Hit men traveled light.

I wiggled the locked doorknob, wishing I'd finagled a key card from Phoebe first. Jogging to the reception desk and back might have killed five minutes, plus I didn't know if her shift had ended yet. A cleaning cart was parked on a patio down the row, so I switched to plan B.

I poked my head into the open door. "Tia?"

The cleaning woman looked up as she bent over to plug in a vacuum.

"Hi. You're Phoebe's little sister, aren't you?" I ambled inside, voice and toes bouncy. "I thought you'd be down here. I'm Ashley." I had no idea whether this was Phoebe's sister or not, but even if I was wrong, it gave me an in.

She propped her arm on the vacuum handle, her change in carriage making the maid uniform suddenly incongruous. "You that TV lady, huh? I see you all the time."

I shrugged elaborately. "That's me." I held her eyes, smiling as I padded closer. "Listen, I locked myself out of my room, and I don't have time to run back and wait for someone else with a key." Every other word rose with a question mark. I even wrung my hands a little. "Would you mind?"

Tia reached into her pocket, her key card glittering in her fingers. "What room?"

"Thirty-one."

She lifted her eyes. "Thirty-one?" Her voice went flat, and I felt my smile twitch. "Funny—I was in your other room about an hour ago."

I looked down, my head thrown to one side. "O-kaay." If I could blush on command, I would have. "Let me explain." My thoughts raced. I wondered what was about to come out of my mouth. "Maybe Phoebe mentioned this guy I'm really interested in?" I shot her a confidential smile, girlfriend to girlfriend. "Well, I wanted to sneak into his room and surprise him. You know—" I strung out the vowels and thrust a hip out. *"Surprise him."*

Tia inspected me dubiously: damp, unbrushed hair, knees grated with scabs, fang marks running under the collar of my blouse. Not a look likely to seduce. "Hope you got some of that frilly stuff on under that."

My posture melted as I strained to remember whether Melissa had left her suitcase open when we'd left for St. John. Or had Tia seen the room after Cosway's crew had been ransacking it? She saved me from my stammer.

"Why the cops bothering you anyway?"

I dropped the girl routine and met her eyes for real this time. "They're framing me for murder."

Her expression didn't change, not a flicker of surprise. The guidebooks claimed the local temperament was mellow, but I thought they were just numbed by Cosway and five hundred years of his colonial predecessors. "Who's in Thirty-one?"

"The guy who killed Shilling's bodyguard."

She still wasn't shocked. The key card dangled in her fingers. "I'll be done in here in ten minutes. That enough time?"

I took the card. "Better be." The ferry left St. John every thirty minutes. If McGuffin had caught the one after mine, he could have been at the dock already, his soggy shorts dripping on a taxi bench. Unless I'd seriously injured him and he was still clutching his throat in the water. A pang of guilt, even concern, rose through me. "Thank you."

Tia muttered at her vacuum. "You wash up on shore tonight, I never met you."

My knees gave a nervous twinge. "One more favor." I propped my purse on the table and dug my cell phone out. It hummed as I punched a direct line to McGuffin's room. "You see him coming, hit redial." I held the mouthpiece under her chin until she accepted it. "I only need a half minute warning to go over the balcony."

Tia fingered the display lights. "Nokia 252." She looked disappointed. "Nextel is better." She pocketed the phone in her pouch and added, "You finish the bathroom in Twenty-nine when you're done." She pointed at the cleaning supplies in the bottom of the cart in case I'd missed them.

I wasn't sure if she was joking or not but nodded my assent. My life for a toilet. I'd made worse deals.

I poked the key card into the slot twice before facing it right side-up. A light the size of a needle head clicked green. Tia watched me from her doorway as I skulked inside.

This row of bungalows angled up a slope so the rooms had second-story balconies instead of patios and entrances in the rear instead of oversized closets. Otherwise, McGuffin's was identical to mine. He had left both sets of drapes drawn. My heart played a drum roll as my eyes adjusted to the dimness. I was inside the lair. I breathed through my mouth, frightened of an imaginary smell, the decomposing bodies rotting in the back of the cave.

All I needed was evidence, something Cosway couldn't refute in a court of law. I crept across the carpet, cringing with each muffled crack. Could the room be booby-trapped? The closet stood open, empty except for a single sports coat, attractive cut. I checked the pockets and found a single ticket stub from a movie theater in Manhattan, one I sometimes visited myself. I pictured the two of us in the same darkened row, our dates and a dozen empty chairs between us.

A novel rested on the bedstand, a bookmark protruding around the midpoint. I picked it up, stunned that anyone could be reading *Northanger Abbey,* the only Austen novel Hollywood never corrupted. His airline ticket and Lovelund reservation were tucked in a white business envelope with a dry cleaner's logo printed in the return address—probably one of Richard Shilling's more obvious money-laundering operations.

Next, I tiptoed to the bureau and ran my fingers

along the teeth of his suitcase—no hair-thin triggers. I held my breath and threw the mouth open.

A pair of colored briefs sprawled on top, docksiders jammed into separate corners. Unrolled socks snaked around the edges. The man did not know how to pack. A mangled copy of the *Village Voice* jutted from the top compartment. It was open to the Personals. Was he looking for dates or target practice between assignments? I skimmed down his column of checks, impressed that he had avoided all the ads with bust and waist measurements. He had circled a couple, including a SWF35 who promised intellectual stimulation and long jogs with her dog—a guaranteed discard from my bachelorette pile. McGuffin shared some of my soft spots.

I began unwebbing the tangle of clothes, choosing clumps to search. My fingers brushed something flat and smooth on the bottom. I dislodged a shoe and spied a woman cupping her bare breasts, her hair obscuring the bottom edge of the *Playboy* logo. Not the sort of evidence I had in mind.

I started rummaging in the upper compartment again, then remembered that both Randy and my mother had mentioned the same article. I wiggled the magazine out, disturbed by the fact that my parents had something in common with a Bachelor #2. The model leered at me, pouty-lipped and bedroom-eyed. She could have been next week's bachelorette. I flipped past the vodka ads to the table of contents and skimmed down until my finger paused under the title "Permanent Vacation: What your travel agent doesn't know about the Mafia's hot business spots." Glossy-skinned nudes flashed at me as I turned to page twenty-four, wondering whether it was more prestigious to have an article placed before or after the centerfold.

The title sprawled off-center in a bold typewriter font, while the black-and-white photo made Charlotte Amalie resemble an exit on the Bronx Expressway. I checked for a byline, half expecting to find Margaret Parker's name, but the credit box at the bottom of the page argued a case for anonymity, citing the author's fear of retaliation. A blowup of a corpse dripping from a fishing net underscored the point.

I skimmed the article, an account of warring crime families vying for control of the Islands. The author stopped short of identifying Richard Shilling by name, but the "powerful American millionaire" was unmistakable. Apparently, Shilling had usurped the Islands' indigenous Don years ago and had been conducting a relentless campaign against insurgents since. Those who obeyed him, he lavished with graft. I presumed Cosway was at the top of that list, although the article meticulously avoided accusations against the local police. Anyone who broke line with Shilling received a more permanent form of persuasion.

I looked at the body in the fishing net again, a bloated arm dangling through the weave. So this was McGuffin's handiwork. I shook my head and grimaced my amazement. Were all hit men so vain? He probably kept a scrapbook of AP clippings of all his unsolved murders at home, mementoes to show his parents when they visited.

My knuckle brushed something hard as I slipped the magazine back under the swimming trunks. I pictured an electric razor or camera case, but a short metallic barrel jutted under the shoe. The saliva in my throat turned bitter as I peeled a shirt back and gazed at the pistol. It wasn't one of those oversized Howitzers macho cops in summer blockbusters wielded. It was smaller, travel-sized, an easy fit for even Melissa's mini-purse, perfect for undercover work. Apparently real hit men didn't suffer from size anxiety.

My hands started shaking as I returned the shoe and red briefs. I stared at the elastic band, wondering if I'd left fingerprints, some of that convenient evidence Cosway said had a way of showing up when needed. I could feel the DNA flaking from my skin.

I backed away from the suitcase and caught my breath, surprised to find that it had risen to a staccato quiver. What had I thought I was going to find here? McGuffin's "To Do" list with a check mark next to "Kill Zelda's bodyguard"? The only loose end McGuffin had on this island was me. I should have been phoning lawyers, not pussyfooting through a snake pit. I padded toward the door, hoping Tia hadn't burnt up the battery on my cell phone yet.

My hand was reaching for the knob when I heard the lock click. Every nerve in my body sparked as the door swung toward me.

15

Do You Sleep in the Nude?

When I was sixteen years old, my mother skidded her old VW Beetle off our driveway with me in the passenger seat. I remember watching the world roll over in slow motion, my adolescence passing before my eyes.

I watched the same montage now. I had another twenty years to cover before the door hit me in the face. If McGuffin was going to murder me, I hoped he did it before I relived my freshman year in college.

The knob scraped my shirt as I swerved for the bathroom. Three steps and I was perched inside the tub. The front door slammed as I tugged the curtain half-closed. Had he heard me? I felt the Beetle's seat belt gripping my waist.

McGuffin strolled past the bathroom door without glancing in. He rattled in the outer room, sounding intentionally nonchalant, probably double-checking the gun cartridge for bullets. I peered around the edge of the curtain, biting my tongue when his foot struck vinyl. He might have had the gun in his hand—or a bazooka for all I could see. I pictured bullet holes tearing through the plastic, my blood splattering the white porcelain.

Something damp hit the floor, and I nearly screamed. I pictured something dead, a swath of carved flesh. When I opened my eyes, a shirt sleeve lay under the towel rack, the maroon weave darkened from dampness. I glimpsed an elbow, a flash of bare shoulder, then I heard a zipper and a grunt as he wrestled the wet fabric down his legs. A drop of water pricked my shin as the shorts plopped across the tub ledge inside out, a pair of briefs knotted through them.

Had he stripped down as a precaution, a means to reduce evidence, fewer blood spots on his clothes? I braced my heel against the soap dish, ready to punt McGuffin's testicles into his spleen. I hadn't made varsity soccer in high school for nothing. If I could knock him off his feet, I would vault over the balcony blind. A broken ankle suddenly didn't seem too bad.

The toilet lid clattered as his shadow sunk. I saw the pink of his skin through the translucent plastic where his knee brushed the curtain. He slumped forward in a Thinker pose as the muffled hiss of water against water resounded against the tiles. He really did pee sitting down.

The phone rang as he finished, the curtain fluttering as he stood. I could barely hear his voice over the flushing water.

"Hello? Hello?"

Phoebe's sister was a little slow on the draw.

A moment later, the phone clattered against the nightstand or bureau, and I could hear nothing more until the toilet stopped whining. I discerned sounds that might have been mattress springs, but I couldn't be sure. Voices under the balcony? The hum of the sea beyond that? I squatted in the tub to relieve the ache in my legs. Though the shower was identical to mine, Lovelund's ubiquitous coral pattern adorning the tiles, it possessed a masculine air now. McGuffin had stood naked in the same spot, probably only a couple hours before. I studied the tiny bar of soap bent to the shape of his fist, unsure if I was repelled or tantalized. The tub was cleaner than any guy's I'd ever seen, but then that was probably Tia's doing.

Minutes passed as I checked and rechecked the tan line on my wrist, where I wished I had strapped on my watch. Was he asleep? Did hit men take naps in the middle of the afternoon? I lowered my foot to the floor with tightrope caution. Surely he heard me. He was waiting, grinning, barrel tracing me through the wall.

I held my breath and inched my head around the doorframe, my left eye as round as a periscope. The curtains fluttered in front of the window and the suitcase lay open, but otherwise the room appeared unchanged. Had he slipped out? I crept forward, then froze as a murmur rose from the bed. I could only see the bottom edge of the mattress, the bedspread draping evenly to the floor.

After a second sleepy groan, a bare foot stretched into view. The toes curled and uncurled, sole facing up. I didn't exhale until they stopped moving.

Even if I woke McGuffin by opening the door, he couldn't have reached me before I was outside, my screams for help echoing down the row of patios. The thought made me bold. I wanted to know what he looked like asleep. I usually didn't bother staying in a man's bedroom long enough to see him in sunlight.

I pressed my hair behind my ear and traced the length of his leg up the bed. He wasn't naked after all. I recognized the pair of briefs from his bag. He lay with one leg pulled close to his stomach, the other straight. There was a divine arch to his thin back, an arm vanishing under the pillow. I could only see part of his face, the crescent of a closed eye. He reminded me of my cousin's demonic toddler, innocent only in sleep.

Laughter outside yanked my head back. The door to the adjacent room rattled and slammed, two voices murmuring through the wall. It was my cue to leave, but I stood paralyzed when I registered the creak of mattress springs behind me. I heard McGuffin yawn and the crackle of stretching joints. I wanted to bolt outside but could only stare over my shoulder as he shuffled into view.

His eyes were downcast, fingers rubbing his mouth while he bent over the refrigerator. Glass bottles clinked, and he straightened with an O.J. in his grip—not a gun at least. He wrenched the cap off and tilted the bottle back, filling his mouth. His eyes blinked once without registering me, then an electric shock twisted through him as he spewed juice over the carpet. He coughed, arms flailing, as the O.J. bottle rebounded off the dresser. When he regained control of his body, he dove for the open suitcase and gripped the gun in both fists.

I didn't recognize my own scream. It sounded like something dying, an animal impaled in a trap. The noise didn't stop until my lungs were empty and my ears rang. McGuffin's gun drooped as I fingered my stomach for bullet holes, confused that I wasn't shot. We gazed at each other, waiting for something to happen.

A fist struck the door outside. "Hey! Is everything all right in there? Hello?"

"Yes, just a minute!" McGuffin sounded friendly but indisposed, the voice of a man throwing on a bathrobe. I braced as he charged at me. My fists tightened, ready to sock him in the throat again, but his hands stopped on my shoulders, barely grazing my skin as he nudged me to the side. I moved away from the door, but he continued guiding me sideways into the bathroom. Our knees touched as we entered. It might have been a dance step, except for the gun barrel touching my arm.

"Hello?!"

The knocks kept getting louder. He surveyed the bathroom, deciding where to hide the gun. He looked at the sink, looked at me, then tucked it into his briefs. His chest pressed mine as he reached over my shoulder for a towel. His arms were thin but muscular, that intoxicating scent now mingled with salt. The bathroom seemed to be shrinking around us.

"Open this door!"

Several voices had gathered outside the bathroom window. McGuffin wrapped the towel around his waist as our eyes met wordlessly. He pulled the door closed behind him.

The last knock was cut short. "May I help you?" I didn't recognize McGuffin's voice at first. The bashful quiver sounded real.

"We heard a scream." Footsteps thumped around him. Someone in flip-flops hovered on the patio.

McGuffin stammered like Hugh Grant. "I—I'm sorry—my wife and I, we, well, we were—"

"Where is she?"

After a pause a gentle knock sounded by my ear. "Honey? Honey, these nice people want to make sure you're okay?"

"Ma'am? Can you open the door, ma'am?" I pictured a paramedic, a pair of firemen in bermudas ready to batter through the wood with axes.

"Just a second." McGuffin had a bathrobe draped on a hook behind the door. I threw it on, gripping it closed at my neck to cover my blouse and wondering why I was helping McGuffin. Playing along with him meant I might find out more information, but it was the game, the fantasy that swept me up. My arms tingled where he had just touched me. I twisted around the door as I pulled it open. "I'm—I'm fine, thanks."

My knights errant transformed into two short guys with beer guts. A woman twittered in the doorway behind McGuffin. Tia might have been back there, too.

I cleared my throat. "Sorry—for all the, ah—" I shrugged shyly, the embarrassed newlywed. "Noise." I think I really was blushing. McGuffin's eyes opened the widest, the gun making him hunch forward. I imagined the touch of metal against genitals. "We were—I was just—"

The idea registered with the first guy, and he elbowed the second, chuckling under his breath, apparently picturing me screaming through an orgasm. They eyed McGuffin enviously, mouth spreading lewdly, as I shut the bathroom door.

Their laughter faded outside as I hung up the robe. Sweat stains dampened my armpits, my heart still rattling, but I was too curious to be frightened. Had I just glimpsed the real McGuffin, or was the bashful routine just the calculated ploy of a bloodthirsty predator? Either way, he impressed me.

I knocked for some reason before creaking the door open again. "Honey, did those nice people leave yet?" Stupid last words. Maybe he just needed time to twist a silencer onto the end of his gun.

McGuffin stood across the room, half dressed, his briefs still visible through the zipper of his khaki shorts. He buttoned a shirt furiously, unaware that he had misaligned the holes. The gun lay on its side on the table in front of him, barrel pointed lazily in my direction. He threw his shoulders back when he spied me. I couldn't tell what he was thinking, but I'd seen the same expression on guys in single bars, the same grooming sweep of his hands down his shirt. Normally I would have crossed my legs at him and smiled, but I had no bar stool and didn't have the faintest idea what the rules of engagement were. He was working up his courage for something, a little nervous to be talking to me at all. I was, after all, Zelda's top employee, woman enough to leave him gasping on a rocky reef. I was beginning to enjoy my secret identities.

He rubbed his hands together before beginning. "First of all, I owe you an apology. I was out of line when I insulted you. We are both professionals. We should be able to understand each other and our respective agendas without coming into unnecessary conflict. I hope we can put that earlier unpleasantness behind us and move on." He bowed slightly, his demeanor brimming with forced respect and cordiality. "Perhaps we could negotiate a new agreement?"

His fingers searched for the missing buttonhole as he spoke. I pointed, and he looked down and started rebuttoning. I had no idea what he was talking about but smiled as though accepting a drink at a bar. "Perhaps." Whatever he had to say I wanted to hear.

He stood sideways as he fixed his shirt, confidence rising in his manner despite the awkward pose. "Well, we both know what *I* want."

If he wasn't a professional killer hired to terrorize Zelda Shilling, then I didn't know what the hell he was doing tailing her around the Islands. Tangling with mobsters wasn't most people's idea of a relaxing vacation. The man liked flirting with danger. We seemed to have that in common. "Don't be coy," I said. "Spell it out."

"It's simple enough. Shilling's scared. I need her calm, unguarded."

"So what can I do?"

"Tell her to trust me."

I pressed a hip against the bureau, pretending to consider. "Why would I want to do that?"

"My employer is willing to pay."

"And what are you making on this?"

"About thirty thousand." Was that the going rate for murder these days? Randy would have puffed out his chest and strutted around the room, but McGuffin seemed indifferent to the figure. Whatever his business was, he wasn't in it for the money. "I'll split it with you, fifty-fifty."

"Just for telling her to trust you?"

"And looking the other way when I get her alone."

Melissa was screaming in my head: *Oh my god! He's*

going to kill her! But I wondered if there were more to the story. That half-smile was alluring but not exactly sinister. "When will you—do it?"

"Right now if possible. When can you deliver her?"

I considered my bluff, hoping to put him off at least a few hours. If he was planning to shoot me, Zelda or anybody else, I wanted a room full of camera-toting tourists there as witnesses. I folded my arms. "Six o'clock. Bluebeard's Castle." Maybe I could use Randy and Melissa as human shields.

McGuffin looked startled. Getting Zelda's main handler to double-cross her was supposed to have been harder. "Okay. Great." His hands met in a single clap. "I'll be there."

My arms untangled, but I didn't know what to do with them. Did conspirators shake hands? I imagined two *Who Wants To Be A Blind Date* contestants hugging awkwardly under spotlights. We needed the host to smooth us through the dead air and into a commercial break. I wanted to ask him a dozen questions: How did a nice boy like you end up in a business like this? I imagined my arms around him on a metal cot during prison conjugal visits. If he was a homicidal sociopath, who better to rehabilitate him than me?

Instead, I turned in the foyer and asked, "Why do you trust me?" It was the most honest question I'd ever asked a man.

McGuffin's shrug was almost audible, his voice a laugh. "I don't."

I nodded as if that cleared things up.

16

What Do You Do When You Realize You've Made Two Dates for the Same Night?

Tia's cleaning cart had migrated up a door. She was hovering in the archway as I approached, the cell phone in her palm. "Sorry. I think I talked to your mother."

I fiddled with the speed dial before dropping it in my purse, not sure which of us had screwed up. "Thanks anyway." Wrong numbers drove my mom crazy. She was probably dialing the police that very moment, convinced that her house was being staked out by Puerto Rican bandits.

"Did you find what you need?" Tia's hand remained out. I dropped the key card in her palm.

"I have no idea."

She started rolling the cart over the threshold. "Don't worry about the toilet."

"Thanks." Then I remembered: "Hey! Room Fifty-nine needs champagne."

She shot me the same ambivalent expression everyone else on this island kept giving me. I would have asked for a bottle myself, but I was hurrying to my row of bungalows, hoping Melissa and Randy hadn't left for town yet. My professional conscience had reared its thorny head again. What would my producer say if he knew I'd scheduled their dinner with a potential killer? I was still chaperoning after all. I doubted McGuffin could mistake Melissa's blonde mop for Zelda's, but you never knew. He'd mistaken my brown bob for a mobster's.

My room was empty, but Randy's curtains remained drawn. Something held my fist back before I knocked. My ears perked as a muffled sound lilted through the glass, human and rhythmic. The curtains hung an inch apart, so I couldn't help seeing Melissa's knees jouncing above Randy's pale hips. Their bodies rippled in unison. Melissa's eyes and teeth were clenched while Randy made all the noise.

Here was a scene you never saw on *Who Wants To Be A Blind Date*. For all its sexual titillation, the show was essentially a Puritan organization. All talk, no action. Horny single people watched it because they weren't getting any. My most sacred duty was making sure the contestants didn't either. Half of our advertisers would have pulled their spots if word of this leaked out. We were already pimps in the eyes of the religious Right. If Melissa yelled rape, the network was done for.

I tripped on the patio table as I stumbled back to the path, wishing I'd packed my camera. A few Polaroids on my producer's desk and I would have that raise Donna and I never got. Or wasn't that shooting high enough? Blackmail the Board and I could be producer. If everyone around here thought I was so sinister, maybe I could smuggle some of that home with me. I was tired of trotting in place my whole life.

The world rolled under my feet like a treadmill, bungalows on each side, the gift shop, the boathouse, the sea marching toward me, wave after plodding wave. I stepped off the path and steadied myself on the back of a bar stool, feeling turbulence in the ground's spin. Maybe Mr. McGuffin was rehabilitating me.

"Something stiffer than an O.J. this time?" The bartender from this morning tilted toward me, her mouth's curve neither a smile nor a frown.

"Bloody Mary."

She stabbed a stalk of celery into the glass before sliding it toward me. She knew which tab to put it on and watched me swallow a long sip. I relished the burn in my throat. So a corrupt police chief was framing me for murder, Zelda Shilling thought I was trying to kill her, and a man who may or may not have been Richard Shilling's top gunman was meeting me for dinner. The afternoon was shaping up better than my typical Saturday.

I was not a usual bar-stool talker, but I had an urge to spill my story. I tried to catch the bartender's eye again, but she stared doggedly at the bar top as she wiped it, her arm the color of the stained wood. If she wanted to avoid my chitchat, she had the length of the bar to retreat to, but she hovered within earshot, feigning invisibility.

I opened my mouth to speak, but words came from behind me: "I know what you want."

My knees retracted as the stool at my side creaked with the Amazon's weight. I'd never seen her so close before, and I found it disorienting, like staring at a doctored photograph, the background and foreground subtly out of sync. "I'm sorry?"

"I said, I know what you want."

The thought intrigued me. McGuffin offered money; I wondered what the opposition could muster.

"And I know Zelda will never give it to you." She propped a Nike on the chair rung and slid back in her seat. This wasn't a fly-by threat; she was here to talk. "Call it pride or loyalty or business ethics, but you'll never get it."

I didn't mean to sigh so heavily. "Get what?"

"The name."

"The name?"

"I haven't asked her. I just know. She'll never betray him." She glared at a couple giggling at the other end of the bar. They might have had listening devices wired into their swimming suits.

I ventured my best guess: "Richard?"

Her brow creased. "No." She glanced over her shoulder again, then moved closer, hand gripping the bar. "Her *contact.*"

I closed my eyes and took a long cleansing breath. "Okay. Listen. My name is Ashley Farrell. I work for *Who Wants To Be A Blind Date*. I'm a—"

"Chaperone. Yeah, I know the whole line. It's a good one, but let it go already. I'm ready to deal." She gave yet another shifty squint across the patio, while the bartender stood polishing the same glistening glass. "Zelda doesn't know I'm doing this. And as far as I'm concerned, she never will. This is between the two of us."

My forehead slumped into my palm. "*What* is?"

"I'll give you what you want, and I'll make sure Zelda stays out of trouble." She chortled contemptuously. "Not that she'd take the risk again. You've got her shaken up pretty good. But I'm going to need some guarantees first. After this, Richard leaves her alone. Permanently. No threats, no strings, no nothing. It's got to be a clean break. Can you get that from Richard?"

The sky blazed a violent blue above our heads as I rolled my eyes. "Lady, I couldn't get the time of day from Richard Shilling. I've never met the guy."

She was unfazed. "I know there's no direct line of communication. I worked your side of the table long enough." If she leaned any closer, I'd be looking down her shirt. "But I also know you have certain operating freedoms. I trust Shilling would abide by your call if they passed the right message up to him. All I need is your agreement. Will you think it over?"

"There's nothing for me to think about." I was about to confess: I'm a patsy, a decoy; your man's in Thirty-one with a pistol in his briefs. But the Amazon cut me off.

"Then it's a deal? All we have to do is tell Zelda. She'll want to hear it from you. In person."

"I thought this was our little secret?"

"It is. Just tell her that Richard is satisfied and you're pulling back. Then you get your man."

I raised a hand to protest, but my jaw clamped shut. Something clicked. I saw Tia's key card, a green light the size of a pinhead: *My man.*

"Okay. I'll do it."

The Amazon stood, her mouth almost bending into a smile. Those were the only underdeveloped muscles in her body. "I'll tell Zelda you're on your way up—I don't want you to scare her. We'll be on the next—"

"Not yet."

She jerked back as though on a leash. "Why not?"

"I'm busy." I held up my glass. Not even half empty yet.

She looked peeved but played along. "When then?"

I gave her the poker face my father had taught me when we played chess: "Six o'clock. Bluebeard's." I was using my old strategy: get all the big pieces out and see what happens.

"We'll be there."

I called over my shoulder as the Amazon thumped away, "Tell Zelda she's buying."

17

Do You Treat a Woman Differently after You've Slept with Her?

The trek up the path seemed shorter. I was debating what to tell Melissa and Randy when I spotted my police shadow trotting in my direction, a sheen of sweat brightening his complexion. He looked both startled and relieved to see me. He veered onto the grass for me to pass, but I swerved with him.

His cheek twitched when I forced him to meet my eye. "What's your name?"

"Ah . . . Gebre." He stiffened his mumble. "Officer Gebre."

His elbow recoiled as I came nearer. I would have loved to read the armed-and-dangerous description that Cosway had fed him, something to tape on the outside of my cubicle to keep the secretary from hassling me. "Officer Gebre, would you like to join me for dinner?" I rattled off the time and place for the fourth time in an hour. "You can tell Chief Cosway he's invited, too." I patted him on the shoulder as I passed.

What the hell? I was going for critical mass. Cosway was going to find out one way or another. If my banquet at Bluebeard's didn't flush matters out, at least my last meal would prove eventful.

I composed a note in my head as I strode to my bungalow.

Dear Melissa and Randy:

Mafia shoot-out at six. Stay in and order room service.

XXXOOO, Ashley

I gave Randy's patio a wide berth even though his drapes were still closed. I listened before sliding my door open, hoping they hadn't switched rooms for a firmer mattress or cleaner sheets.

Melissa's top and swimsuit dangled over a chair back as the sound of water rattled from the bathroom. No sign of Randy's trunks. I tiptoed across the rug, praying they weren't back there together. Randy's bouncing buttocks flashed in my head when I blinked.

I grabbed a Lovelund pen and stationery from the nightstand, but my ballpoint halted above the paper when I heard a whimper over the white noise of the shower. Not a quiver of pleasure but a sob.

"Melissa?"

I rapped gently, feeling steam on my face as the hinges creaked. Melissa was balled against the wall, naked, her hair soaked black, tendrils splaying on her shoulders. She looked up with one tear-puffed eye. The other she pressed behind her hands.

"What happened? Tell me!"

Sobs bubbled up when she tried to answer. I kneeled and peeled her hands back, each finger as taut as a scab. Her eye socket pulsed red, and I saw two or three knuckle marks where the bruise was still darkening. I didn't wait for an explanation.

Randy's patio door was unlocked. It ricocheted in its slot as I stomped through. He poked his head out of his bathroom. A splotch of shaving cream clung to his chin, and his hair was wet and combed back. He took one look at me and held his hands out.

"Hey, look, don't get mad at me. It just sort of happened. Ask her yourself." He pointed through the wall, more or less at the spot where Melissa was balled on the bathroom floor. "If you were so worried, you shouldn't have left us alone in the first pl—"

I shuffled my steps like Mia Hamm and rammed my foot into Randy's crotch. He snapped together like a mousetrap, lungs emptied in a single huff. A thread of spittle hung from his chin as he sunk down the wall. His eyes were open but unfocused. He didn't seem to be breathing.

I'd listened to boyfriends—usually other people's boyfriends—proclaim the tender, even hallowed nature of their testicles, a pair of Achilles' heels swaying exposed by God's perverse wisdom. It had always struck me as an elaborate gender neurosis. Whatever its root, Randy had an advanced case. He lay L-shaped on the floor, hands buried between his thighs as he wheezed.

He deserved worse. I would help Melissa file assault and battery charges, a guaranteed death knell for *Who Wants To Be A Blind Date*'s ratings.

Melissa entered barefoot in her bathrobe. Her hand dropped from her eye as she glimpsed Randy. "Oh, my

God. What did you do?" She shouldered past me, face wrenched with worry. She sank to Randy's side, her hands fluttering, afraid to touch.

My mouth worked up and down wordlessly for a moment. "But your eye . . ."

She mumbled at first, then screeched, "I hit the towel rack!" Her whole face was red now. "I was getting out of the shower!"

My blood flashed hot. I stammered an apology, but Melissa ignored me. She was caressing his hair, sniffling as though he were dying right there on the rug. I imagined ambulance sirens in the distance.

Randy twisted his neck up, lips twitching. I thought he was trying to speak. Melissa pressed closer, but he nudged her away. Then he opened one eye at me and rasped, "Get out."

Okay, so I had a slight tendency to jump to conclusions. But my heart was in the right place. I shivered as the breeze dried my sweat. I still considered leaving that note in my room, though there wasn't much point. They wouldn't come anywhere near Charlotte Amalie, let alone Bluebeard's, if I was there. Melissa would have her clothes moved into Randy's room long before I got back. If I got back.

I beelined to the Lovelund entrance circle and found a driver reading inside the only taxi, an unfolded newspaper drooping against the steering wheel. The passenger window was rolled down—they always were—so I knocked on the hood and pointed toward town. He nodded but kept his place on the sports column.

I climbed in back and crossed my feet on the opposite bench, my fingernails clicking on a steel support. I had no excuse to rush, except that I preferred not to spend my last hours on earth in a converted livestock truck.

A woman's voice shouted from the lobby just as the gears ground into first. The taxi lurched as Parker skidded onto the bench beside me. She looked up and smiled in recognition. "So I hear you had quite a run-in."

My feet slid off the bench as we careened around a curve. How had she heard about my conversation with McGuffin? Or did she have contacts in the police department?

"With Shilling. On the ferry?"

I exhaled a laugh. "Oh that." I'd forgotten Melissa's moment of drama, probably the turning point in her flirtation with Randy. If it hadn't been for Zelda, he would still have been waddling around with an erection. "Is it going to be part of your news story?" "Mob Queen Slaps Bachelorette" didn't strike me as *Washington Post* material.

"I'm surprised, that's all. I would've thought you'd had enough of her after last night. Unless you like fishing dead bodyguards out of the water."

"I thought you said they were newlyweds." I kept my voice flat, curious about where she'd take this.

"I did some snooping since then. Grapevine says she's down here for a *business* meeting." She pronounced *business* the way Zelda pronounced *fucking*, a dozen connotations trailing behind it.

"Selling off more of her husband's company secrets?"

"Or worse." She watched the trees thin as new buildings blurred by and the road quieted to asphalt. She was waiting for me to ask.

"What do you mean?"

Her face brightened as she slid nearer. "Mr. Shilling has enough skeletons to fill a dozen walk-in closets. And the ex knows about most of them. We think she came down here to meet up with an FBI operative and spill the beans." She shook her head at the thought. "Personally I think it's a suicide run for both of them."

The hair on my arms pricked. "Shilling wouldn't really kill her, would he? They were married for what, twelve years? You can't just throw that away, can you?" I was almost pleading.

"Honey, I know the TV won't touch the full story on Richard Shilling, what with all of his philanthropist foundations, but the man's as dangerous as they come. He payrolls the best hit men in the business. The dead bodyguard was a warning shot. If the wife doesn't wise up, he'll pop her and anyone who looks at her."

The taxi squealed to the first traffic light, and our fingers touched as we grabbed the same railing. Parker stood, knees bending against the motion of the truck. She looked me dead in the eye before stepping over the bumper. "If the Feds do have an agent down here, he's as good as buried."

The taxi clattered forward as I slid down the bench, trying to keep her in view. I wanted to shout a dozen questions at once, but Parker disappeared in a belch of exhaust smoke.

Do You Arrive Early and Risk Looking Eager, or Do You Make Your Date Sweat a Little and Come Late?

A three-hundred-year-old tower loomed behind me. Bluebeard must have picked this restaurant for its view. I could see the whole bay and enemy vessels approaching for miles. The two cruise ships docked at Charlotte Amalie blazed like Christmas trees.

I'd staked out a chair with a view of both entrances and waited an hour for the tables to start filling. John, my waiter, was brewing me a new pot of decaf. After a second visit to the bathroom, I'd settled on my strategy, a kind of zone defense dependent on who walked through the doors first. I hoped to keep Shilling and McGuffin apart in case Cosway showed up. If he spotted them talking, things could get ugly, but if I worked the middle, relaying information between them, everyone might get home in one piece—winning me the eternal gratitude of the Federal Bureau of Investigation.

My first impression of McGuffin was my best. He

was no killer. I knew a hit man wouldn't wear Gap shirts. Parker claimed the FBI had sent an agent down to meet with Zelda, and McGuffin was now my leading contestant. It made sense, the way he was orbiting around her, waiting for an opportunity to approach. No wonder he had berated the Amazon out on the peninsula; he'd just lost his breakthrough informant.

My only problem was Cosway. He knew if Zelda blabbed to the Feds, her husband was going to take a big fall, flattening him and the rest of the St. Thomas underworld. McGuffin I assumed could take care of himself, but if I juggled this wrong, I would be spending the remainder of my fertile years in a Virgin Island jailhouse as Cosway's fall guy.

I clutched my cup, bracing myself the way I would before a big interview. A chaperone wasn't so different from a secret agent. This was a lateral career move, a way of tapping some of that inner potential my parents liked to drone about. My mother always said I loved law enforcement. I had a crush on Columbo when I was ten, Rockford at twelve. McGuffin fluctuated between those two poles, a tough guy too cunning to flaunt it. I hoped we could have a real date after this was over. My mom would tease me, saying it was only the thrill of adventure while she dropped hints about bridal patterns. My colleagues would make lewd handcuff jokes.

The waiter poured fresh coffee into my stained cup as I noticed outlines in the vestibule, two figures, neither one tall enough to be the Amazon. The hostess motioned toward a center table, but Randy spotted me and pointed. He gave me a reluctant wave and tugged Melissa's elbow. I didn't recognize him in the white Oxford. Most of my bachelors never thought to pack a tie.

Melissa's expression looked painted on, the inch of foundation over her bruised cheek aiding the effect. She tottered in her pumps and avoided my eyes. Randy was walking funny, too. He took the seat furthest from me. Melissa beamed a hello but kept looking out the window. She seemed jittery.

I tried to force myself back into chaperone mode, wondering how I was going to juggle them, too. "I'm glad you made it. I was afraid I'd be eating on my own tonight." There was a nice thought.

"Are we late?" Melissa yanked her wrist up and looked at a watch I'd never seen her wear before.

"No, no, you're right on time." To the minute. I hadn't thought Melissa was aware of the concept of punctuality.

She hid behind the menu the waiter handed her, while Randy pondered his, glass-eyed. They must have decided I was their only ticket off this island. Cross me and they'd never get home. There were different laws down here. Probably dozens of *Who Wants To Be A Blind Date* winners vanished every year.

I considered shooing them back out. If I barked, I was sure Melissa would scream and bolt, but they did provide a useful cover. I could impress McGuffin with my resourcefulness.

"So." Randy cleared his voice. It sounded higher. "What do you recommend?"

Before I could answer, the vestibule brightened again, and the tinted glass swung open. My heart rose when I recognized the jacket from McGuffin's closet.

The *Who Wants To Be A Blind Date* curtain swung into the flyrail, Bachelor #1 standing center stage. The walls and floor vibrated; engines hummed. The hairs on the back of my neck stood erect with electricity.

Every bachelorette I'd ever chaperoned huddled behind my chair: *He really is handsome.*

The hostess tried to steer him toward a side table again, but he froze when he recognized me. I was weightless, my chair plummeting a fraction slower than the rest of the room. I braced for his approach, but he pivoted and mumbled something to the hostess as he headed for the bar.

Melissa followed my eyes. "Isn't that the guy from—"

Randy pressed his hand against hers; he'd been watching, too. "I think the chateaubriand looks good." He pronounced it phonetically.

I slid my saucer away and stood. "I think there are cheeseburgers on the children's menu."

McGuffin sat with his back to me, his spine straightening with each clop of my shoes on the wood floor. The bartender had already opened a Red Stripe for him. The froth curled at the mouth of the bottle untouched. He watched the row of liquor bottles as diligently as a moviegoer ignoring the stranger rustling into the seat beside him.

"That's not really your name, is it?"

"What?"

"McGuffin."

He pursed his lips. An aura of masculine toiletry products wafted around him, deodorant, shampoo, shaving cream. The strands of hair nearest his scalp were still damp; he didn't pack a blow-dryer either.

"So what do I call you?"

"Andrew's fine. Andy, really." He looked me in the eye, not afraid to share his first name with a professional assassin, although his jaw tightened when I smiled. I should have explained, put him at ease, but there was something delicious about the error. He thought he was sitting next to a dangerous woman, the drowner of bodyguards, the Big Man's trigger finger. It made sense now, his confusion in the pool lounge, his anger outside Zelda's bungalow, his fear on the peninsula, the negotiations in his room. He thought my job was to keep the foulmouthed Mrs. Shilling quiet and that I was double-crossing Richard Shilling by agreeing to let him near her. He edged closer, apparently enjoying my presence. "Do I get to buy you a drink, or is this simply business?"

"Aren't you afraid of it going to your head?" I was trying for a femme fatale rasp, but it came out nasally, more Cyndi Lauper than Lauren Bacall.

The point of a vulpine eye tooth grazed his lip when he smiled. "I'll take my chances."

Words to live by. Years at *Who Wants To Be A Blind Date* and my heart could still flutter like any bachelorette's. It would take a bay larger than Lovelund's to drown the romantic lurking inside of me.

McGuffin gestured, and the bartender deposited a second Red Stripe at my elbow. "I phoned my employers this afternoon. They were pleased to hear you'd had a change of heart."

"As pleased as you?"

He studied my face as he considered his answer. I thought his eyes paused on my lips. "I'll be honest with you. I've been in this line of business for a long time now, and I've never run across anyone quite like you. You are not the woman I was expecting."

Typical male compliment; make me fish for details. "Disappointed?"

He held my stare while he took a first sip of beer. "Hardly."

I wondered if this was the sort of assignment the Bureau usually gave him, wooing wayward women for the good of public policy. Maybe I was just the week's conquest. My moment in the spotlight might be as brief as Melissa's, but I still savored it.

"So how'd you become an agent, Andy? College job fair? Answer an ad?" I couldn't help teasing him a little. I pictured him in his underwear waving that adorable little gun at me. I hadn't known they made men's briefs in paisley print. A whole new world was opening up to me.

His brow flexed into a stack of Ws. "An agent?"

"For the FBI."

"What are you talking about?"

A nervous waver had cropped into my voice. "Then you're a private investigator or something?" Had Parker gotten her story wrong? If the Feds weren't down here, then who the hell was I flirting with? This wasn't the game I thought I was playing. I cleared my throat, trying to sound nonchalant. "Did one of Shilling's rivals hire you?" By rival I meant corporation—not syndicate. I didn't want to know that Zelda's planned contact and the killer were the same person, that McGuffin had been leaning on Zelda Shilling not to shut her up but to make her blab. "Who do you work for?"

"You don't know?" His eyes flashed over my shoulder as he tilted back in his stool. "The *Washington Post*," he said. "*New York Times*. A lot of freelance."

I wasn't sure what my face was doing, but it seemed to disturb McGuffin. Andrew, I meant. Agent Andy. "You're a . . . a . . . a—" Nope, I couldn't say it.

"I'm a reporter." My incredulity sparked his anger. "A writer. You must have known—"

My finger silenced him. "And you're working on a . . . ?" I raised my eyebrows, waiting for him to finish the sentence.

"Story."

"About?"

"What the hell do you think? It's a follow-up. You must have read my first piece—" He swallowed the end of the sentence, afraid of giving away information. He no longer knew who he was talking to either.

"In *Playboy?*"

His face brightened. "Yeah."

"No."

My bar stool spun. Had Zelda arrived yet? Were Mafia gunmen storming the castle? I pictured a rain of bullet-splintered glass spilling from the window frames.

"Why the hell are you asking me this stuff? You must—"

My whisper crackled, "*But you carry a gun.*"

Andrew studied me as my fingernails clutched the edge of the bar. He was trying to piece together the same puzzle. Neither of us fit. "Yes, I carry a gun." His tone was growing flippant. "I'm a pretty good shot at the shooting range, too."

I could have stomped on his toe. The one time in my life I wanted to be rescued, and this was what I got, a newsman with an attitude. Where was my knight in armor—where was the cavalry?

Melissa and Randy were whispering over their place mats. I should have grabbed them by the scruffs of their necks and shoved them outside before either Cosway or Zelda showed up. The only strategy I had left now involved cupping my hands and screaming, "Fire!" If there was an evening flight and Cosway was still willing to let me go, I would be on it. This little chaperone was done playing with mobsters.

I looked at Andrew, unsure whether I should berate him or apologize. It wasn't his fault. Like every bachelorette before me, I'd made my best guess, imagining him into the man I wanted him to be. The blunder was mine. I swigged a mouthful of beer and thumped the bottle next to his arm. "Thanks for the drink, cowboy."

He rose from his stool with me. "You're leaving?"

Unlike Melissa and the other seventy bachelorettes before her, I didn't have to suffer a whole weekend for my mistake. There was no host here forcing me to hug him.

"Sorry, Andy, but this just isn't what I'd—"

My lips froze as I noticed a figure in the entranceway. This time I knew who it was going to be. I knew it before our eyes met, before Parker winked at me. Her face was a coiled grin. I could feel the ground rolling over the roof of my mother's Beetle as I realized that I was staring at the bodyguard's killer. She had orchestrated this all.

Andrew stared at me as I spun back on the stool, my head facing rigidly forward. I whispered through my teeth, "Do you have it with you?"

"Excuse me?"

"*The gun*. Do you have it with you?"

"No." He looked annoyed. "Concealed firearms are illegal in—"

"Then why the hell did you pack it?" I grabbed his wrist and pulled him closer to my mouth. He tensed as though I might bite off his ear. "Do you know that woman?"

I kept my grip as he twisted his neck around. "Of course. That's Wakefield." He waited, but the name meant nothing to me. "Zelda's other bodyguard."

"What?!"

I twirled and saw the Amazon striding between the tables, Zelda in tow. Her eyes widened when she registered McGuffin beside me. I ignored her and surveyed the room, amazed that Parker had vanished so quickly. Had she ducked outside, through the kitchen, to the rest room? As far as I knew, the whole restaurant was rigged to explode.

"I have to go."

Andrew leaped to his feet. "I'm coming with—"

"Sit."

His expression was skeptical, but he couldn't hide his grin. "You're not really . . . ?" He was amused by his error but not exactly disappointed. I wasn't the fantasy he'd imagined either. An undercover reporter infiltrating the Mafia had to love the lure of peril. Without my aura of danger, I figured I'd vanish from his radar, but he kept smiling at me.

"Neither are you." So he wasn't my dream man any more. The fact didn't seem so bad. My hand grabbed his lapel, and I pulled our faces together. I gave him just a quick smack on the lips, but I felt it down to my toes. "Bye."

The waiters were pushing another table beside Melissa and Randy. Wakefield glowered at me, her mouth twisting as though she'd swallowed something raw. "I see you have already met Mr. McGuffin." According to her plan, she was about to introduce him to me so I could shoot him. She wasn't the only one scrambling for a new strategy.

I pushed my way to Mrs. Shilling. "My name's Ashley Farrell. I work for *Who Wants To Be A Blind Date.* I don't know anything about your husband—"

"Oh, for Christsakes—" Zelda yanked Wakefield's sleeve. "You said she—"

My voice reverberated off the ceiling. "Listen to me! I don't know what's going on. I've been used. This is some kind of setup. I think you're in danger." Conversation in the restaurant ceased, and the people at the next table rose nervously. Wakefield and Shilling shared the same expression, their chins back, nostrils flared.

I wanted to explain more, but a blue uniform appeared in the window. The door slammed open, and a dozen boots pounded the carpet. The cops jostled place settings as they surrounded me, hands on their unhooked holsters. I recognized two from last night. The one with the wedding ring mumbled my Miranda rights as Officer Gebre unhooked handcuffs from his belt. He turned me around gently and slipped the metal around my wrists.

"Good evening, Miss Farrell." Cosway strolled through the double doors last. His uniform looked tailored, creases ironed, badge crowning a chest of colored insignias. He had the Islands' publicity to worry about, too.

"What the hell is going on?"

He motioned benignly at the tables of patrons as he approached. An evidence baggie dangled from his thick fingers. "We found Kevin Anderson's wallet in your suitcase." He held it up as though performing a magic trick for the crowd.

"Who?"

He smiled for his audience. "Why, the man you killed, Miss Farrell. That poor bridegroom you drowned in Lovelund Bay."

The tourists gasped at the spectacle. This was going

to be the high point of their vacations, a Caribbean morality play.

Officer Gebre nudged me politely forward. I glimpsed Melissa and Randy, shocked that they didn't look shocked. They were the only people in the restaurant still perusing their menus. Shilling and Wakefield were heading toward the ladies' room. I took a last glance at the bar before my entourage escorted me out into the sunlight.

McGuffin was gone.

19

After You Surprise Me by Picking Me Up after a Bad Day at Work, Where Do You Take Me?

Gebre ducked my head into the rear of the police cruiser. A faint scent of vomit rose from the hard plastic seat as I squirmed backward awkwardly, arms locked behind me. He made sure my toes were clear before slamming the door.

Orange sunlight rippled on the car hood as his boot steps receded into the muffled hum of the outer world. I closed my eyes and noticed that my breath was held, my lungs weighed down. I could have been underwater.

If I just sat still, smiled, kept my mouth shut, maybe this would all blow over. I felt as if I were back in high school, feet flat on the floor of the principal's waiting room. Popular girls always got off with warnings. Who could resist those contrite sniffles, those perky breasts heaving? It was the weird ones, the outcasts and hooligans who got it. The ones like me.

I twisted onto my knees to see through the rear

window. A couple of uniforms loitered near the restaurant entrance, a few others near the swimming pool patio, the tower looming above them all. It looked absurd, an enormous chess piece. I strained to see down the sliver of alley beside it, but couldn't.

The driver's door opened, and I rolled off my stomach. "Gebre."

He turned, his face cross-hatched by the squares of net dividing the front and back seats. "I don't know what you know, but you could be an accessory to murder." He regarded me with one eye, a light stubble framing his baby-round cheek. "You work for a mobster. Your chief is on Richard Shilling's payroll." This was not the cool, reasoned voice of persuasion, but it was the best I could muster. I couldn't prove it was true. Only Cosway and I knew I was innocent. "A person's life is in jeopardy."

The word triggered a spasm in my chest. I was the one they'd taken alive. My hands writhed in the cuffs as I heard Parker's monotone in my head: *Sometimes they insert the needle under a fingernail.* They could do anything with me, dump my body anywhere. No one would miss me until the limos arrived at the airport tomorrow afternoon. I could be lying bloated on a shore by then, my corpse ruptured on a rock. How many days would I bob there? Who would bother to check my scalp for puncture marks? I'd have no stomach left to pump.

Gebre seemed to read my thoughts. His chin extended in a good-natured smile. "Don't worry, ma'am. This won't take long." The voice sounded a little affected but sincere. I tried to feel reassured, but the promise worried me. Was my best hope a quick death?

I was debating who at the office would telephone

my parents—probably Donna—when the passenger window darkened. The door clattered, and Cosway's stomach filled the opening. His cigar tip brushed the dashboard as he sat down, the back of his seat curving toward my knees.

Then I heard the first gunshot. I thought it was engine backfire, but it continued, three distinct claps through Cosway's open door. The pauses were evenly syncopated, professional. I imagined the gun in Parker's hand, a string of smoke unraveling from the barrel. Was Zelda sprawled in a puddle of blood in the back of the alley?

"And that," announced Cosway, "is what happens to snitches."

I assumed he meant her, but then Wakefield appeared in the parking lot, Zelda Shilling safe at her side. They hurried toward a taxi parked on the opposite side of the road, passing an officer who made no attempt to stop them. I strained to see the opening of the alley again, bewildered by the gunshots. Who had they killed?

Cosway glimpsed my expression and sniggered. His door slammed as Gebre twisted the ignition and pulled out of the parking lot.

"That's quite a pair you got back there." I could see the yellow stubs of the Chief's teeth as he turned in profile. "Reggie and Melissa." Randy, he must have meant Randy. "Are all of your couples so loyal?" His voice rose: "*We knew there was something wrong with her from the start.*" It was a good imitation of Melissa's Jersey whine. He kept chuckling, his face wrinkling with dark lines. "I'll have to show you their testimonies. They're damned funny." He drew a breath through the cigar, the tip brightening, then dulling.

"What did you tell them?" My voice was loud enough but shaky. I pictured Melissa and Randy signing their names at the bottom of a typed affidavit, practice for a future wedding certificate.

"Guess." Victory had made him chatty.

"I murdered the bodyguard." Anderson. He had a name now.

Cosway worked his head up and down with the air of an encouraging therapist or game show host. "What else?"

"That I worked for Richard Shilling. That I was using them as a cover while I stalked Zelda."

Cosway almost clapped. He beamed at me as though sharing a joke. "They believed it instantly." The cigar spilled ashes as he gestured. "I told them they were Mrs. Shilling's only hope. If they would play along, keep you at ease, we could flush out your partner."

I didn't understand the word at first. My domestic partner? My significant other? The handcuffs tightened when I heard the name McGuffin in my head. I was center stage again, the host supporting my elbow as the curtain rose on the truth. They had wanted Andrew all along. If I hadn't told him to meet me at Bluebeard's, if I had never broken into his room, never sat down at his table, never smashed my breasts against him in the airplane, he would still be safe. The three shots from the alley were for him.

Cosway saw he had lost his sparring partner and adjusted forward, head still nodding with that chuckle. A plume of smoke surged at the windshield and collected around the shotgun mounted above his head. Gebre appeared unfazed by his boss' confession. He'd probably zippered the dead man's wallet in the evidence bag. All in a day's work.

I lost track of the roads. We might have been anywhere. My arms tingled when I shifted, numb from their handcuffed weight. I wondered if Andrew and I would wash up on the same beach, limbs tangled together in our only afterlife.

I didn't look up when the car stopped. I'd slipped into hostage mentality. If I was real quiet maybe they'd forget I was back here. Cosway's door creaked as he heaved himself out, the air battering me when it slammed again. I expected Gebre to follow, but his hand held steady at two o'clock on the wheel, gravel crunching as he drove on.

Of course. The boss wouldn't witness his own crime. Leave that to the aspiring underling. *Who Wants To Be A Blind Date* had a dozen interns just like him. My blood churned with the engine. I should have been weighing my life, radiating psychic atonements to all my loved ones and enemies. Instead, I found myself mentally ransacking my closet, debating which dress would look best on my corpse.

My body tensed as the car idled to a stop. I expected a clearing in the woods, broken glass shimmering in the weeds, maybe a dilapidated gas station, but when I forced my eyes to the passenger window, I saw an old woman in a miniskirt walking a schnauzer past a fire hydrant. Behind her a couple dunked biscotti into mugs, a Starbucks sign looming above them. Gebre was drumming his thumbs on the wheel. It sounded like a rhumba beat.

"Where are we going?"

He looked up and smiled into the rearview mirror. "The precinct, ma'am."

"What happens there?" I felt relieved for an instant. Then my brains switched film projectors: rubber hoses, glaring lights, metal-tipped boots pacing behind my chair, the table bare except for my typed confession and the uncapped pen. I would last ten, maybe eleven seconds.

"Well, I don't think I can get the public defender in this late on a Saturday. But he'll see you first thing in the morning." He considered it for a moment, then added, "After church."

A trial! My God, it sounded almost reasonable. I could see the black robe, the wood paneling, the guards at every exit. Even the Salem witches got that. "Does he work for Shilling, too?"

Gebre fidgeted and met my eyes in the mirror for the last time. His shoulders stiffened as he stared out the windshield. The car jerked ahead when the light changed.

It's Our First Weekend Away Together: Where Do You Book the Room?

Something scuffled under the cot in the corner cell. Otherwise, I had the place to myself. I'd found the driest patch of concrete to sit on, my back against the bars. A continuous drip echoed from somewhere in the darkness behind me. It was a slow beat; love ballads kept playing in my head. The Virgin Islands weren't spending their tourist dollars on penal infrastructure.

No minute hand hung from the clock face, but if I strained, I could make out the hour. It had inched under the three the last time I'd craned my neck. *Who Wants To Be A Blind Date* was on. If I were in my apartment, roaming with insomnia, I would have been watching. Weekends were the worst, my drawn blinds changing color with the street lights below, as I stared dead-eyed from my love seat at the TV. Sometimes the scent of my own perfume lingered around me, the residue of another abortive date—sometimes only the stale fumes from the microwave. Either way I was alone.

I preferred old episodes. Cocky contestants grew sympathetic after I had witnessed their downfalls. In retrospect, the nudges and high fives among the bachelors looked more desperate than arrogant. I was more likely to notice how a bachelorette's knees bobbed, her giddy hope tugging at my heart. She was still innocent.

That was the joke about the show, the tension that kept viewers tuning in: *The bachelorette always picked the wrong guy.* She didn't get to hear the bio blurb until after she had eliminated the contestant and stared dumbly as lawyer and doctor escaped from the lineup. The schlep who was left was cute enough—they were all cute enough—but he was never *the one.* He couldn't be. The act of choosing obliterated possibility. Her fantasies would linger forever in the wings as she strained to hear the footsteps of the departed.

Take Melissa, for instance. The choice should have been obvious, Bachelor #3. He had looked down as though blushing when the audience roared at an innuendo. The fireman from Colorado had been a close second. He had looked sincere when he'd crooned the Hallmark poem on his knees. But all Melissa had heard was his nasal drone. The guy with the deepest rumble for a voice always won. Even I wasn't immune. I used to gaze adoringly at my car radio whenever my favorite DJ spoke, until one appearance on a local telethon and the illusion was ruined. The square jaw of my imagination vanished under a row of double chins.

A bachelorette made her choice in minutes, but a dream was made in an instant. No man could ever measure up to his pseudonym.

I pulled myself up on the bars, buttocks numb. I hoped that McGuffin was sleeping somewhere more comfortable. The thought made the hairs on my arms rise. I tried to convince myself that the gunshots from the alley hadn't meant anything. Parker could have fired and missed, bricks chipping as Andrew slipped around a corner. Or they could have been warning shots, enough to pry him from behind a Dumpster, hands held high and empty. But I saw him when I closed my eyes, his bullet-riddled body bobbing restfully beyond the breakers. It was another reason not to sleep.

This wasn't the pang of love or even infatuation clawing at my heart. It was guilt. I should have flown the island when Cosway told me to, not tailed bodyguards and ferreted into private rooms. I had nearly crippled two men in one day, leaving McGuffin clutching his throat at the end of the peninsula, and Randy wheezing by his bathroom door. What was I doing? So my job had left me teetering on terminal boredom—did I think I could cast myself as my own hero, an action princess rescuing nobody but herself? If it weren't for me, Andrew would still be alive.

The thought spurred me into pacing. If I'm alive, I told myself, he could be, too. My heart leaped every time a noise echoed from the outer hall. I'd heard his footfall a thousand times, Gebre leading Andrew by handcuffs. Sometimes he looked battered, picturesque cuts on his forehead, at the corner of his mouth. Sometimes he was grinning, a roguish groom striding down an aisle of bars. If I could just see him one more time and apologize for getting him killed.

Unlike Melissa, I hadn't gotten the chance to redeem my mistake. Bachelorettes never fled through the stunned audience for the exit. They were obligated to face their decisions, suffer a weekend to prove themselves wrong. I think that was why I'd accepted the chaperoning job in the first place. I'd wanted to see what happened after the lights and music faded, after the romantic trappings were stripped away. And though week after week my cynicism triumphed as the winners parted with a terse handshake at an airport curb, I still longed for the exception.

I jerked wide awake when the lights blinked on. The noises were real this time. The far door rattled, and Parker strolled in. I waited for other footsteps, Andrew's, another officer's, anyone's, but the hallway behind her remained barren. She still wore one of her JCPenney outfits, the mobster soccer mom. I'd expected a complete transformation, either slinky dress or guerilla fatigues, cigarette holder in her teeth, but only her gait seemed different. She had always looked confident, but now she had this sexy thing going, too. Her heels scraped the cement like stiletto blades.

I stumbled on the cot leg, realizing that Cosway had probably sent her to dispose of me. For the thousandth time I skimmed the walls for an escape route, praying a crack in the concrete might suddenly give way. I should have spent the last hours tunneling with a cot spring.

She folded her arms as she watched me tremble, so I sucked in a staccato breath and mirrored her pose. If I couldn't feel brave, I could still act it.

Parker pivoted a heel as she spoke. "I knew Cosway was wrong about you." Her feet avoided the puddles as she paced, a stream snaking between her shoes.

"But he had me going at first, especially when you showed up behind Anderson on the Lovelund path. I figured you saw me in the bushes. I should've shot you then, but I'd gone to such trouble to stage Anderson's drowning I didn't want to spoil it." She smiled sheepishly, as if admitting a fashion error.

"When one of my moles in the Bureau said they were sending an agent down here to meet with Zelda, Cosway convinced us you were it. He's had his eye on you for awhile. Thinks the FBI has been working up your chaperone cover for a couple of years. He even thinks you're responsible for that *Playboy* leak, that you made it look like an inside job to stir up trouble between him and Richard." She rolled her eyes. "Cosway is an idiot." Her demeanor invited my camaraderie, two girls gossiping. Then her gaze sharpened. "I knew you were nobody."

She let the toe of her heel touch the edge of the water as though testing its temperature or fluidity. The puddles shimmered with rainbows under the exposed bulbs. "I let him lean on you for a while—I still can't figure why you didn't catch the first flight off the island this morning." She flashed a half-smile at me. Was it amusement? Admiration? It vanished with her shrug. "But then you were so convenient. Once Zelda thought you were me, I had free rein. Never saw a patsy run better interference. You're the best fall guy I've ever had."

Something wasn't right. Did professional killers detail their crimes before disposing of a witness? Why was she talking to me at all? If they wanted me dead, I'd be dead, not caged up sweating the seconds before my execution. Was Parker so confident, so egotistical that she needed to demonstrate her impunity? Or was there more to the story than I had realized?

"What the hell do you need a fall guy for?" I padded to the bars, arms flapping. What's the point of being cowed on your deathbed? "Bodies wash up all over this place. No one investigates. Isn't that the point of controlling the chief of police?"

For an instant, Parker looked almost embarrassed. "I liked you." I wasn't sure if I saw a quiver of vulnerability running across her mouth or if she were holding in a laugh. "When you didn't run, I knew I could use you. Light a fire under your ass and you'd do something interesting." She shrugged. "You led me to McGuffin, didn't you?"

I winced audibly. Andrew had been smart to fear me. I might as well have pulled the trigger myself. When I closed my eyes, I could feel the press of his lips against mine. That was all it took, one kiss in the garden. I wanted to ask if he were dead, but I knew Parker would dictate every detail, his blood-drowned gurgles, the way his face slowly whitened. I could feel the breeze drying his open eyes. Three distinct shots echoed in my head.

Parker started pacing again. She'd gotten something sticky on the sole of one shoe. "You were the perfect decoy right up to the end. McGuffin, the whole restaurant, everyone had their eyes on you and Cosway parading around like a pair of second-rate magicians. No one noticed me. When McGuffin skulked out the kitchen he thought he was home free."

I ratcheted in my breath. "And this is my reward?"

She looked around, waving a finger. "Oh, these are just temporary accommodations." She used the apologetic tone of a customer-services operator. I waited for the punch line—that I would be comfier in a canvas bag at the bottom of a swamp. "I told Cosway to lose Anderson's wallet."

I didn't register the name of the dead bodyguard at first. Then my jaw unhinged. Losing the wallet meant losing the evidence against me. I glared at her. Was this just another game?

Parker chuckled. "Cosway was pissed, but he knows a court case would stir up more media attention. Nobody gets tried for murder on this island." It might have been one of those statistics from the tourist manuals. "The morning shift has orders to release you." She beamed at me as she strolled toward the door. "Think of it as payment for a job well done." Her fingers fanned as she waved good-bye, the door clanging shut behind her.

I waited for the lights to blink out, but they never did.

21

Can I Count on You to Be There When I Wake Up in the Morning?

I didn't recognize the officer who unlocked my cell. He grunted something and turned to leave as the door screeched and almost hit me. The bars collided with the cell wall and reverberated like dented chimes. I assumed I was to follow.

He stood me in a doorway and vanished. Several cops sat at desks as others bantered beside a derelict watercooler, their laughs as dull as coughs. A clock on the lobby wall had a minute hand but no hour, and it clicked four times before someone handed me a manila envelope with coffee rings on its front.

Two earrings, a Lovelund key card and my wristwatch slid out. My purse arrived separately, zippered into an unmarked evidence baggie. I signed something and stood several minutes before realizing that I was free to leave.

The salt in the air stung my eyes as I shuffled down a street of closed shops. I could still feel the jail bars against my back as I walked the four blocks to the tourist district, then another four to the edge of the pier, where I knew a row of taxis would be parked. A driver finished his Egg McMuffin, pawing a magazine on his hood while I waited.

The muffler sounded like it was spraying gunshot. I slumped in the back, as calm as a corpse. If I knew my producer's home number I would have rung him up and resigned. In eight hours I could be alone in my apartment, a Lean Cuisine hissing in the microwave, while I skimmed the Want Ads, pretending I'd never heard of anyone named Andrew McGuffin. He was just some reporter who'd gambled his life away trying to land a once-in-a-lifetime interview with a mobster's ex-wife. It's not like I knew the guy. We never even finished a drink together. What did any of it have to do with me?

Exhaust plumed around me as I climbed out and trudged past the reception desk without glancing up. My sandal straps had rubbed blisters on both my heels, but the pain seemed distant. I was my own ghost.

The curtains blew through the patio door to our bungalow as I poked for the opening. The bed was empty, the sheets streaming from the mattress in a suggestive tangle. The torn condom wrapper on the rug may or may not have been mine. Melissa and Randy must have left the bungalow unlocked when they went out for an early swim, apparently feeling safer with me, the resident killer, behind bars.

I pulled my top off and chucked it at the wastebasket, then unfolded the last change of clothes left in my drawer, wishing I could burn the odor of mildew out of my hair. I shoved the other remnants into my bag and threw Melissa's suitcases open on the bed.

I considered marooning the two of them, but then I would have screwed up the last remaining detail of the weekend. I'd gotten an innocent man killed; I could at least shepherd my wards onto a plane. Once they were airborne, they were on their own. I wrestled on my shirt, hands groping for armholes, as I staggered toward the bathroom.

The sound of running water behind the closed door stopped me. You would never have guessed there was a water shortage from the number of showers people took around here.

"Melissa?" That was my mother's tone again. I waded through the steam and yanked the shower curtain back the way she had always done to me.

Randy gaped, as though reliving a scene from *Psycho*. All I saw was matted hair and white lather, his arms covering his crotch from fear, not modesty. He slipped, clawing at the slick walls as he plunged under the stream. I waited until he landed before peering over the tub ledge.

"Where's Melissa?"

He blinked. Water sprayed off the side of his head. "She wanted to swim before breakfast."

"You know we check out at ten?"

His chin started bobbing and didn't stop. "Yes."

"Good." I shoved the curtain back.

One of the blisters popped as I worked my sandal back on. I blotted the heel on the sheet and kicked off the shoes by the door. It was viciously beautiful outside, chlorine blue sky, breeze like a rotating fan. I would have sunk the whole damned island.

A morbid whim tugged at me, and I allowed myself the luxury of self-punishment. My legs led me down a familiar row of bungalows, the sun sparkling on each gold number, Twenty-seven, Twenty-nine. I stood at Andrew's door, staring at a blank slate of wood, not so much as a peep hole to peer back.

Maybe that was why I had chased him around the Islands for two days, inventing and reinventing him as I went, my fantasies safe as long as he remained at a tantalizing distance. I may have been too jaded for fairy tales, but a part of me still longed to be rescued by a prince, that stranger who would remain forever perfect, never to devolve into a snickering bachelor on a contestant chair.

This time yesterday he would have been inside, sipping coffee, shaving maybe, wet curls clinging to his neck. I closed my eyes and willed the world back. My hand rested against the wood and snapped back when the lock clicked open. It wasn't latched.

"Andrew?"

Could he have been inside? Maybe Parker hadn't wanted to leave a messy corpse smear behind Bluebeard's, another dead vacationer for the local press and tourist bureau to overlook. I read somewhere that hit men fired into the eyes to minimize cleanup. Closing mine only focused the image: Andrew's empty sockets gazing at the ceiling, blood soaking into the sponge of his pillow. If Parker had taken him alive, it would only have been to murder him in the privacy of his own room.

The room appeared empty, unchanged. I inspected the bathroom but spied no bodies, no killers lurking in the tub. The bed was still made, but a slight rumple remained where Andy had rested on the spread, the faintest outline like a faded police chalk line.

My bare toes squished into the carpet. I grimaced and held my breath before looking down, expecting a bloody puddle, but the pattern in the carpet obscured the wet stain. I knelt and rubbed my fingers warily into the spot, then sniffed them. Orange juice. Tia hadn't made her morning rounds yet.

There was nothing here to prove that Andrew was dead. A corpse would have been better, cold stiff fingers to grip. This was worse, an absence large enough to drown in.

The unzippered suitcase grinned at me. I knelt and slipped my fingers into the plush shadows before parting the jaw. These were Andrew's remains: a couple of pairs of briefs, a creased dress shirt I hadn't seen him wear. A navy blue sock tried but failed to match its darker mate.

I knew what lay underneath the shoes but peered at the glossy cover anyway. The magazine slapped against the bureau top as my fingers dug again. Belt buckle, shoe heel, fountain pen. Where was the gun? I yanked out a fistful of clothes but found nothing. Andy had said he didn't have it on him at the restaurant. Had he lied? I overturned the suitcase and rifled every pocket and lining until I was satisfied they were empty.

I checked the bare table, remembering how the barrel had lain by his hip while he'd buttoned his shirt. A new hope seized me as empty drawers rumbled out of their sockets. If the gun wasn't here, then Andrew had had it last night. A Lovelund stationery pad slapped the pillow and landed in a pile of pamphlets. A Bible somersaulted over the bed as I rifled the bedstand. If Andrew had had it last night, he might still be alive. He could have fired the three gunshots from the alley last night, downing Cosway's men as he escaped.

I ransacked the bathroom in seconds, the contents of his toiletry bag ricochetting in the tub. Nothing was taped under the toilet lid, nothing submerged in the rusty water behind it. Where else could he have hidden the gun? He would have wanted it out of sight but accessible in case I or some other Mafia henchman visited his room again.

My toes sunk into the drying orange juice as I padded back into the bedroom. Glass bottles rattled as I yanked open the mini-bar. Perrier, Red Stripe, Pepsi-Cola. I reached under the freezer compartment and grabbed a plastic shopping bag tucked behind the candy bars. It felt heavy, cold to the touch. I imagined a frozen donor organ wrapped in dry ice.

My fingers tensed as they slipped inside. We had played this game in elementary school, only with blindfolds. The metal stung my skin, but the handle was woodier, curving to my palm. I thought it was called a snub nose, the kind police detectives carried on '70s reruns.

War widows got dog tags, flags wrapped into triangles. My mother still had the mining cap her father wore until the cave-in. I pulled the bag away and glared at the gun. This was what strangers got.

It didn't mean anything. He had the same chance of being alive as before, though knowing the odds, the thought failed to warm me. I flexed my numb palm, the chill from the gun rising up my wrist.

If I hadn't been so blind to him, so bent on projecting my own fantasies—roguish assassin, intrepid FBI agent—I might have discovered something better. Forget romantic hyperboles, the guy was risking his life exposing crime syndicates. What more of a hero could a girl want? Could I even rise to that level? A quiet life of corporate banality hadn't prepared me for this.

When my mother's Beetle had rolled over the embankment on our driveway, I had assumed I was going to die a sixteen-year-old virgin. But my foot had still wedged itself against the dash. I remember debating the best handholds while my window glass crunched inches from my face. The desperate were crafty. What did odds matter?

I felt myself rising as though inside an elevator. My stomach sucked in as I tucked the gun into my shorts, the handle frigid above my panties. I had business to attend to. Until I actually saw Andrew's body draped under a tarp on a picnic table, I wasn't giving up.

My problems had begun with Zelda Shilling, and I still hadn't collected a single favor from her. All I wanted was confirmation, proof that Andrew was dead. If Parker and Cosway had finished him off, they would have made sure Zelda knew about it as a warning.

Andrew's door slammed behind me as I tramped toward the plusher end of the resort. The gun kept slipping, the barrel jabbing my thigh. How had John Travolta and Samuel Jackson kept those Magnums in their boxers in *Pulp Fiction*? A pair of honeymooners on the path divided in front of me, their fingers unlinking at the last instant. The next couple steered onto the grass. Shilling's row of bungalows lurked under a scrap of cloud. I rapped on the glass.

The latch gave when I squeezed the handle. Did everyone think the island was safe just because

Cosway had thrown me in jail? Wakefield's Amazonian arm drew the curtain back as I slid open the glass. She didn't have time to look surprised.

"I want to talk to Zelda."

"She's not available."

I pulled the gun, not caring how many carefree tourists witnessed it. "I want to talk to Zelda." The stunted gun tip almost touched her nose.

Wakefield backed up step by grudging step. I didn't need to follow her glance to see the other gun on the table. It was bigger than mine but out of reach. If she hadn't mistaken me for an overzealous bellhop, I'd probably be dead.

Zelda appeared in the bathroom door, her face half made and a Lovelund towel wrapped in a beehive around her head. The eyeliner in her hand sank as she recognized me. At this point, I didn't know if she thought I was a hit man, a reporter, or the Islands' resident lunatic. She erased the startled look from her face and glowered at me.

"What do you want?"

"Where is he?"

Her lips fluttered. "Who?"

"McGuffin."

"How the hell would I know?" Her surprise sounded genuine.

"You were supposed to meet with him. This was all your doing."

I pointed the gun at her without meaning to, the barrel a severed fingertip. Shilling backed into the door edge but maintained a cool grimace. "He contacted me. He hid messages in my dry cleaning till I wrote back and agreed to meet with him. The last envelope he sent had a plane ticket in it and reservations for this godforsaken resort." She gestured at the walls. She'd never spent a night in one of Cosway's holding cells.

"Why—"

My cell phone chimed in my purse, and the three of us froze. Shilling and Wakefield exchanged glances after the third ring. I knew who it was, the secretary pressing his headset to his ear, a pen tapping his blotter. He'd called the same time yesterday, having gotten a lot pushier since the producer appended the word "associate" to his job title. Wakefield inched toward the table, her hands hovering at her hips in a gunfighter's stance. She inched back when I pointed the gun at her kneecap.

After the seventh ring, I submitted, juggling the phone in my left hand, the gun still raised.

"What?"

"Once again you neglected to call." It was a little song, high and prissy. "How many warnings can I give you? I have an unfinished press release waiting on my screen. How am I supposed to—"

The syllables strained through my teeth, "This is not a good time—" I hesitated. "Pat." That still wasn't it. "I will call you back."

"Call *me* back? Now that's an idea! Do you know how many times—"

I clicked the phone off, my eyes never leaving the gun on the table, then squinted at Shilling, trying to regain my lunatic edge. "Why did you meet here?"

"I don't know. It was his idea." She was trying to feign composure now, the eyeliner pencil twisting in her fingers like a cigarette. "I was mad at Richard. I wanted to get back at him." Her face flashed sudden irritation. "I was supposed to meet McGuffin on St. John when you killed—"

This time I raised the barrel on purpose. "I didn't kill anybody!"

Wakefield spoke in a monotone. "I guess that's why they arrested you."

"That was a setup. They framed me."

"So why did they let you go?"

The gun was already drooping despite my scowl. She was right. It didn't make sense. Parker had murdered the other bodyguard just to get Andrew's and Shilling's attention, the way I might type off a snitty memo on office e-mail. She killed for a living. Why would she let me go? The Anderson frame job was irrelevant. I was a witness, or at least an awkward rumor, an eraser smudge on her CV. You didn't scale that high in the Shilling pantheon by acting on whims of compassion. I was alive for a reason. Parker and Cosway wouldn't have left a loose string flapping—unless they needed help tying it.

Wakefield and Zelda kept staring at me, waiting for another question, another threat. I mumbled an apology and crammed Andy's gun back into my shorts. Wakefield lunged for hers, but I had already backed onto the patio. I walked away slowly, daring her to shoot me in the back.

22

Do You Like It When Girls Compete for You?

Cosway's men had vanished from the resort, and no police cruisers lurked in the staff parking lot. Gebre was probably directing traffic, coaxing tourists onto the walkways. I climbed into the first taxi as it was pulling out and asked the guy next to me where we were headed. St. John sounded as good as anywhere.

The first step to winning, my father had once coached me, whether at softball, chess or gazing over the scattered shards of a jigsaw puzzle, was simple: adopt the good-natured assumption that you will. The trick wasn't psyching out your opponent, but yourself. Amateur or not, I was going to outsmart the crooks who had played me for a pawn.

My plan—if you could call it that—required that Cosway was still having me watched. I'd led them to Andrew already. Once they had him, I should have been useless, a piece shucked back into the box. That one fact buoyed my conviction. If Parker hadn't killed me, then she must have had a reason, a new use for me. Why else would she have divulged all of that information in the jail except to manipulate me further?

It was a thin scrap of logic, but I'd pinned my hopes to it. If Andrew had gotten away, if he had ducked down the alley as the bullets whizzed over his head, then Parker and Cosway had botched their assignment. The *Playboy* reporter was still on the loose. They could have the airport and docks patrolled, post a man at every boat rental hoping to pick out a thirty-something white guy from the deluge of identical tourists. Or they could follow me. Parker knew I'd try anything to help McGuffin; she'd sharpened my guilt to be sure of it. If they tailed me long enough, they hoped I would lead them to him again. We'd had enough time alone at the bar to work out a secret rendezvous plan, something I wished had occurred to me at the time. Now all I could do was wander the Islands, hoping to flush information out of my hypothetical pursuers.

No polyester uniforms skulked at the Red Hook pier either. I pictured the married cop fetching Cosway's morning coffee while I climbed aboard the ferry. The waves were choppier than usual, St. John vanishing under the stern, then popping back on a seesaw. The woman next to me paled as her head bobbed up and down. Another couple quoted storm reports, but I didn't catch whether one was coming or going. I gripped the railing for balance, but my stomach held solid.

No tourists loitered on the St. John dock as we nestled into our moorings. The first ferry ride of the morning carried barely a quarter passenger load. Honeymooners never woke before ten. The Islands boycotted daylight savings down here. Cruz Bay was still a ghost town.

My fellow passengers teetered across the gangplank while I eyed them one by one. There wasn't a shifty face among them, but I knew better. Those were assault rifles bulging from their beach bags. The shy ones lingered, peering down the short block with uncertain frowns. The initiated marched toward the rental huts and Jeep lots, pigeons scattering from their paths. No one stole glances at me.

Was I expecting Parker in a trench coat and wig? A pair of Groucho Marx glasses? I wasn't working with rookie cops anymore. These were professionals. If they didn't want to be seen, then I wasn't going to see them. The same was true with God or bacteria. I just had to pretend they were there.

I stalled in my seat until a crewman with a ponytail asked if I needed help. I met his eyes, probing for hints of deception, but he only blinked and smiled. If I waited any longer, I was afraid he would start hitting on me.

The gangplank shuddered under my weight while I trudged across, debating my next move. My logic seemed sound, but I was relying more on faith. I wished I could ring Andrew on my cell and get advice from a pro. What would the seasoned crime reporter do at this point?

A kid in an apron flipped an Open sign as I crossed the block to a vegetarian cafe. I sat at the outermost table, visible to the entire street, and ordered a steaming bowl of adzuki beans and pickled radish. Couldn't get more conspicuous than that. My stomach contracted with the first spoonful, then calmed. I hadn't swallowed anything since the decaf at Bluebeard's.

Pedestrians glanced at the bowl but ignored me. None had the air of a Mafia criminal except the overweight father haranguing the owner at the counter. He didn't understand why his ten-year-old couldn't get a cheeseburger. The whole family wore matching biking shorts. I tucked an extravagant tip under the water glass and headed for the Jeep rental, hoping someone else would follow me.

I had never excelled at attracting men, so I didn't know why I assumed this would be any easier. At least singles bars had rules of etiquette. If you rubbed against someone long enough, he would eventually take you home. I would have walked nude through the tourist shops if I'd thought it would work. But I opted for the opposite approach.

The cashier at the Jeep rental lot took his time, expecting a husband or boyfriend to materialize to sign the credit slip. I grabbed the keys out of his hands. My tires left tread marks on the asphalt, the back of the National Forest sign bouncing in the rearview mirror. A homely girl could sit alone at a bar for half an hour, then hook three guys just by weaving for the exit. If Cosway was anything like the last guy I'd dated, he would think my avoiding him was a turn-on.

The road dipped and rose like a wrinkled sheet as I angled into the curves, pretending I had somewhere to go. I made a game of it. There were cars tailing me, and I had to lose them. The Jeep moaned as I shifted into the next hill, but nothing surfaced in the mirror.

St. John was the runt of the the Islands, so I had to circle back after ten minutes or plunge into the Atlantic. A pair of grazing cows cut off my adrenaline flow. I idled to a stop while they lulled in the road, munching on bouquets of weeds poking between the no-passing lines. Honks only slowed the meal. I slouched and watched the sky. Every cloud posed in the shape of police surveillance helicopters.

Step two of winning required systematically guessing what your opponent was going to try next. In chess, it was simple; whoever saw ahead the greatest number of moves won. I beat my dad for the first time when I was thirteen. He was so proud, he took me out for ice cream and signed me up for soccer summer camp. We never played again.

I watched my bovine companions chewing methodically, their udders gently swaying, trying to remember that last time I'd stepped foot on a soccer field, or any field for that matter. What had I done with that ancient softball mitt? I sat, mentally scouring my apartment, unable to locate even a chess board. My twenties seemed improbably distant, obscured by a hilltop cresting prematurely. When was the last time anyone had called me spunky?

I extracted my phone and punched "1" on the speed-dial, the last resort of every derailed girl sleuth.

"Hello?"

"Hi, Mom."

"Ashley, hi, what's wrong? I thought you were in the Islands." She sounded breathless, probably having jogged from the garden again, though she'd answered before the third ring.

"I am. I just wanted to—" To what? Ask my parents if they thought of me as a couch potato, check whether my life looked as boring from the outside as it felt from in here? I heard my father's voice, the sound of bed springs creaking. I didn't think they slept late on the weekends. "I'm sorry, did I wake you up?"

"Not exactly, dear. But tell me what's wrong?"

I think I actually gasped, "Oh, God," and covered my eyes. I hadn't interrupted them having sex since I was ten. "It can wait, really, it can wait. I'll call you tonight or something."

I wanted to hang up but she blurted back, "Ashley, don't be ridiculous. What's going on? You sound upset."

"No, I'm okay." There was the problem. Perpetually okay. "I guess, I don't know, I wanted advice, I think."

"Advice?" The awe in her voice overwhelmed the flattered delight. "You haven't asked me my opinion about something since—" The receiver hummed as she thought. "Since that boy across the street asked you to your first dance."

I didn't think I'd asked her then either. "What did you say?"

"Don't go."

"Why not?"

"Because I didn't think you really liked him."

"I thought you were just being prudish. Wasn't he older?" I remembered him vaguely, clean-cut, a little jockish, a proto-bachelor for *Who Wants To Be A Blind Date.*

"You had a crush on that other boy. What was his name? You used to make me drop you off at the mall after school so you could try to see him."

Don Sposato. He and his friends always hung out near the Dairy Queen. I never worked up the gall to speak to him. I just kept putting myself in his way, hoping he would notice me. "I have no idea what you're talking about."

"Well, you didn't listen anyway."

"I'll keep it in mind next time I want to—" I looked up, the light in my head as bright as the sun shimmering off the hood. Even the cows had surrendered the road to me. "Mom, thanks, I'll call you later. You're terrific."

Twenty minutes later and I was coasting into the Trunk Bay parking lot. Nostalgia had spurred me to a new leap in logic. Cosway didn't need to follow me if he knew where I was likely to go. Zelda and McGuffin had met here yesterday. Cosway probably had all the big tourist locations staked out, figuring Andrew would want a big crowd to blend into.

I retraced Shilling's footsteps into the tourist center and probed the cafeteria for spies. A short-order cook prodded a pair of sausage patties with a metal spatula. He rubbed his eyes with the back of his wrist, grease vapors wafting across the counter. Okay, probably not one of Parker's associates.

A party of Japanese tourists occupied the nearest picnic table outside. I remembered where Shilling had sat and took Wakefield's spot on the bench, checking under the deck for movement. Parker might have been under there, peering up my shorts through the slats, but I doubted it.

I was doubting everything. Maybe Parker had let me go for the reason she'd given me. She liked me. What did I understand about the moral ambiguities of professional killers? If Andrew hadn't gotten away, then my options narrowed. I could ring Cosway, schedule an appointment, and shoot him in his office with the snub nose, ruining the nicest uniform in the precinct. If his men didn't use me for target practice I might get parole in thirty years.

The thought of Andrew kept me going. He might be hiding out somewhere, hungry and exhausted, waiting for Shilling's people to zero in on him. What the hell did I have to complain about? I'd spent the last two years too afraid of a drop in salary to quit a job I hated. I wondered how well *Playboy* paid, doubting Andrew gave it much thought. If I did make it home, I would send my résumé to some of those public channels I'd always snubbed.

The clock in the lobby read ten to nine, a little more than an hour until check-out. I wondered whether Randy and Melissa had phoned room service to alert the authorities that an escaped killer was roaming the Islands. I wondered if they knew how to phone room service.

I checked my watch. If someone was watching—maybe that Japanese mother in the pink sunglasses—it was good to look anxious, counting the seconds until my imaginary rendezvous with Andrew. My watch read five till. I looked again, minute hand centering the eleven, then squinted through the lobby glass again. It was still ten of inside.

My watch was never wrong. I had every clock in my apartment synchronized to the Weather Channel, every digital second flashing in unison. I approached the Japanese family, hoping one of the kids understood English, and pointed at my watch like a mime.

"The time?" My lips moved in slow motion, exaggerating each syllable. "Do you know the time?"

The girl glanced at her Mickey Mouse. "Yeah, eight fifty." Few cabbies had thicker New York accents. I thanked her and headed for the rest room, my paranoia aflame.

The door knocked against the wall as I bent and checked for Parker's feet under the stalls. I pictured her perched on a toilet seat as I shoved each door back, metal reverberating against metal. Two days of gangsters and I was getting a little crazy. The woman at the mirror left without drying her hands.

I unclasped the watchband and set it on the sink ledge. It was moderately expensive, a present from my father a couple Christmases ago. I angled it toward the lights and realized that I'd never seen the two tiny gouge marks along the edge before.

After splitting two nails trying to pry the watch open, I dug a fountain pen out of my purse. The glass cracked under the pen tip, but the face wouldn't budge. I was starting to work the gun out of my shorts when a girl in a mini-dress strolled in, her spiked heels pounding like hoofs.

"Can I see one of those for a minute?" She looked down to see that I was pointing at her left foot. My other hand was outstretched.

"Uh, I guess." The automatic hand dryer rattled on as she balanced against it, teetering on one foot.

It took three blows to pop the watch face off. The girl gawked over my shoulder, as I handed the shoe to her upside down. "Thanks." She accepted it and exited without using the toilet.

Realizing that a gear or two had already rolled down the sink, I sealed the drain and scrutinized the jumble of metal. My nose hovered an inch above the porcelain. I didn't know what the hell I was looking at. None of the miniature wheels inside the watch were moving. I had already started concocting excuses for when my dad asked why I had stopped wearing it. Silver clashes with my prison jumper.

I flipped the face over, ready to sweep the heap into the garbage can, but something clung to the back of the open lid. It pricked my thumb and fingertip as I pried it out, a lopsided sliver of black electronics, garishly clashing with the gears' Victorian purity. I'd read an article in my dentist's waiting room about pet tracers that were shorter than toenails and could attach under flea collars so affluent pet owners could rest peacefully at night. I held the tracer up to the window, glorying in its existence—at last tangible evidence of God. Parker must have installed it while I was dozing in Cosway's cell, probably the reason they took me there in the first place.

If there was a microphone in there too, maybe I'd shattered her eardrum battering the watch open. I dropped the tracer back into place, hoping I hadn't damaged it with my handiwork, and pressed the watch closed, minus a few stray parts. It jingled in my pocket as I walked. My dad would never know the difference.

I wondered why strangers were smiling at me, until I noticed my grin reflected in the exit door. If they were tracing my steps, then they were hoping I'd lead them somewhere, presumably to Andrew, as I had the first time. *He was alive.* I wanted to shout it in the parking lot, fire the gun in a victory strut, but I turned toward the beach instead. Technically, my life had just gotten more complicated. That was a Mafia tracer tickling my thigh.

A family of snorklers waddled up the sand, and I returned their greetings and headed for my favorite peninsula. The vegetation looked furrier, almost blue in the cloud shade. I'd never planned an ambush before. This was a weekend of firsts.

I'd edited dozens of contestants' mini-bios, dredging them for interesting life tidbits, slashing out mundane details and underlining any inkling of adventure. I was following my own advice for a change, revising as I went. A part of me longed for my love seat, feet propped on a folder of applicants as I watched other people take chances with their lives.

Part of me didn't.

The wind scoured my face as I walked the low road, one eye searching for the sandal I'd lost out here yesterday. Every bush rustled as I approached, tree limbs waving. I thought I glimpsed Andy every few feet. They had gambled wrong. I had no idea where he was hiding and was no more capable of leading Parker to him than taking her to Richard Shilling. But if she was tracking me, I might surprise her and get some of my own questions answered.

I passed the rock where Andrew and the Amazon had rendezvoused. Dozens of sniper roosts overlooked the shady spot. An entire precinct of St. Thomas crooks could have hidden in the brush. I stalked to the end of the peninsula: flat, no cover, water clawing at its edges. Only an idiot would cut off her only escape route. At least I hoped Parker would think that. If I wanted to surprise her, this was the spot.

An invisible gear rolled off my pinky and fell soundlessly into the weeds as I fished the mangled watch out of my pocket, praying the tracer still worked. I arranged the remaining pieces on a rock in the center of the clearing. Ants investigated it, a new altar fallen from the sky. Hopefully Parker would think I'd left it out there for her to find too, while I snuck back to the parking lot unnoticed.

My cell phone chirped while I backed away, and I yanked it out, afraid of drawing sniper fire from the trees. "What now?"

The secretary tried for a menacing rumble. "You didn't call back."

I considered placing the phone next to my watch and smashing it with the gun. "What do you want?"

"You didn't phone me last night either." If I told him that I'd spent the night in jail, he would have asked how I had squandered my free call. "You can't keep shirking your responsibilities like this, Ashley."

I bent and craned my neck to see the path. Presumably Parker would use it. I couldn't picture her in snorkel gear. "I've been a little busy."

"I know. I rang your room three times last night after I gave up on your cell phone. What'd you do, bury it?" I pictured the manila envelope with my phone inside ringing in the back of the precinct evidence room. "Rollins wants to know where you were."

Rollins was the latest in a long, undistinguished line of *Who Wants To Be A Blind Date* producers, all of whom rewarded office snitches. "You talked to the producer?"

He didn't answer. I thought I heard his breath quicken, but it might have been the ocean amplified from my own mouthpiece. I might have been pressing a seashell against my ear.

"Why were you talking to Rollins about me?" I didn't care—I had already written off my job as a happy casualty of the weekend—but I didn't like being the secretary's stepping ladder.

"It came up, I guess." I could see the cord to his headset knotting around his fingers as he squirmed.

"Look, don't blame me. You're the one screwing around on company time."

I shuffled out of view of the path and started inspecting the rocks for a hiding place. "Yeah, I'm just out here skinny-dipping, Pete." It required discipline, but I got it wrong every time. "Do you want something?"

"I told you. This press release has to leave my desk today. I need a scoop on the couple. How are they doing?" He dropped his voice conspiratorially. "I mean, you know, are they *hitting it off?*"

He really wanted to know if they'd fucked yet, but he didn't know how to ask a woman that. I propped my elbow on my other arm and peered at a distant yacht. "Melissa has a black eye, and Randy is still walking funny."

More waves echoed back at me during a shocked pause. Then he chuckled like a kid pretending to get a dirty joke. "Oh come on, tell me something I can print."

"The island is overrun by syndicate operatives. They control the police department and kill with impunity. I'm being stalked by one this very moment."

He exhaled a sigh of infinite tribulation. "Fine. That's fine. I bet Mr. Rollins will think that's funny, too."

"Tell him and you're dead." The waves drowned his last words as I spotted a good hiding place in the rocks and hung up.

I inched down the ledge, trying very hard not to puncture my spleen with the gun barrel. I rested it carefully on a dry patch of rock before easing into the water. If I ducked my head, I turned invisible. This was the spot where I had downed McGuffin, my first deadly Mafia assassin.

The shallow waves lapped up my legs, the eddy warming quickly. The sun climbed from one to three finger widths above the hilltops while I counted gulls. I considered pulling my blouse off for a headrest, thinking it might help to even my tan lines, too.

I wondered whether all investigative work was this thrilling, hours killed in anxious boredom. How long had Andrew tailed Zelda, memorizing the nuances of her New York routines, before attempting to contact her? He must have spent weeks in surveillance before slipping the message into her dry cleaning. And then how long did he wait for a response, parked outside her skyrise, watching for one of her maids to drop off the next load of laundry?

At least he had a more comfortable seat.

When I needed two hands to measure the time, I started to worry. Maybe the tracer was dead. Electronics weren't usually quality-tested with spike heels. Maybe I couldn't tell a tracer from a watch battery. My judgment of character had been off this weekend.

One of my legs had fallen asleep, and it tingled as I shimmied my butt off the rock ledge to poke my head up for the thousandth time. I nearly yelped as I ducked back, almost knocking the gun into the water as I grabbed for it. Someone was there. I peeked an eye over the top of the boulder to study a figure crouching over my watch shrine. A woman. Parker. I couldn't see her face, but her head was shaking with amusement.

I clasped my hand around my other fist and elbowed over the rock. Her back was still turned, but I knew she sensed me, her hand slithering for her gun. The wind had died to a faint stirring.

"Don't fucking move." The snub nose grew suddenly heavy. The barrel drew lines up and down her back, my finger nowhere near the trigger. "Turn around. Slowly."

She waited, then called over her shoulder so I could see the corner of a smirk. "You told me not to move."

I cocked the gun, and she turned.

"Put your hands on your head."

She did, but with a Simon-says roll of the eyes. "Is this really necessary?" I tried to climb up the rocks without lowering the gun. Not easy. I must have looked pretty ridiculous, water dripping off my soaked shorts as I stood.

Parker sighed, then pointed with her chin. "You know you have the safety on?"

Without looking at the gun, I aimed to her left and pulled the trigger. The handle yanked my fists up with a cymbal crash that rattled through my marrow. Parker stared at me, the muscles in her neck rigid. The bullet must have missed her head by a yard, but she wasn't smirking any more. "Someone probably heard that."

"I doubt it." I used the barrel as a pointer. "Let me see your gun."

She wiggled her shirt up like a stripper and revealed a black holster webbing around her white bra. The gun was bigger than Wakefield's.

"Take it out. Barrel first."

After a minute of contortions, the nose swung between her fingertips, and I gestured toward the yacht anchored off the bay. "Aim for the boat."

She wound up the throw as well as any pitcher. I wonder if she'd played girl's softball as a kid, too. The silence before the splash drew my glance away. When I pointed at her arms, she raised them again.

"Now what?"

"Tell me where he is."

She tried to shrug, but it was hard with her hands on her head. "Who? Cosway? Probably still in bed—"

She shut up when I closed one eye and aimed at her mouth. She was afraid I might fire by accident. So was I. I inhaled and steadied the gun. The whole game rode on this hand.

"No. McGuffin."

"If I knew, why would I be here?" She frowned the same way Rollins did when he was annoyed with one of my contestant recommendations. "I still can't figure out how Cosway's men blew it." Something between chagrin and admiration flashed across her face. "That reporter ambushed the three of them in the alley before I got back there."

The truth was too much. I swallowed and tried to keep my voice even. "He got away? Andrew got away?" It had been a hunch at best, a kind of prayer. I'd been playing make-believe.

"Thanks to you. You're the one who tipped him off."

My smile burst out with a gust of air from my lungs. I might have knocked Parker over with a hug if I didn't think she'd knife me. God knew what else she had hidden in that bra.

Her grin mirrored mine, only with a sardonic twist. "So we're after the same guy, huh? It's kinda touching." She didn't look touched. Her eyes settled on the gun barrel, which I'd let droop a little, and I raised it as if scolded. "I guess this is your chance to knock off the competition."

Was she suggesting I shoot her, eliminate her before she could get to Andrew before me? We each raised an eyebrow. "That your advice?"

"All's fair."

She had let an amateur pin her down at gunpoint. Maybe the humiliation was too much. All the other gangsters would tease her during recess. I thought of the tragic monsters of lore, the Frankenstein creature wandering across the North Pole to immolate itself in a final act of penance. But her face looked more bored than remorseful.

"Throw me your car keys."

They skidded between my feet. I considered kicking them into the water, but it would have taken the Jeep rental place a week to replace the ignition. "Start walking."

I kept twelve feet and the gun barrel between us. She made it halfway across the clearing before I stopped her. "One more thing."

She looked back, arms drooping from her head.

"Where's Richard Shilling?"

Her disbelief appeared sincere. "You really don't know?"

I wasn't sure I wanted to, but he was the only piece missing from the chess board. Parker unlaced her fingers and pointed behind me. I assumed she was bluffing, a corny TV villain gimmick, but then I noticed her chin was angled over the rocks. The hairs on my neck straightened into needles before I looked.

Shilling's yacht protruded from the waves like a mountaintop, its metallic hull glistening as if snow-capped. It looked more stationary than St. John, the ocean rotating around it like clock hands.

If You Called to Ask Me Out and I Wasn't Home, What Message Would You Leave?

Parker didn't drop her hands until we arrived at the beach. I'd already jammed the gun back into my shorts—a tight squeeze in wet denim—hoping no one would notice the bulge. I expected Parker to sprint back for her keys at the other end of the peninsula, but she slowed her pace, waiting for me beside a pair of snoring sunbathers.

I veered to the other side of the beach blankets, trying to keep Parker at a safe distance. She followed me up the walkway, smiling whenever I glanced back. She looked like she was taking a stroll to the food vendors, bringing back soft drinks for the husband and kids. No one would have pegged her for a killer. When I reached the parking lot, I broke into a trot, the keys jangling from my fingers. The Jeep stalled twice, while Parker watched from the edge of the asphalt, waving as I pulled out.

The roads seemed more treacherous, more spiraling each time I drove them. I returned my Jeep and jogged to the pier, twisting my neck to check the rental lot every other step. The next ferry swarmed with tourists huddled at the gangplanks like sunburnt refugees.

I shoved on board and glared at the crew until they unhooked the moorings. Maybe that was Parker strolling through the town square; maybe it wasn't. I took a seat near the front and watched St. John recede. With any luck, I'd never see it again.

After squeezing past an elderly couple, I flagged the first taxi on the St. Thomas side, the exit bar rattling as the driver tried to spill his passengers on the turns. The people across from me gripped their bench nervously, but I had bigger worries. Andrew alive was no more accessible to me than Andrew dead. Resurrecting him might have proved a lesser miracle than smuggling him off of Cosway's island. Assuming I could even find him. I was on parole from Purgatory, my guilt only temporarily assuaged.

The Lovelund entrance loomed like a pastel mausoleum as I jumped out of the taxi and strode past the reception desk. Phoebe caught my eye. It was past checkout time.

"Don't ask."

"I'm not."

I hurried to my bungalow, hearing frantic shuffles as I slid the patio door back. Melissa and Randy sat on the edge of the bed, feet flat, both of them breathing anxiously. The suitcases stood in a line by Randy's leg, the smallest, my carry-on, placed respectfully at the front. Randy folded his hands on his lap while Melissa sat gripping her purse on her knees. They were terrified.

I tried to smile, wondering how long they had rehearsed my return. "Change of plans."

Melissa jolted when I clapped my hands.

"We're staying another day!"

Neither moved. They regarded me as though I were a demonic activities director, the words "another day" registering as "eternity in hell." Randy squeaked, then cleared his throat. "*Who Wants To Be A Blind Date* will pay for that?"

Melissa's eyes widened in horror: *You fool, she'll kill us both!* She probably thought I'd murdered the entire Virgin Islands police force during my escape.

Randy's neck tightened as I touched his shoulder. "Don't worry about it, bucko. It's on me." *Who Wants To Be A Blind Date* wouldn't have paid for an extra minute on my parking meter. "So smile and enjoy yourselves." They stared uncomprehendingly as I motioned at the open door. *"Now."*

They jumped in unison, Melissa pressing her purse in front of her breasts to shield herself. Randy pushed her through the door first as her strangled whisper wafted back on the breeze. "I don't even think she works for the show.

I unzippered my bag, curious about which of them had folded my dirty laundry, then grabbed yesterday's shorts and changed. The gun had left a reddened gouge under my belly button, like a bad C-section scar. I checked the cartridge, hoping the seawater seeping through my shorts hadn't ruined the shells. As if I could tell. After wiping it with the dry half of my shirt, I dropped the gun in my purse.

If I had been in New York this weekend, I would have made my obligatory phone call home by now, chatting to my mom about nothing, trying to twist an uneventful week into diverting stories. If a date turned out dull—they usually did—I would lie and say I'd spent the night in with a video. For once, I'd have something to tell her.

The phone book had found its way back on the nightstand shelf. I flipped through the Cs. Conway, Cooper, Cotter. No Cosway. I dialed an outside line for information and waited to be told there was no listing, although I thought the operator wavered, her voice tinged with curiosity.

A detail had been buzzing in the back of my head since I'd left Zelda Shilling's bungalow. It grated on me, a string bending out of tune, the orchestra hammering over it. I knew Zelda didn't belong at Lovelund. The nouveaux riches hate the bourgeois. She'd come because Andy had told her to meet him here. The anonymous *Playboy* reporter who had every thug in the Islands after his scalp had told the crime lord's wife to meet him in the heart of the enemy stronghold. Granted, there was a perverse logic to it—who would have dreamed to look for him on St. Thomas?—but it didn't add up. Andrew had a better reason for coming here. He must have felt safe, and I thought I knew why.

I dialed the police precinct, imagining how Andrew McGuffin, dauntless investigative reporter, would handle the conversation. "I need to speak with Chief Cosway."

The voice coughed, then grumbled, "Not available. Call back." I liked his directness. Maybe I could get him an intern job.

"How do I get a message to him?"

The background hummed with noises—voices, a daisy wheel printer. "What about?"

"It's in regard to his *vacation* plans." I was trying to allude slyly to the title of Andrew's article, "Permanent Vacation," thinking it would spark some interest.

The snort deafened my ear. "His what?"

Okay, plan B. I just needed this guy to ring his boss. "He and I spoke last night about going to New York for a weekend to shoot an episode of our show *Who Wants To Be A Blind Date*. We think he'd make a great contestant." I almost said informant. "But we need a definite answer within the hour."

"Look, lady—"

I raised my volume but kept Parker's cool monotone. "Just give him the message. My producers are not patient men." Before he could protest, I dictated my cell phone number, then slammed down the receiver. The technique had worked once with a guy I wanted to date.

The wet shorts and panties drooped over the back of the chair. They were half dry before I gave up on the idea that Cosway was about to call back. I never was good at waiting by the phone. I needed a new source of information and so shuffled outside toward the bar.

Melissa and Randy huddled at a back table with a pair of tumblers between them, no paper umbrellas. Their hands were laced, the tops of their foreheads almost touching. Anyone else would have assumed they'd weathered a hundred storms together, two lovers bound forever. I pretended not to notice them and sat at the bar, relieved to see that the new bartender had Sunday off. Uche stood in the corner, holding the lid of the mixer down as it shrieked. He popped off an Amstel Light cap on his way over.

"Hear you're the luckiest lady in the Caribbean."

I took a swig and smiled innocently. "How's that?"

"A ride in the chief's cruiser is usually a one-way ticket. They call that jail Cosway's Morgue."

My fingers ran up and down the bottle neck. "Just the man I wanted to talk to you about."

"Not much to be said. You're more of an expert."

"How about an address?"

His head flopped to one side. "One night wasn't enough for you?"

"I mean to his house."

"Ah, hell, everybody knows that. He's got a big ole thing up in the hills." He flicked a finger over my head. "Worth a fortune." I pictured a World War II bunker with armored turrets.

"Tell me how to get there."

Uche plucked a cocktail napkin from the top of a stack. He mumbled as he drew, waving his finger around for clarity. No street names, just slash marks. The napkin resembled a sketch of someone's palm.

I squeezed his hand. "Thank you, Uche."

"Your funeral."

I swallowed another mouthful of beer out of politeness and strode out without looking at Melissa and Randy. My phone rang on my way up the hill. I huddled under the shade of a palm tree, watching the leaves' shadows on my legs.

"Hello?"

"Is this phone secure?" I didn't recognize the voice, too deep to be the secretary's, too young to be Cosway's. Then it clicked: the police chief wouldn't talk on a cell line.

I probed the grass for microphones. "No."

"Where are you?"

"Lovelund Resort."

"*Where* in Lovelund?"

The lobby perched on the hilltop. "Near the reception desk."

The phone clicked, and I slipped it back and jogged the rest of the way.

Phoebe looked up as she sipped something cold, ice rattling inside the Styrofoam. "So how are you?" She spoke the way guests at funeral parlors greet grieving family members, words communicating less than expressions. The whole staff must have known my saga.

"Ask me again in a minute." I drummed the counter, idly anticipating a lightning strike.

"Do you—" The phone cut her off. She spoke into her headset. "Lovelund Resort—" She froze, her eyes moving to look at me. "Just a minute." I pointed at the office behind her, and she nodded. "Nobody's in there."

The room looked more like a storage locker, Lovelund's grimy underbelly. A phone rested on a dented box lid in front of a wood bench. After locking the door, I watched my finger hover above the blinking light for a long moment.

"This is Ashley Farrell."

"You got a problem, honey?" Cosway's voice was unmistakable. The air thickened with the smell of his deodorant and the wet odor of the dead man on the picnic table behind me.

I swallowed and played my hand: "I bet you were surprised to see Parker last night. She followed me to the restaurant." If my theory held, Cosway hadn't expected her to show up either. I had originally believed they worked as a team. Now I was betting that Cosway had his own agenda.

"Parker? Who's that?" He still assumed the line could be bugged. He probably thought an FBI agent was whispering directions in my other ear.

"Richard Shilling's main gunman. The one in charge of hunting down the reporter who wrote that article. You know, the one in *Playboy*."

He grunted. "I don't *read* pornography."

"You don't have to. You write it."

There was no answer. Either I'd baffled him with a random insult or I had just hit bone.

I cleared my throat and did my Parker voice again: "I'd like to drop in for a chat. Phones seem to make you nervous."

He stayed quiet so long that I thought the line had been cut. "Come near me, and I'll blow your head off myself." His voice was softer, thinner, but the threat still shivered my neck. I watched the light on the phone pad blink dead and wiped my lips before cradling the receiver.

I'd had worse phone interviews.

24

You Just Met the Girl of Your Dreams, but Your Place Is a Wreck—Do You Invite Her Up?

The trip to Cosway's would require a real taxi, but I grabbed a tourist shuttle into town first. Parker didn't have much cause to follow me now, but I'd gotten used to the secret agent mentality. I wove through the shopping district and flagged a cab on the outskirts. It was a renovated Pacer, a Christmas tree deodorizer swaying in the air-conditioning.

"Where to?"

I handed her the cocktail napkin. "What can you make of this?"

"Cruz Bay Rum?"

"Other side."

She frowned, rotating the square clockwise. "This a drawing of somebody's hand or something?"

I'd understood enough of Uche's directions to give her a street name. She flashed me a look in the mirror and nosed into a lane of traffic. In ten minutes we'd nudged out of Charlotte Amalie, the street grid giving way to hilly turns. The Pacer's engine whirred as we corkscrewed higher, the tree branches closing over our heads. I glanced at the bare patch on my wrist, feeling as if we'd traveled twice the island's width already. I'd forgotten St. Thomas was an extinct volcano, a mountain of ancient ash packed fifteen hundred feet high. You could have said the same about me a couple days ago.

The car strained to a crossroads and halted, tree trunks visible through every window, but no street signs. "Why are we stopping?"

The driver pointed. "Private road."

"You can't take me closer?"

"Are you expected?"

Her fingers tapped as I counted exact change. She didn't look at it. The exhaust dissipated in the breeze as her cab ducked over the hilltop.

I felt for the gun handle in my purse before walking, the metal incongruous with the floral pattern obscuring it. The bulge strained open the unzippered mouth. My life wasn't as tidy as it used to be.

If I guessed right, I had nothing to fear. Andrew hadn't. He'd strolled onto St. Thomas impudent as Columbus. He and Zelda might have met anywhere on the planet, but he'd chosen Cosway's backyard because he'd felt safe. And why wouldn't he? The Mafia underboss had leaked him his last story.

That was my hypothesis at least. Yet to be tested. If I was right, Andrew was safe inside, protected by the crooked arm of the law. If I was wrong, Cosway would probably mount my head on his study wall.

It was probably better to be obvious, so I stayed to the center and kicked up as many stones as possible as I trudged up the pebble road. At least Parker wouldn't be here. She would have sniffed under every rock on the island before tracking Andrew to the top of Cosway's volcano. If I was right about the police chief, he hadn't expected Parker to show up at the resort in the first place. If she found out that he was leaking information to the press to undermine Richard Shilling's control of the Islands, Cosway was as good as dead. I was betting he had three of his own men murdered behind the restaurant in order to convince Parker that McGuffin had gotten away.

Something shimmered through the branches, and I tried to make sense of a reflected skyline. Uche was right; Cosway did live in a palace. The wall of windows stretched three stories high. The rest of the building took shape as I neared: balconies, circular deck, four-car garage. The acrid scent of chlorine wafted from a pool I couldn't see. It wasn't hard to guess why the jailhouse was collapsing.

I expected armed guards in every treetop. Weren't these guys supposed to keep a regiment around them? I made it halfway up the driveway before I spotted the first lookout sitting in a deck chair, asleep. It never worked this way in the movies. Another tidbit for the tour books: the Virgin Islands really were mellower. I pictured Andy and Cosway inside sipping Red Stripes in front of the TV, their damp swim trunks soaking into the cushions.

I considered waving and calling hello until I glimpsed something by the lookout's feet. I stretched on tiptoe, shifting to see a hand protruding between the railing slats. The body was motionless. I continued on tiptoe.

The window behind the sleeping man yawned a circle of shards, cracks webbing from the row of bullet holes. The guard's shirt clung to him, dark with moisture. I should have sprinted back down the driveway. This time last weekend, my worst problem was a bachelorette's lost contact. Now I was staring at my second corpse in two days.

The deck stairs creaked as I climbed. The sleeping man's hands rested on a rifle in his lap. He would still have looked asleep except for a dime-shaped hole in his shirt pocket and the V-shaped spatter on the deck behind him. The blood looked black against the fresh coat of paint. My toes curled as I stepped over another dead man's legs. I wished I were wearing fishing boots.

The sliding glass door was an empty frame, but I worked the handle, the pebbles of glass clinking from its path. Cosway's last threat rang in my head, but I called anyway. "Andy?" It came out a whisper. I prayed he wasn't here.

It was worse inside. I counted four corpses in a glance, some in uniform, some not. The puddles were small, mostly soaked into the carpet—the same pattern my parents had chosen for their living room. I focused on the hands and tried to look without looking. Andrew's fingers were long like a musician's. They wouldn't have blurred into the carpet's dark tones.

More bodies waited in the next room. The kitchen cabinets belonged in the back of a shooting gallery. I paused over one uniformed body, recognizing the gold wedding band resting against the gun handle. I couldn't tell which direction he had been shooting from, inside or outside, good guy or bad guy. The distinction was starting to lose its meaning.

My voice grew louder as I stopped flinching at the exit wounds. "Andy?"

Cosway's sprawled behind the counter, two owl-eyed holes staring through his shirt. A bottle of whisky sat on the counter, a full glass beside it, not a drop spilled.

"Andy, it's me, Ashley. Ashley Farrell. It's okay. You can come out now."

I toured every room, searching under beds and the backs of closets. Andrew wasn't sprawled beside the bedstand with half of his head shorn off, and he wasn't balled in the bathtub waiting for me to rescue him. He wasn't anywhere.

I sunk onto Cosway's toilet seat and stared at the wallpaper, quaint ocean pattern matched to the shell-shaped sink. My hands smelled of blood when I rubbed my face. Everything smelled of blood. The air was salty with it. I started pacing; Cosway's bathroom accommodated a surprisingly wide circle.

A cordless phone rested on the toilet tank—an intimate glimpse into Cosway's former working style. I wondered if he had been sitting there when he'd called me. I tested the dial tone. Who was I going to call? Half of the police force was already here, and I didn't know who the other half worked for.

I stabbed zero. James Earl Jones rumbled in my ear, and I asked information for the local TV station. For an extra fifty cents the automated operator dialed the number for me.

"Hello, this is WVIS, Charlotte Amalie."

"I'd like to report a—" What should I have said, a murder, a shoot-out? I cleared my throat. "A massacre."

There was a long pause. "A what?"

I gave an approximate body count and the address, then hung up, remembering to wipe the receiver with one of Cosway's hand towels, the same shell pattern as the wallpaper. I would have to recommend it to my mother.

The walls darkened as I stood again. I looked up as a cloud settled over the skylight.

Do You Kiss and Tell?

I didn't want to be spotted leaving a crime scene, so I opted for a brisk jog through the woods back to Charlotte Amalie. Cosway's road was better maintained than those below it, but all I needed was a ditch to follow. It's hard to get lost when everything goes downhill. My new life philosophy.

When I reached the outskirts of town, I started sticking my thumb out at passing vehicles, knowing that this above all else would traumatize my mother. I even tried smiling coquettishly, brushing my hair behind my ear the way Melissa had a thousand times this weekend, but the first two cars only sprayed gravel at me.

A driver in dreadlocks eventually stopped and pointed me to the back of his pickup. My love of life rekindled every time he fishtailed around a gravel curve. His shocks were gone, too. I watched the trees turn to billboards, then spied a resort taxi idling at a red light. I banged on the side of the truck and hopped out.

It was a longer-than-usual ride to Lovelund. A pair of spinster aunts—or were they an elderly lesbian couple?—kept quizzing me on island cuisine.

"Try Bluebeard's, ma'am."

I touched pavement before the taxi bucked to a stop. My plan was still vague, but I suspected it would involve the gun I was fingering in my purse. The absence of Andrew's corpse at Cosway's meant he could still be alive. I pictured him in the back of a trunk, face bouncing against a tire jack. With Cosway dead and Parker out of sight, my only hope of reaching Andrew now was through Zelda.

I scattered azalea petals as I cut into the grass. A couple glanced at me blandly: *Oh look, it's that funny running person again.* Shilling's patio door stood open, the curtains billowing in front of it as I slashed inside, purse cocked.

Tia peered up from her vacuuming. She looked surprised, less by my entrance than by my existence. She stomped the vacuum off. "Hey, I heard you were still alive."

No pistol on the table, no diamond earrings on the nightstand. My body tightened as though in free fall. Zelda was gone.

"So what did they do to you?" From the way she was eying me, lobotomy was high on her list of guesses.

My purse swung behind me as I sprinted to Andrew's bungalow. The patio chairs overturned in my wake, and I skidded into the open door. A woman stood unpacking a suitcase on Andrew's bed. She jumped, blouses dangling from her fingers, as a man stuck his head out of the bathroom.

I wanted to howl and chase them out at gunpoint, but I backed up instead. "Sorry. Wrong room."

I could only jog to the reception desk, the ground feeling insubstantial under my heels. The wind had picked up, and couples in sight-seeing gear eyed the sky nervously. Phoebe said nothing as I staggered behind her counter. The checkout book lay open, and I slapped the pages, running my finger down the column. Zelda Shilling, 10:45. Andrew McGuffin, 12:30.

I looked at Phoebe.

"It wasn't him. Two guys settled his bill. Put his luggage in the back of a private car." She was pointing at the empty sidewalk. "I'd never seen them before."

Probably two of Richard Shilling's thugs tying up loose ends. "What about Parker?"

She turned the book back a page. "Checked out last night."

I mumbled something and wandered away, the grass darkening in front of me. I could hear my father consoling me after a bad game, his hand patting my uniformed back. *You played a good game, Ash. I bet you'll get them next time.* Not much comfort to Andrew McGuffin. Parker had already cleared the board and left with her winnings. I had nothing to do now but tie up my own loose ends.

I knocked as unmenacingly as possible at Randy's patio door. A bruised eye peered between the curtains. Voices murmured behind the glass, then a finger released the lock.

Melissa and Randy faced me on their feet, his arm looped around her protectively. The TV blinked over the rumpled bed as the news anchor bellowed, agitated about something. They had probably been holed up in here since morning, dreading when I might show up again. They both flinched as I reached into my purse. Did they know I had a gun in there?

"These are your plane tickets. Call reservations and reschedule for tomorrow morning. It's Monday. It shouldn't be a problem." I set the envelopes on the table.

"You're not leaving with us?" Randy frowned to suppress his elation.

How could I go back? How could I pretend none of this had happened? Manhattan was a dream, my apartment a fairy tale tower. All I had to do was click my heels and sleep forever.

"I'm not leaving."

I was about to make a dinner recommendation when I noticed the TV screen again. A man in a bad suit stood in front of Cosway's house. The reflective siding was unmistakable. He boomed into an orange microphone, "—the worst in Virgin Islands history. There are no confirmed casualties, but we have reason to believe that Chief of Police Raymond Cosway has been killed."

Ambulance lights rotated in the glass behind him, and we were told that the mayor would make a statement after the commercial break.

I mumbled as I left, "Try Café Normandie. Great kids' selection."

My room felt stuffy as I splashed water on my face and examined my reflection. Yesterday's scratches had thinned but darkened, some mad surgeon's handiwork. I hoped they would never fade. I tried to imagine myself back at my desk, back on my love seat, at a restaurant listening to some date drone about his job. Where could I go to escape myself?

The door rattled, and someone was standing inside when I tramped out of the bathroom. Somehow this didn't startle me. The woman appeared familiar, but I didn't recognize her until I remembered how she had slid a vodka and O.J. toward me. I'd never seen a Lovelund bartender in a pants suit before, bureaucratic gray oddly picturesque among all the pastel.

"Hello, Miss Farrell." I pictured a bar rag in her hand. The jacket changed her shape, even her features. Latina? Middle Eastern? She was prettier than I remembered, exotic enough to blend anywhere. "I'm Special Agent Rachel Haboush with the Federal Bureau of Investigation." She produced a badge and opened it with a practiced flip of the wrist. It could have been a plastic kid's toy for all I cared. We shook hands, Haboush squeezing mine with unnecessary violence.

"Would you like something to drink, Agent?" I was making a joke—you know, the bartender cover. I wondered how much of her time she spent pretending she was someone else, how many nights alone in her apartment pouring over Most Wanted headshots.

"No, thank you."

The accent threw me, an almost New England inflection now. She seemed intent on making eye contact, probably the result of an FBI training seminar. I'd learned the same trick at a corporate in-service.

"I would like to talk to you about Andrew Olmstead. You probably know him by his alias. Andrew McGuffin."

I looked away, afraid she was about to tell me where the body had been found. "Aren't you worried about being seen? Lovelund employees don't usually drop in on guests."

"The operation is dead." She looked at the walls and offered a sigh as dramatic as Melissa's. "It died at 1:20 this afternoon when Shilling's force moved on Cosway. We watched most of it on our surveillance camera. It lasted four minutes. It would have been shorter if Cosway hadn't been mixing himself a drink when Parker surprised the lead guards."

I hadn't realized that I was being recorded when I'd entered Cosway's. I pictured myself tiptoeing across a color monitor, a room of seasoned agents snickering every time I winced at a corpse. "What do you know about her?"

"Margaret Parker?" Haboush scowled. "She's wanted for murder in Portugal and Greece, but there's not enough evidence to extradite—even if Shilling's lawyers weren't the best. She knows how to watch her step. She was wearing a baggy jumpsuit and a pink ski mask when she hit Cosway's." Her mouth twisted, either with amusement or irritation. "We link her to at least six murders in the U.S. Another ten on the probable list."

"Did you know I was almost one?"

She did.

"Is Andrew?"

Her shrug conveyed both disinterest and lack of information. "Olmstead came down here to meet with Zelda Shilling and his then-anonymous source. We tailed him in hopes of learning the informant's identity." She shook her head with contempt. "Now we know it was Cosway."

"Why didn't you just ask?"

Haboush's voice rose. "Olmstead wouldn't tell us.

Reporter's confidentiality. We wanted the information to prosecute Shilling. Olmstead wanted to publish *stories.*" Her nostrils flared at the obscenity. "We had no idea that someone so high up in Shilling's organization was working against him. Cosway knew enough on Shilling to put him away for life."

"So now what?"

"Now?" She threw her hands up. "Now nothing. We go home." She turned as though actually leaving but rotated into a pace instead. "When Olmstead and Shilling's wife started sending messages to each other we thought we were on to something. We'd approached her a dozen times, but she wouldn't talk to law enforcement." Her eyes swept across the room but seemed to register nothing. "Now she won't talk to anybody. And Cosway is dead. Every leak is plugged." Her heel dug a line in the carpet. "I've wasted four months on a bad hunch."

"But Andrew is alive?" It was a question.

"Yeah, but he's useless to us now."

"But he's still alive."

"Maybe. For a little while." Haboush wasn't looking at me anymore. "They won't want his body turning up around here, not after this mess. They've probably ghosted him off the island already. Wait a week and he'll show up in a car wreck, high blood alcohol content, no link to the Islands at all."

I felt my fingernails digging into my palms. "And that's okay with you?"

She looked up, vaguely surprised. "Nothing I can do about it. We can't even get a warrant with Shilling's name on it. His lawyers are already pressing two harassment charges. Olmstead should have talked when he had the chance." She reverted back to witness interrogation mode, the accent leveling. "Which is why I've come to you. You've had multiple contacts with him in the last forty-eight hours. With Mrs. Shilling, too. We were hoping you could add something to our reports."

The muscles in my jaw tightened as I glared at the rug. Haboush waited, unaware of the lava shifting under us.

"For instance, what exactly did Olmstead say when he told you he was meeting Zelda? Was he working on a specific angle? Did he already have some information?"

My eyes closed. I swallowed before I could speak. "Get out." It was more a hiss than a whisper.

Haboush was startled, but her voice remained even. "You've seen what these people are capable of. I'm surprised you wouldn't want—"

I was fantasizing about the gun in my purse. "Get out." If she wanted information from me, she would need a subpoena first.

Haboush stood for a moment and then reached inside her jacket. I'd gotten used to people pointing guns at me, but it was only a business card, its whiteness darkening her fingers. "The Bureau operator will forward your call to my cell phone if you should change your mind." She rapped the card against the dresser top. "I hope you will reconsider." She set it facedown like a poker deal and slid it across the wood toward me.

I waited till she was on the patio before flipping it over. Rachel Haboush.

"Hey!"

She looked back expectantly.

"Where is Richard Shilling?"

It wasn't the question she had in mind. "I'm afraid I'm not at liberty to divulge that sort of—"

"Is that really his yacht off St. John?"

Her expression faltered. It was all the confirmation I needed.

"Thanks."

Haboush hesitated on the walkway, grimaced, then stormed off. I watched her until she vanished around the far bungalow, the thunder grumbling overhead.

I Can Tell My Dreamboat by His Anchor—How's Yours Hung?

My phone clamored in my purse while I sat on Melissa's bed, channel surfing. *Little Women* was on AMC. The Katharine Hepburn, not the Winona Rider version. I was trying to cast Parker, Zelda, Melissa and myself as the four sisters, but I kept coming out as Beth, that selfless martyr of femininity. Hepburn was leaning over her death bed that very moment. It seemed like a bad omen.

I clicked off the remote. "Hello?"

"Where the hell are you?" There were probably two limos double-parked in the arrivals circle at JFK at that very moment. I suspected that one of the drivers had finally dragged himself inside to skim the flight times before calling the secretary in a panic.

"Who is this?" I tried to sound flustered, the way my mother did when she thought a telemarketer was an obscene caller.

"Oh, I'm—I'm sorry." I heard his Rolodex clank back open. "I'm trying to reach an Ashley Farrell?"

"Wrong number." I hung up and watched the rain on the patio. The bushes bristled as the wicker chairs slowly changed to gray.

The phone chimed in my hand.

"Ashley Farrell."

There was a pause as he debated whether it was the same voice or not. "Ashley, this is Percy at the office." See? Already more polite. "The guys just called in from the airport. They say no one was on the plane. Is that right?"

I took a moment to consider. "I doubt it."

"You—doubt it?"

"It doesn't make sense. Why would the airline fly an empty plane?"

There was that pause again. I could almost hear him blinking. "Where—I mean—what's the problem?"

Where would I have begun? I shifted the phone to my other ear and slipped my shoes back on. I'd waited long enough. "No problems here. But I've really got to go. Bye." His voice squeaked before the beep.

I dropped the phone in my purse and checked Andrew's gun again. It looked peculiar lodged under the floral wallet. My parents had never owned a gun in their lives, but they'd sent me brochures and e-mail addresses for every distributor in the U.S. They'd expected me to be murdered my first week in Manhattan. I told them the odds were twice as good that I would commit suicide.

Haboush's card glowed on the bureau. I'd almost phoned her twice, but I was a lousy bluffer. She would never have believed that Andrew had passed on all of

Cosway's evidence to me, let alone gambled a rescue mission in a trade. I held the card up, mostly white space, black Helvetica letters. Mine was nicer, a little pink Cupid smirking in the corner. That's what the FBI needed, a mascot. I slid the card into my pocket and grabbed my purse.

The rain was sporadic but sharp on my back, my blouse filling with tiny wounds while I jogged. Phoebe was chasing Visa receipts in the breeze as I caught my breath in the lobby. She didn't notice me wave good-bye.

The taxi driver looked up, surprised to find a tourist at his window. He twisted the ignition as I shouted the name of the boat rental. He called back to make sure he'd heard right. As far as I was concerned, this was ideal boating weather. The racket would drown out the sound of my motor, and I would be harder to spot in the rain.

When I closed my eyes, I could see Shilling's yacht shimmering like a mirage in the waves. Haboush had said they wouldn't want Andrew's body found near St. Thomas. The yacht was the best way to smuggle him out of the area. Shilling knew he was immune from search warrants. My only fears were that they had pulled anchor or that Andrew was already wrapped in chains with a bullet in his head. I didn't know which Shilling would find more annoying, a live hostage or bloodstains on his deck.

My phone chimed as we rolled toward town. I pressed it to my cheek and mimicked the producer's personal assistant. "Mr. Rollins' office."

I heard an intake of breath, then a huff. "God damn it, Ashley, quit screwing around. Are you getting on the next flight or not?"

The secretary's voice sounded more muffled and tinny than before. I pictured him trapped inside his desk drawer. "I'm afraid I'm not."

He didn't answer for a while. He probably hadn't considered that possibility. "Well, why the hell not?"

I watched the rain dripping under the canopy edge, wondering if I could convince him the potholes were air turbulence. "Because I'm in the back of the limo right now."

"No, you're not." It was a guess; he couldn't be sure.

"Would you like to speak to Melissa? She's right here."

He considered it, his brain moving in slow, methodic lurches. "No, no, that's okay. I'm sorry I bothered you. The guys must've just missed you, huh?" His voice rose when I didn't answer. "Well, I'll just call Rollins, tell him everything's okay after all. So long." The receiver clicked as the taxi turned and a puddle streamed under the dented door. If only Richard Shilling would be as easy to manipulate.

"Once it starts raining, it never lets up." That's what the guy in the boat rental shack told me as he misspelled my name, the rain tapping a syncopated beat on his roof. I had to jog to the ATM, because the magnetic strip on my MasterCard was bent. I didn't want to charge this on the corporate card in case *Who Wants To Be A Blind Date* refused to pay.

My shirt pulled wetly against my shoulder as I scribbled my name. He studied it before sliding me the keys, though he knew he was lucky to be getting any business at all.

I killed an hour in a coffee shop waiting for the last hint of daylight to die. The tourists frowned at the gray horizon and kept their cameras in their bags. I ordered a second decaf so the waiter would stop scowling at me. Strings of steam rose against my chin as I debated Andrew's preferences. Black, one sugar. There was a great cafe two blocks from my apartment. I'd take him there on the off chance that we both survived the evening.

I was about to risk my life for a man I'd spoken with maybe a half dozen times, each conversation ending in unique disaster. Sure I was attracted to him—I still flushed at the memory of our first tongued-tied encounter over the Atlantic—but so what? He was handsome, undeniably so, and in ways outside any list a *Who Wants To Be A Blind Date* producer could dictate on a memo. I'd forgotten what real attraction felt like, that rush of blood, that quiver in my gut realigning my center of gravity. But that's not a thrill a girl usually breaks her neck for. Maybe I wasn't so different from Melissa or Randy. I wasn't desperate, I was bored, ready finally to exchange my life.

I looked at my purse, that perfect, little Kate Spade resting on the table in front of me, a centerpiece in permanent bloom. I'd carried it clamped against my ribs on subways, down sidewalks, up elevators, my world organized inside a floral still life. I was so efficient, burdened only by the essentials. It was a risk-free existence, one I might have perished in forever.

My purse produced a muffled ring, heads turning as I extracted the phone. "Yes, dear?"

"You are so dead." The secretary was breathy with indignation. "The drivers are still at the airport. Where are you?"

"I'm taking a personal day."

"Where are—where are—?" He didn't even know

the names of winning couple #71. "You've got two people to deliver, Farrell. You can't just—"

"They're booked for the morning flight. That's the best I can do. Good-bye."

His tiny insect voice screeched as I pulled the phone from my ear, "Do you have any idea how pissed—" This time I turned the power off before dropping it back. It would be fun to trumpet my resignation speech in the producer's face tomorrow, but twenty-four hours was a lifetime away. I pushed my mug away and started for the door. It was dark enough.

The rental guy had an umbrella handy for our walk down his pier. He pointed at the last motorboat bobbing in the row, the small gray one with rust marks on the floor. My deposit would have paid for it twice over.

He held the umbrella as the boat wobbled under my feet. I wadded the tarp on the dock and felt for the second paddle. No bailer either. The engine didn't look that different from my father's John Deere. I poked the primer bulb a few times and yanked the cord. It kicked in on the fourth try, the owner continuing to mouth directions. The prow tilted as I waved to him over my shoulder.

I'd counted the bullets in Andrew's gun after digging change from my purse. Five. That was how many holes the married cop had had in his chest. I steered between Mandahl Point and Thatch Cay, glancing at the resort lights burning along the shore. A million years ago it would have been lava glowing.

All my trips to the Islands and I had never rented a boat. The producer deemed it too risky. The waves were spaced like the peaks on a carnival ride. I imagined the feel of rust on rails, wood beams groaning apart. My neck snapped with each slap as I veered north into Pillsbury Sound, visualizing the map on page twelve of my guidebook.

I couldn't see the hull of the yacht yet, only the deck lights hazy above the water, St. John a dark mound behind it. I closed one eye and aimed the prow like a rifle sight, remembering how the U.S. had bought the Virgin Islands for fear of German U-boat attacks. My plan was simple. Andy's five bullets and I would scale aboard Shilling's battleship and accomplish what Haboush's trained FBI team would never attempt. My father had stopped whispering advice in my ear hours ago.

The rain pellets lost their needle sharpness as I eased off the throttle and steered under the row of portholes, imagining a cannon mouth behind each. It wasn't the all-protective downpour I'd envisioned, but who would want to roam the deck in this mess? I stared up at the railings of a ghost ship, hoping that Shilling's lookouts stayed inside.

After cutting the engine, I paddled the last few feet, the yacht's hull rising perpendicularly from the water as my tiny boat sloshed beside it. An anchor chain rose from the waves, its other end vanishing into an opening high above me. After knotting my moorings through a chain link the size of my fist, I unzipped my purse and wedged Andrew's snub nose into my bra for quick access. I'd never worn my blouse buttoned so low before.

My toes squeezed into the first link, the chain clinking against the gun as I pulled myself up the side of the ship. My arms were aching before I ran out of chain, my body too wide to slip through the anchor opening in the hull. I paused, not exhausted or frightened enough to miss the absurdity of my appearance, a wingless Tinkerbell flapping like laundry in the rain. If I just let go, the waves would catch me. I could be back on shore in minutes, steaming in a bathtub within the hour.

The strain in my muscles urged me on, the novelty of pain invigorating. I was no slacker on the aerobics matt or the nautilus bench, but this was different. I wasn't peddling to stay in place anymore, my heart rate artificially elevated. For the first time in a long time, I felt thoroughly alive.

The bottom of a lifeboat dangled above me, and I stretched until my fingers gripped its edge. A deep puddle had collected across its tarp, so I splashed as I muscled over the top. My clothes were already soaked through. I stood and peeked through the yacht railings. Raindrops spattered the deck, but no thugs. I straddled the railing and drew the gun, the metal warm with my own heat.

The ship appeared lifeless except for a few lights glowing from the other end of the walkway. I threw my second leg over and skittered under the awning. I hadn't felt how wet I was until I was out of it, hair clinging to my neck, streaks of water tickling my legs. A puddle trailed me as I inched toward an open doorway and spied a metal balustrade leading down. The rain grew louder as I descended.

My sense of ship anatomy came from *Titanic*, but I hadn't expected Shilling's yacht to include the same red carpeting. My sandals squished against their shadows as I crept to the first of a dozen doors extending from the foot of the steps. I gripped the handle and yanked, my gun aimed at a stack of towels. Sheetless beds lurked behind the next two doors. No one was tied in the shower stalls.

The vent in the fourth room vibrated with music. It sounded distant and metallic, like the speaker on my clock radio. Linda Ronstadt maybe. I leaned closer, trying to place the direction somewhere below me.

I descended another level, but the next hallway appeared as empty, the row of identical doors stretching like an optical illusion. Shilling could have entertained an army on this ship. I skipped the linen closet this time and pressed my ear to each door until the music swelled. It was k. d. Lang, not Ronstadt.

I affected a cheerful knock and cocked the gun. I wasn't about to shoot anybody, but it helped the pose. I was an actress now, blocking my way through a new scene. I'd seen the dullest bachelorette manage it, an assistant director leading her from point to point across the sound stage an hour before the audience doors opened. Only there were no chalk marks on the carpet here, no guides but my own astonished nerves.

My arm started to droop as k. d. broke into the second chorus of "Big Boned Gal." I debated knocking again, unsure if I had been heard over the music, when someone finally clumped inside. I tightened my grip as the door opened.

"Don't move—"

Wakefield lifted her head, and we both jolted. She and her dead bodyguard buddy were probably the last people I expected to find aboard. Her bathrobe was tied sloppily, and her hair lay flat on one side, but she looked wide awake now. "What the hell are you—?"

The gun barrel shut her up. "Let me in."

The room seemed smaller with two bodies inside—especially when one was Amazon-sized. I backed

Wakefield to the shower, trying to keep her arm's length between us. Not easy.

"Where is he?"

"Who?"

"Olmstead."

"Who?"

I was tired of this conversation. "*McGuffin.*"

She didn't say anything, but I could see she knew. Zelda Shilling's personal bodyguard was taking an evening off aboard Richard Shilling's private yacht. She knew a lot.

I gestured at the bed. "Lie down."

It was hard hog-tying her with a gun in my hand, but I managed. Her muscles shifted like tennis balls under her skin. The robe belt held her until I could double the lamp cord between her ankles and wrists. She didn't resist. "Just be careful where you point that thing, okay?"

She was right. My arm was shaking. How long could I keep up this act? If Richard Shilling himself stormed through the door, I would never have pulled the trigger. The sight of blood revolted me. My hands always covered my eyes during the gory sections of movies. I didn't even rent thrillers.

The tape deck sang by my foot as I sat on the single chair, resting the gun in my lap. "So do you work for Richard now?"

Wakefield scraped her chin against the mattress, searching for a comfortable position. "The nature of my employment has recently changed."

"You double-crossed Zelda."

She eyed the barrel tapping against my thigh. "Why do you even care?"

I wanted to blurt something about loyalty, honor,

integrity. I pictured Cosway's open mouth, his cheek resting in blood. How many people had been murdered in that house? Did the married cop's wife even know she was a widow yet? "Where's Andrew?"

Wakefield tried to point with her chin. "Two halls down on the left." She decided it was easier to rest with her ear flat. "I forget the room number."

"He's—*alive*?"

"Last time I talked to him."

My clothes left a puddle on the chair as I stood. "Where do you keep your socks?"

Wakefield hesitated. "Near the bottom by the shoes." My fingers groped inside her duffel bag. I found a pair of sweat socks and unballed them. Bodyguards were lighter packers than hit men.

I held one to her mouth. "Open." She scowled, then stretched her jaw like a patient in a dentist's chair. It seemed rude but prudent—what I imagined Andrew would have done. "Can you breathe?"

She approximated a shrug.

I listened at the door before creeping out, leaving k. d. crooning as I flicked the light switch. I wanted to lock Wakefield in, but the door latched from the inside. I hadn't thought to check for her gun until I was halfway down the next hall. The weight would have popped my bra straps anyway.

This time I found a laundry room and a storage closet stacked with broken deck chairs. Only one doorknob jiggled locked in my fist. Assuming Wakefield hadn't lied, Andrew was behind it. I pictured him handcuffed to a water pipe, water rising by the minute.

I remembered passing a fire axe and doubled back. I stuffed the gun between my breasts again, thankful that an emergency bell didn't sound when I yanked the axe free. The head felt too heavy, but the handle had a pleasing curve. Wakefield could have been sending me into a trap—Richard Shilling might be lounging in a hot tub on the other side—but I didn't care.

A well-timed roll of thunder rumbled as the axe arced over my head. The door handle popped free and bounced past my foot. I wiggled it back into the hole and felt the door give when I turned. The room was black except for the lightning flashes through the porthole, the door clicking shut behind me.

"Andrew?"

I inched forward, feeling for the bed I had glimpsed. My toe hit it first. I noticed that I was still carrying the axe and rested it on the foot of the bedspread. It grazed something under the sheet. A leg pulled away sleepily. The curve of a hip emerged, my eyes adjusting to the red glow of a clock radio.

My fingers searched until they found flesh and a patch of soft hairs springing from his chest. Oh God, let this be Andy. The stomach was too shallow to be Shilling's. The bed creaked as I perched by his side.

"Andrew?"

I squeezed his shoulders and shook as he twisted toward me, still asleep. He now had an arm around my hip and another groping on my lap. He wasn't handcuffed.

"Andrew."

I could see him now. His cheekbone and the edge of his jaw were outlined in red. What I couldn't see of his lips I imagined. I leaned closer, afraid of being heard through the vents. "Andrew, wake up." A hand was working up my back. I couldn't help wondering what he was wearing under the sheet. Or how long Wakefield's lamp cord would hold. The rain on the glass sounded like titillated applause. "Andy, *please* wake up."

His hands pressed warm through my wet blouse. I hadn't realized I was shivering until that moment. His fingers found a bare patch, and I tightened my grip on his shoulder. He was half awake now, but unwilling to abandon his dreams. My back bent, my cheek hovering over his.

"Andy, we have to go."

He mumbled something, but all I understood was the breath on my neck. I wanted to surrender when his hand touched the gun. His arms stopped moving. After an instant of uncertainty, he jolted up, his shoulder knocking my jaw as he rolled for the lamp. He toppled it, but the bulb didn't break.

"Ashley?!" He sat up, his eyes pivoting between me and the axe by his leg. Despite his confusion, there was a spark of delight in his voice. He registered my soaked, half-open blouse, and the sheet fallen from his chest, a swath of his red briefs exposed. His mouth widened into the same grin he had on the airplane, a mix of concern and amusement. "Well, this is a surprise."

I was back in a fairy tale, my sleeping prince returned from the dead. My heart beat faster than it had as I had dangled from the hull.

"I didn't think I'd see you again." He reached forward and combed a wet curl from my cheek, tucking it behind my ear. His fingertip was calloused but the gesture was tender. Until that moment I wasn't sure he was even attracted to me.

I took a breath and pulled back. "We've got to get

out of here." His suitcase lay on the chair, yesterday's clothes draped over the back. I tossed them at him. "I've got a boat waiting."

He stared at the shirt in his lap as the seriousness of the situation sunk in. "No, this is crazy. It's too dangerous for you."

He yanked the shorts on as I turned my back, listening at the door to prevent myself from watching. I wanted to ask him whom he thought he was fondling in the darkness, if I was the dream made flesh. But I held my tongue.

"You shouldn't have come."

"I had to. I got you into this mess."

"The hell you did." The bed creaked as he stood. He sounded angry, but I sensed concern, too. That or he was worried what the other manly *Playboy* writers would say when they found out a girl had rescued him.

"If I hadn't drawn Parker to you—"

"Then she would have found me some other way. This is my problem."

"You know they're planning on killing you, don't you?"

"I spent a year in Bosnia, two more in Iraq. I know how to take care of myself."

I drew the gun before looking back at him. Shirt misbuttoned again, hair comically disheveled. He flinched when I gestured at his crotch with the gun. "Pull your fly up."

"Ashley—"

I rose an admonitory finger. "Follow me."

"I—"

I pressed my mouth against his, ostensibly to shut

him up. His lips tasted warm and savory with ocean salt. I didn't give him time to return the kiss. "Please stop talking."

He chuckled under his breath, amazed that he was giving in to me. "Okay," he whispered.

The hall was still empty, no sound emanating from either end. This should have been the easy part: backtrack to the stairwell, leap over the railing, fire up the boat, motor to freedom. I held Andrew's hand, already picturing us in my favorite Manhattan coffee shop. He was probably an espresso man, double, maybe triple. I'd have to dig out the instructional manual for my coffee machine. Weekends we'd sleep late, read the papers. Fight crime by night.

Andy's arm grew rigid against my pull.

"What's the ma—?"

I heard a gun cock as a shiver tightened my spine.

Parker sang out, "Don't move, hon."

27

Would You Take a Bullet for Me, and If So, Where?

I was wondering which had given us away, Wakefield or the mangled doorknob, when my body lurched forward. My legs had a mind of their own. I threw myself in front of Andy, arms spread to catch the spray of bullets. It was a little melodramatic but apparently sincere. I hadn't even thought of my mother when the Beetle was rolling over, and here I was ready to sacrifice all. Parker's gun was aimed at my left breast.

"Don't hurt him. I'll give you anything you want. Just let him go."

My bank statements flashed before my eyes. I had no idea how much Parker charged to kill somebody—let alone to spare them.

Parker stared at me, blinking wide-eyed as she let her gun droop. Her first laugh bubbled up as a giggle before building to a roar. She had to lean her hand against the wall. All of her teeth showed as she breathed in snorts, her gun bouncing, the barrel aimed at nothing. She didn't even care about the snub nose still in my fist. "God," she gasped, "you're too much."

I was too stunned to speak. I should probably have shot her while I had the chance, but the laughter was literally disarming. Every time she glanced up at me, she burst into a new round of gasps. I was missing the joke.

"Okay, that's enough." Andy's voice grew gruff. He pulled his gun out of my hand and waved it unconvincingly. "Are you going to turn us in to Shilling or not?"

Parker caught her breath. "Who, me? No, no, Mr. Olmstead, I surrender." She raised her arms, the gun bobbing by its barrel. "Don't shoot, don't shoot."

His face toned with the red carpet. He grabbed her arm and shoved her toward his room. "Get in there."

I snared his sleeve. "The lock's broken." We all stared at the missing handle as I tried to remember where I'd dropped it.

"That's okay. I'll count to a hundred."

He pushed her into the laundry room. Parker watched, grinning, as I yanked the string from the rim of a hamper bag.

"Don't you want this?" She held out her gun.

I took it and fiddled with the switches until the cartridge dropped out and almost hit my toe. Andy finished tying her to a vertical pipe while I flung both parts through the porthole. She held her hands out as though receiving a manicure.

"Want me to show you how to do a double half hitch?"

She touched my arm before we left, her eyebrows bending earnestly. "*Good luck.*" Then she cracked up again, forehead bumping against the pipe. Her laughter stalked us down the hall.

We passed Wakefield's closed door as k. d. Lang eased into a softer tempo. I tiptoed back up the stairs, expecting the rest of Shilling's henchmen to descend upon us, but we reached the deck unnoticed. The rain still drummed the awning as I peered up and down the walkway.

"Come on."

Andrew thumped behind me as I grabbed the railing, relieved to find the motorboat still lashed to the anchor. Why hadn't Parker alerted anybody else? I didn't understand her sense of humor and didn't want to see if Shilling would either. "Quick. We have to go over." I listened for gunmen in the mist as Andrew raised a leg up. How much longer could our luck last?

"Why don't we just—?"

I shoved him over the side. His arms twirled as he splashed, his head reemerging with a sputtered cough. I aimed for the opposite side of the motorboat, landing almost as gracelessly. The boat rocked as I clambered in, Andrew's shoulders rising and falling from the other side. He couldn't get a grip because of the gun in his hand. That and it sounded like he'd swallowed a lungful of sea water.

He clung a moment and laughed, rivulets draining into his eyes. "A little warning next time?" Water dribbled from the barrel as he handed it to me.

"Sorry." I tossed it into my purse and helped him up, the pair of us flopping like walruses into the keel. I wanted to say that his body felt good against mine, but the paddle was gouging my spine, and he'd kneed me in the shin. Our elbows splashed through a half foot of water as we groped up. Another hour and the boat would have been submerged.

I wrenched the engine cord, bracing as the motor sputtered and belched and rolled dead. I yanked again, waiting for a row of snipers to appear over the deck railing. Andrew watched patiently. "Mind if I try?" Usually that sort of here-let-me-little-damsel arrogance was guaranteed poison to me, but under the circumstances I was more impressed by his calm.

The engine hacked to life on his third tug. He half sat, half fell on my foot as I twisted the throttle. I didn't care if anyone heard us as long as we were out of shooting range when they reached the deck. The waves had thickened in the last half hour, our stern dipping deeper with each. I felt like a trout swimming upstream to spawn.

When Shilling's deck lights began to blur, the yellows and whites bleeding together in the rain, I started breathing normally again. Andrew's hand rose to touch my elbow as his other clenched his chair plank. I loosened my grip on the throttle and leaned against his leg. His fingers were as cold as mine.

We could have landed near the Red Hook pier on St. Thomas, but the ferry captain might have spotted us and radioed the authorities if he thought we were in trouble, a motorboat lost in the storm. The same went for the rest of St. Thomas, the shore bastioned with resorts. One well-intentioned tourist pointing at us over his champagne bucket and our escape was ruined, the waiters racing to dial 911 to better their tips. Jost Van Dyke, the nearest of the British Virgin Islands, lay only seven miles north, but as far as I knew, Richard Shilling ran that police force, too. We needed somewhere desolate.

Andrew straightened when I steered a wide circle back in the general direction of the yacht. "Changed your mind about me?" He had to shout into my ear.

I squeezed his leg. "Trust me!" I kept the yacht to a low blur at my right as I rounded toward St. John, knowing that the town of Cruz Bay would be packed with soggy tourists but the National Forest would be empty. The biggest danger was running aground. St. John's mountains merged with the storm clouds.

I cut the engine when I thought we were close to Trunk Bay, but the waves crashed against the shore still dozens of yards away. Andrew gestured me away from the pull cord and wedged himself in the prow with the single paddle. He alternated strokes, muscles tightening and bending, his shirt wet and translucent. This was turning into the best vacation of my life.

I leaned into the dark, straining to glean possibilities, willing matter to coalesce from nothingness. I'd spent my adult life honing the opposite skill, closing opportunities before they could open. Every introduction was a test, every man a bachelor, a contestant to be vetted. I was an expert at weeding out flaws and failings, tugging at the weakest threads. It protected me from the imperfect relationships I never let begin, let alone evolve, the chances I never had to take, satisfying no one but the tyrannical producer in the back of my skull. My life had been safe, ungrounded until now.

A strip of gray sand emerged from the mist. "Look!" I felt like Columbus. Andrew nodded and kept paddling.

We shoved the boat half into the weeds. My ruined purse bulged as I tilted the water out and followed Andrew up the beach. We ran with our hands over our heads as if we weren't already soaked, the sand like freshly poured cement under our shoes. A lost snorkel mask lay half buried where Melissa and Randy had spread their Lovelund towels the day before. It seemed a lifetime ago.

Andrew tried to blaze a trail through the bushes before I tugged him toward the steps at the back of the beach, avoiding the loose board at the top. He never let go of my hand. The trees afforded some cover, but we needed a dry spot. I stared mournfully at the locked visitor's center, knowing every window was wired to an alarm system in Cruz Bay.

Andrew stumbled across an empty rental shack, and we climbed over the cashier counter and collapsed against the back wall, using a deflated raft for a love seat. My body shivered, but I was content against Andrew's ribs, both of his arms circling me. I felt absurdly safe. Who would look for us here? I'd done it. I'd rescued Andrew. I had rescued myself. I twisted my head up.

"Aren't you going to thank me?"

He freed his hands, his fingers tracing my temple and cheek. When he found my mouth he kissed me. His lips seemed to tingle, the current radiating through my body, down to a muscle in my groin I'd never felt before. When he pulled away, my mouth felt impossibly hollow. I probably knew even then that something was wrong, that the rescue had gone too easily, but I couldn't pull myself out of the fantasy. It was too delicious.

The truth was that, despite all my cranky self-confidence, I had never pursued a man I thought might turn me down before. Little wonder I'd never been in love.

Andrew's chest rumbled as he spoke. "Am I your first?"

I squinted at the darkness, his face a half-imagined outline. "My first—what?" Had I plummeted from whore to virgin?

"Damsel in distress." His voice grinned, and I pulled him back to my mouth. This time he tasted salty. My first real catch.

"Hey—do I get to be in *Playboy* now? I mean in your next article?" His chest hairs tickled my arm as I nestled against him. "My mom will have a stroke. You'll have to change my name. I was thinking of something Scandinavian. I've always wanted to be Scandinavian." I pronounced the word the way Randy pronounced French.

Andrew tried to kiss me again, but our lips were pulled into smiles. We laughed into each other's mouths, puckered, laughed more. His breath felt like steam from bread.

I rested my head in the curve of his neck, a perfect fit. Outside, police boats combed the waters; Shilling's hounds sniffed for our tracks. I nuzzled closer. "I'm afraid I'm not much of a knight in armor. My plan peters out about here. I wasn't really expecting to get this far."

He combed his fingers through my hair, untangling tiny knots. "This is fine. We're safe."

"For now. But we have to get off the Islands. That bucket of rust I rented will barely make Tortola."

"Don't worry about it. You catch your plane in the morning. I'll meet you back in New York."

I pushed off his chest. "Are you crazy? They'd arrest me at the airport. Besides, I'm not leaving you again."

My fingers tightened around his arms. In the blackness he could have already been gone.

"Ashley, I'm serious." He found my hands and squeezed them. "They're not going to bother you. Parker is the only one who saw you on board. She's not going to tell—"

"Wakefield, too."

He stumbled a little. "Well, neither of them are going to tell Shilling. He'll think I escaped on my own."

I didn't see how a night with a sweat sock in her mouth was going to motivate Wakefield to lie for me. "So where would that leave you?"

"I've got connections here. I'll get out."

"You mean you had connections. I saw what they did to Cosway."

Andrew's hands stopped moving. The length of his silence startled me. "What did they do to Cosway?"

I remembered peering at a corpse on Cosway's kitchen tiles because it had Andrew's curls. "I thought they caught you at his house."

"No, I—" He struggled with something, a fact he wasn't ready to reveal to me; I could hear it catch in his throat as he swallowed. "What did they do to Cosway?"

I tried to remember Agent Haboush's exact words.

"They killed him. I think they killed half the police department. You're lucky you didn't go there." I meant it as a kind of question, a prompt, but he said nothing. The rain on the shack roof obliterated his breathing. I felt colder now that his arms weren't around me. "Why didn't you?"

His feet shifted as he pried one that was caught in the curve of the rubber raft. This wasn't adding up. I'd assumed that Cosway's men had helped him escape from the restaurant, spiriting him away from Parker. He answered in a weak voice. "It was too dangerous."

"You mean if Parker followed you? You didn't want to endanger Cosway? He was your contact, wasn't he?"

"Yeah. Yeah, he gave me the whole *Playboy* story."

"And he was protecting you?"

He hesitated. "He was." The sentence spoke more than he intended. A strand of hair tickled my cheek as Andrew shook his head in the dark. "Cosway's not the type to take chances. He knew if Shilling got hold of me . . ."

I pictured Cosway's men leading him down a back alley, smiling as they drew their guns. "Parker wasn't the only one hunting you, was she? They'd been ordered to kill you, too."

"Cosway knew he'd be dead if Shilling's people got to me first. They would get his name out of me." He said it as though it were an object, an organ removable by scalpel and forceps. Andrew's confession pricked him; men liked to think they could stand up to torture. I returned my head to his chest, hoping that if we hid long enough, the bad guys would keep killing themselves off.

"The first half of this rescue wasn't as hard as expected. It didn't seem like Shilling was even aboard. Maybe we'll have more of that luck in the morning."

Andrew snaked his arms back around me. "He wasn't." It was an offhandish mumble.

"Who wasn't?"

"Shilling. He went on shore when he heard the forecast."

I lifted my head, having trouble picturing a millionaire gangster huddled in a Lovelund bungalow.

"They own a beachfront mansion on the other side

of St. John. Enormous thing, private airfield, twenty-acre golf course. He bribed the park service to sell the land to him."

I accidentally elbowed him in the ribs as I scrambled up. "Where's my purse?"

"Why?"

"Is this the kind of airfield with airplanes?"

"Yeah. Shilling is a plane buff. Do you know how to fly?" His voice conveyed skepticism.

I flicked his gun aside and grabbed my cell phone. "No, but I know someone who does."

28

What's the Biggest Lie You Ever Told to Impress a Date?

I poked the power switch, expecting to electrocute myself. My phone didn't usually rest in a puddle for an hour. The numbers illuminated Andrew's face, but he didn't ask whom I was dialing.

It rang three times, the lapses between chirps growing longer. I pictured Randy and Melissa out skinny-dipping in the pool, Agent Haboush mixing drinks at the wet bar. She picked up on the fourth ring, her voice hesitant. "Hello?"

"Melissa? This is Ashley."

She inhaled a tiny breath but said nothing. I could sense Randy at her shoulder.

"Have you called the airport about tomorrow's flight yet?"

She answered quickly. "Yes, yes, we did that right away like you said."

My teeth clenched. I wished I hadn't given them their tickets. "Well, they just called me and said they had to bump our seats. But we can still make a late flight tonight. We have to hurry though."

A muffled noise followed as her hand cupped the receiver. She and Randy exchanged nervous sentences, their voices staticky. I heard her hand pull away, but the silence continued a long moment. "Okay." She breathed shallowly. "Should, should we meet you at the—"

"No, I need you to pick me up. I'm on St. John."

I waited for a response, but none came.

"Take the last ferry over. Do you remember where the Jeep rental is?" I pointed as though she could see. "We're at the same beach we went to yesterday. Can you find it?"

She sounded faint. "I guess so."

"Great." I should have hung up, but my hand wavered as I suppressed a twinge of guilt. At this point in the weekend, my bachelorette was usually giving me a heartfelt hug good-bye at Kennedy airport. Mr. Wrong had already escaped to his connecting flight, and she was thanking me for saving her life, buddies forever.

I switched ears. "Melissa, listen. I really need your help. I'm in trouble. A friend of mine is in even worse danger. I know this sounds crazy, but you and Randy are the only people I can trust." My fingers rubbed my temple raw. "But you don't have to do this."

She paused, but not to speak to Randy this time. "Okay." I thought I could hear her chin bobbing as her voice grew more forceful. "Okay, we can be there."

We reviewed the directions before hanging up. I listened to the dead receiver a moment and then dialed the Jeep rental. Unlike my parents' number, I knew it by memory. Melissa and Randy needed an hour to get here, and the office would only stay open if I prepaid. I used the *Who Wants To Be A Blind Date* Visa this time.

Andrew helped me read the numbers even while he was protesting the plan.

It was too dark to find the slot in my wallet again, and something wrinkled when I stuffed the credit card in my pocket. The paper was pulpy with moisture and tore when I pulled. I couldn't see either half of the FBI card but wondered if the numbers were still legible. Even if they were, I wouldn't have dialed them.

Andrew leaned against my arm as I wadded the pieces into my pocket. "What's that?"

"Someone else who doesn't like you."

The rain stopped long before we spotted headlights in the parking lot. Andrew thought I was being overcautious by hiding in the bushes. Shilling could have intercepted the signal from my cell phone. My cousin could do that with her baby monitor.

I saw two heads in the dashlights, Melissa's big Jersey hair glowing like a halo. I was watching for thugs in the backseat when Andrew stood up and waved. Melissa waved back. My suitcase shifted on top of a pile as Randy cut the lights.

Melissa bounded up for a handshake, her natural perkiness having reasserted itself as I introduced everyone. Randy grunted from a safe distance, unsure what to make of Andrew or our drenched clothes. I gestured everyone toward the beach. Randy slipped on the top step. "Where are we going? I thought you needed a ride."

I used my stewardess voice. "No, we've got a boat. The plane's just on the other side of the island."

"What about our luggage?" He pointed through the trees as I hesitated.

"We'll have to come back for it."

He knew I was lying but climbed into the motorboat anyway, Melissa almost pulling him over because she didn't want to get her shoes wet. I watched her heels, afraid they would poke holes through the rust.

Andrew crawled in last, step by reluctant step. This probably wasn't the cavalry he'd expected. I squeezed his hand, but the look of indulgent trust had left his face. He wasn't afraid, but something was straining those metal nerves of his. He muttered a last protest, how we should just take Melissa and Randy's Jeep back into town and lay low in a hotel room. I missed the last part when the engine kicked in. I got it on the first try this time.

The motor blades slashed weeds on the way out. It was easier to steer now because the moon had shaved open a swath of clouds. Melissa and Randy clung to each other in the center of their plank, staring forward as if they were watching a very suspenseful movie.

I leaned into Andrew's ear after we rounded Long Point. "Can you pick a spot near Shilling's mansion?"

He kept staring at the upturned waves in our wake.

"Andrew?"

He held my wrist. "This is a bad idea."

I smiled, trying to tease him back into his old mood, but his conviction held. I couldn't read him any more, the tension in his voice fluctuating between tenderness and distance. I felt like I'd known him better when he was a hit man.

"But will you do it?"

He was silent for ten minutes, then pointed me toward a small boy. I cut the throttle when I glimpsed the lights. The next bank of rocks was backlit, like the outside of a sports arena. The boat coasted into the nearest eddy, and I plopped my leg into the water as the boat lurched between two boulders.

Melissa stared at the water around my thighs. She was wearing white capri pants. "They don't have a dock?"

I jammed the prow in. "It's under renovation."

Randy had the worst spill as we teetered over the rocks. Melissa whispered to him, "What airport are we going to?"

I peered over the rock top, expecting a fortress, but the sight of a real turret startled me. A cannon perched on top of a medieval guard tower. Shilling's mansion was literally a castle, the gray stonework angling into crenelated walkways. Azaleas bordered the flooded moat. Bluebeard would have killed for it.

"Wow," Melissa cooed. "Who lives here?"

"Richard Shilling."

She literally gasped as Randy scowled over her shoulder. "I don't see any airplanes."

I turned to Andrew, who paced behind them. He wasn't interested in the view.

"Which way?"

"I've never been here, but Cosway showed me maps." His hand twitched, as though trying to point against his will. "There should be a plateau at the top of the hill."

We fell into single file, Andrew as the caboose. Melissa stepped on my heel twice, oblivious to the mudholes and mosquitoes. I had to hush her every few yards as she spouted a list of Richard and Zelda Shilling biographical facts: their estimated net worth, how much they gave to charities last year. Randy grunted after each.

The trees thinned near the top of the hill, where swarms of insects pinged against stadium lights, the mist glowing like a UFO landing site. Melissa's voice petered out as we neared. A vast golf course arched and dipped over sculpted mounds, every blade visible in the artificial brilliance. I surveyed the grounds, but there wasn't a golfer in sight. Every rest room on St. Thomas posted warnings about water shortages, so Shilling must have imported private tankers for the sprinkler system. The grass felt as springy as astro turf. I nearly twisted my ankle as I stepped on a golf ball, skittering it toward a sandpit.

The airfield stretched in the opposite direction, its far unlit end extending indefinitely. I stared at the hangar, wondering if Shilling housed a Boeing in there.

Andrew rattled through the brush behind me. "This is too dangerous for you. There could be guards posted inside." He grabbed my arm protectively, ready to drag us all back to the boat.

"How else are we going to get off this island?"

He said nothing.

I led my squad of commandos to the hangar wall. The paint looked as fresh as Cosway's deck, same shade of red, and I expected it to stick to my palm as I peered around the window frame. My reflection peered back.

I tried the doorknob, surprised that it turned. Even Shilling had been infected with that Virgin Island mellowness. I reached inside and pawed for a light switch; the ceiling fixtures blinked in slow bursts.

The hangar was decadently empty, just three prop planes roosting near the door. I pictured Richard Shilling leaning out of the cockpit in goggles and a red scarf, and I debated how we were going to cram four of us in and whether the engine had enough lift. The propellers didn't look much longer than the ones on the boat.

Melissa breathed nervously in my ear. "That's our plane?" She pointed at the third and largest, a Piper Saratoga logo stenciled on its side.

Randy stared as I called back to him, "Can you fly it?" I'd sat through two meals' worth of pilot stories. I didn't care if he could make it around the world. San Juan waited a hundred miles to the west, St. Croix only forty to the south. He could choose. I repeated the question.

Randy blinked. "Can I—?" The idea didn't penetrate for a second. When it did, his jaw started to quiver.

"You're a pilot, right?" I could have quoted the story about his flight instructor taking tips from him their second day out.

"Yeah, but I mean—" He stammered, then looked up, as though searching for divine intervention. "I don't know, with these clouds . . ."

Our chins followed his up. A thread of cloud unwound below the full moon, stars swimming at its edges. The breeze was placid.

Andy rubbed his mouth. "Maybe your friend's right. I wouldn't want to be caught in a storm in one of those things." I didn't think he wanted to be gunned down in Shilling's backyard either.

"Why can't we take a real plane?" Melissa asked.

I sighed. "Because Parker is waiting for Andrew at the airport."

She nodded but didn't get it. "Are you famous or something?"

It took Andrew a moment to answer. "I'm—I'm a reporter."

"Do you work for the *Post*, too?"

"Freelance."

Her eyes brightened. "Are you two competing for the same story? You must have an exclusive on Shilling!" She attached herself to Andrew's elbow as I pushed them through the door. "Does this have something to do with that police chief they showed on TV?" Her voice reverberated against the domed rafters.

His eyes flashed at mine, then dropped again. "Shilling sent Parker to kill Cosway." His voice sounded oddly humble, almost guilty.

"Parker? The reporter?!"

I modeled a whisper for Melissa. "She's not a reporter, she's a hit man. The police work for Shilling, too. Everybody works for him." Her head rocked slowly up and down; the idea seemed to impress, rather than frighten, her.

I glanced back for Randy, but he hadn't budged from the doorway. He looked like an actor frozen in the wings, a prompter hissing his cue. I knew he'd been bragging, but it didn't matter. As long as he could find the on switch, I was happy. If he couldn't land, we'd parachute. I just wanted off this island.

"I don't have my license." I had to lean to hear his mumble.

"It's okay. If anyone pulls us over, we'll say it's in your other pants." He planted his legs when I tried to nudge him forward.

"I mean I haven't taken the test yet."

"I'm not really worried about aviation paperwork at the moment, Randy."

He twisted away from my arm. "No, I can't take the test. I'm not allowed to. I've only booked—" Our eyes met for an instant, then he glared at the floor. "I was going to start lessons this summer."

I staggered back. When I turned and looked at Andrew for help, he and Melissa faced me with their arms raised. I thought they were waving at first, signaling me in semaphore. Then I heard the door hinge creak.

Officer Gebre stood in the opening, his gun aimed with both hands.

29

What Secret Would You Never Share on a First Date?

We marched single file down a tiered path leading to Shilling's pool, while Gebre's walkie-talkie chattered behind us. A part of me was relieved to see my personal policeman again. One of the corpses in Cosway's living room had been about his size but faceless. Apparently, he'd picked the winning side, though I wasn't sure if golf course patrol was a promotion or not.

Shilling's mansion appeared less foreboding from the rear, the castle facade surrendering to glass and terra-cotta. The swimming pool was heart-shaped. I wondered if he employed the same groundskeepers as Lovelund.

Gebre maintained a nervously close distance. I could hit his knees if I lunged backward. He couldn't have shot all of us, and I had the happy delusion that a bullet from his gun would have been less painful than another thug's. If Andrew had glanced back even once, I might have tried it, but he walked doggedly in front, hands bending his head low. Here was a man who had been taken prisoner before.

A figure appeared in the doorway as we rounded the pool's left ventricle. A walkie-talkie hung in Parker's fist as she shook her head. "You never cease to amaze."

They marched us into what I could only assume was a living room, though the ceiling was slightly lower than the airplane hangar's. Indian rugs dangled from the distant walls, and a pagan-looking fireplace towered at the center.

Parker directed us to a matching pair of plush sofas, air hissing from the cushions as they enveloped us in Venus's-flytrap upholstery. Melissa and Randy appeared impossibly distant as they sank on the opposite sofa, the coffee table between us the size of my mother's old VW. I smiled bravely, but their eyes had glassed over. I couldn't catch Andrew's either. His face seemed taut with something more than fear. Anger? Humiliation? He pulled his hand away when my fingers reached for it.

Floorboards thumped behind me, and Wakefield appeared with my purse; it looked miniature in her fist. She held up Andrew's snub nose for Parker to see. "There wasn't anything else in the boat." She looked down at me, unable to fight back a chuckle. The gun and purse dropped onto the table beside Gebre, yards and yards away.

A door rattled on the landing, and our seven chins turned in unison. A tuft of hair bobbed above the banister as Richard Shilling stepped onto the staircase, knotting his bathrobe as he descended. I glimpsed more paunch and hair than I needed to. I wouldn't have recognized him. He was taller on TV, or shorter, the gray at his temples more convincing in photographs. He looked like a remarkably good stunt double.

He waited until he reached the bottom step, his slippered feet soundless on the marble, and smiled broadly at me. "Ashley Farrell. I've heard so much about you." His voice oozed charm. "And this must be Melissa and Randy." He spread his arms in welcome, bathrobe tie straining against his stomach. "Any friends of Mr. Olmstead are friends of mine." He could have been auditioning for a spot as the next *Who Wants To Be A Blind Date* host.

He padded to a drink cart double-parked behind Melissa and Randy. They stared forward, two anesthetized patients as Shilling's tumbler scraped like a scalpel on a surgical tray.

"I hope Meg's made you comfortable. I wasn't expecting company." A brown liquid gurgled from the crystal decanter. "You're lucky you caught me at home. I was supposed to attend a meeting in Madrid today, but when I heard Zelda was vacationing in the Islands—" He clapped a hand to his chest, his heart supposedly surging with romantic impulses. "Well, I just couldn't stay away. You know I proposed to her here?"

He grinned to himself, amused by his own performance. I waited for the glass to reach his lips.

"And how is Zelda?"

Andrew's neck straightened as Shilling postponed his sip, his other hand swirling in the air. "Oh, fine, fine. I think she overextended herself a bit this weekend, but she's recovering."

I imagined her manacled in the dungeon. The wadded FBI card stuck to my thigh as I rested my hand over the pocket. "And yourself?"

"Me?" The question seemed vaguely novel. "Never felt better."

I nodded, frowned, pretended to consider the answer. "That surprises me."

Shilling's head tilted. "Oh?" He was deciding whether to be amused by me.

"I mean a man in as much danger as you are." My legs crossed slowly as both Parker and Wakefield listened more intently. Gebre was out of earshot. I folded my hands on one knee and waited until Andrew's head turned. "Your operations have been under intensive FBI surveillance for the past four months."

Parker chuckled. "Imagine that."

"Did you know they had cameras in Cosway's house?"

She squinted skeptically, ready with another quip, when I cut her off.

"He was mixing himself a drink in the kitchen when he saw you take out the guards on the deck. You look good in pink." Parker's lips opened, but she didn't say anything.

Shilling shifted his glass to his palm, his arms crossing against his paunch. "We're listening."

"They tailed Andrew's every move. They know everything he knows and a lot more." Andy met my eyes for the first time in an hour, his lips parting. If my bluff worked on him, it could work on them. I reached into my pocket for Haboush's wadded card and displayed it like a trophy. "I met with the head agent this afternoon. Her name is—"

"Rachel Haboush." Parker scowled at me. "She dropped her cover this morning. Flew out of here on the six o'clock." Her laugh betrayed relief. "I understand she makes a mean margarita."

"I know. I used one to swallow the FBI tracer she

gave me this morning." It was an absurd bluff, but it was all I had. Unless they had an X-ray machine handy or gutted me on the cushions, they couldn't have ruled out the possibility. "They've been monitoring my every footstep. There's a team of operatives waiting to descend the second you screw up."

Parker's mouth pursed the way it had when my bullet whizzed by her ear on the peninsula. Even Melissa and Randy had emerged from their haze. I looked at Andrew, unsure whether his eyes were wide with hope or horror. He didn't seem to recognize me.

Shilling's laughter broke the silence. "Oh, I like that. That's good." His free arm waved at the walls. "The house is surrounded right now." He nodded furiously, trying to pour the remainder of his glass down his throat. He almost choked. "I hope they bring their own drinks. We're low on ice."

Parker strutted over to the sofa arm and perched next to me. "You know the best way to wreck one of those gizmos?" Her finger swirled at my belly as she leaned closer. "Fire." She stretched the word into two syllables. Maybe the fireplace really had been designed for sacrifices.

Wakefield braced a tennis shoe on the coffee table. "They don't do so well underwater, either. Pressure kills the transmission." She offered this in a helpful tone.

Gebre's hand wavered over his holster as I leaped up, my finger aimed at Shilling. "*Who Wants To Be A Blind Date* is an internationally syndicated show. It maintains a loyal following and consistently wins its time spot. It's the second most popular dating game in television history!"

I left my hand raised as the echo faded, the room suddenly silent. Melissa and Randy gaped like carp as Parker and Wakefield exchanged looks. They really didn't know what to make of me.

Shilling's eyebrows raised. "I know. That's why I own it." He waited for the rest of the explanation. Andrew's eyes followed me, too, but I didn't dare look at him.

"They'll be missed."

Shilling tilted forward. "*Who* will?"

I gestured with my chin. "Melissa and Randy." He looked down, surprised to find them there. "No one's heard of me, but they're winners. Their faces will be televised to hundreds of thousands of viewers tomorrow night." My shin bumped Andrew's knee as I paced around the coffee table. "How could the media pass up the story? A dating game couple mysteriously vanishes during their dream vacation. It'll be the movie of the week."

Shilling's chin doubled as he contemplated this, but I didn't give him time, my arm extending as though introducing a next contestant: "And Andrew. A star reporter disappears after publishing an incriminating article on Virgin Island mobsters! *Playboy* will lead the investigation. It's better than a serialized mystery."

Both my arms were going now. Wakefield backed up to give me room. "You're a powerful man, Mr. Shilling. You control headlines. You trade TV stations like baseball cards. But you can't keep a finger in every leak. The key to power is knowing its limitations." I stood only a few feet from him. I wanted to grab him by the lapels but feared the robe would open, or Gebre would panic and shoot me, so I dropped my voice to a dramatic rumble instead. "If you know yours, Mr. Shilling, you'll let us go."

He studied me without expression. His glass rose to his lips, then lowered when he found it empty. My fingernails gouged my palms as he shrugged and inspected the liquor tray.

"Okay."

My knees twinged. I wasn't sure if I'd heard him right. I looked to Andy for confirmation, but he was rubbing his face in his hands.

Ice clattered into Shilling's glass. "But what was that part about everyone vanishing?"

I watched the bottle tilt in his hand as he poured. One of the ice cubes shattered. "I mean, if you were going to . . ." I didn't want to say it out loud.

"Kill all of you?"

"Yeah."

Shilling belched a single laugh. It rang like a gunshot. "Good God, no!" The whole cart rattled as he dropped the bottle back. "Making Mr. Olmstead's acquaintance is the best thing that's happened to me in months. I never realized how cooperative a gentleman of the press could be. No more worrying about my name popping up between pornographic spreads anymore. Is there, Andy?"

Andrew flinched. "No."

Shilling was wagging his finger at him. "But I do know of some unscrupulous business practices occurring in the Caymans these days. Some of my competitors, I'm sorry to say. A crackerjack reporter like you should get right on that. Your editor sounded very enthusiastic on the phone."

Andrew stared at the crystal urn on the coffee table,

his arms limp at his sides. I struggled to catch my breath. "You've already agreed to this?" My voice was so faint I barely recognized it.

"It was his idea." Wakefield passed beside me, but I didn't look at her.

"When?"

Parker slid off her perch and into my empty seat. "About an hour before that horrible incident at Mr. Cosway's. Andy ratted him out for us. Didn't you, ole buddy?" She gave his arm a familiar slap.

Shilling boomed behind me. "We checked the facts, of course. We're not entirely gullible. I would never have suspected Cosway. He loved that house of his." He gazed philosophically into his glass. "It's so hard finding a balance between loyalty and ambition."

None of this was possible. A Mafia crime boss had just confessed to murdering his police chief. None of it could have been true. Andrew wouldn't have betrayed his contact. I seized his cold fingers. "You went to Shilling?"

He said nothing.

Wakefield's tennis shoes squeaked behind me. "He came to Zelda and me first. He caught us on the way to the airport." She leaned against the sofa back, hands on her hips. "He was desperate. Said everyone was out to kill him."

Parker nodded at that: *We were.*

"He wanted to turn himself in. He said he'd trade his life for his contact's, he'd do anything they wanted, but he needed Zelda's help. He couldn't get near Richard without her brokering the deal."

Andrew's chin perched on his chest as if the muscles in his neck had been cut. "Is it true?" My hand pulled away from him. "You work for him now?"

He didn't face me. "Yes."

My jaw tightened as I tasted bile. This was the man I'd risked my life for? I stood, ready to walk away again, just as I'd done a thousand times—left my half of the bill on the table, hung up after a polite pause. I knew better than anyone else how to walk away from a man. I stared at him, sickened that my heart had ever fluttered in his presence.

I turned to Shilling, who was smiling innocently. "What did Zelda get out it?"

He considered answering, but a heel on the staircase drew his attention. I looked up to face the inevitable. Zelda Shilling gazed from the top step. Her hair was mussed, and she wore a matching robe, the sash barely tied. She looked good. Maybe a few new gray streaks in her bangs, a few extra wrinkles around the eyes, but good. Nothing a blank check couldn't fix. She looked down at her palace court, as mute as a goddess on a pedestal. What was there to say? She was home again.

When Do You Know It's Time to Give Up on a Relationship?

The Atlantic seaboard was a ragged edge under the clouds, the window fogging if I looked too closely. Seventy-two flights in three years and I'd never had a window seat before. This was my first peek behind first-class curtains, too. When I'd arrived at San Juan for the transfer flight home, I'd discovered that our tickets had been upgraded, a parting gift from Richard Shilling. I'd wanted to shred them and scatter the pieces, but Melissa had gripped her reservation stub too tightly. Her delighted giggle had made even the check-in clerk smile.

They had met me at the San Juan airport, bloodshot but grinning. Randy had gotten his first flying lesson after all. One of Shilling's men had shuttled them over in the very plane I'd coveted in the hangar. After spending the night partying at Shilling's, they were anxious to tell me everything. Wakefield—they called her Becky now—had used a bullet shell to play quarters with them, and Melissa had won. She produced the souvenir from her makeup kit and made me hold it. I was back in their good graces. They'd tell this tale to their grandchildren, Grandma's and Grandpa's night with the mobsters.

Melissa's pillow was now wedged against her window, her legs shifting on Randy's lap as their snores punctuated the engine roar. I envied their sleep, wishing I could exorcize last night from my thoughts.

Zelda had tightened her robe belt and descended the stairs in hostess mode, scolding Richard for not serving the guests drinks. He looked indulgent. If he still had plans about dumping three of the guests into the Atlantic, then his wife's whims won out. They were newlyweds again.

He began charming his victims into collaborators instead. Melissa didn't know whether to be flattered or terrified when he took her hand and escorted her to the entertainment center. Soon Ottmar Liebert was strumming from the mounted speakers. Servants materialized with cold cuts that looked raw and vaguely human, and he grinned devilishly as he toasted us with vintage cognac. "To long life."

Melissa shuddered with each sip, but kept smiling. I let mine drain back into my snifter as I studied her face for signs of poisoning. She giggled, and Randy got chatty after his second glass. Andrew's sat untouched on the serving tray.

He and I had migrated to opposite edges of the sofa, a wide, cushioned gulf between us. Zelda nestled into the gap, her bare calf scraping mine; neither of us had shaved our legs that morning. She started asking me about the glamors of the TV business.

"I always wanted to be an actress, didn't I, Becky?"

Wakefield nodded across the table as I watched Andrew wrestle out of his seat. He seemed oddly uncoordinated, his direction random. He eventually retreated to a corner, wincing whenever servants approached him with food trays.

Zelda spilled into his space and pitched ideas for TV shows. She had concepts for two comedies and a *Who Wants To Be A Blind Date* spin-off; a new divorced couple would appear every week as the contestants tried to woo them back together. Apparently I was perfect for the host. I listened, paralyzed except for my nodding chin. None of this was happening.

When Zelda snared Randy into the conversation, her robe opening precariously as she wedged him in beside her, I retreated to the kitchen. Melissa's giggles rose from the hall, where Richard had escorted her to his trophy case. I kept waiting for a muffled scream and a thud.

The spigot splashed into my cupped hands, and I doused my face twice, then dried it with a kitchen towel still stiff with the manufacturer's creases. I noticed Gebre lurking in the doorway as I held a glass under the water. He waved but kept his surveillance distance. A job was a job.

Wakefield glanced at the glass in my hand as we passed in the hallway. "Enjoying yourself?"

I wanted to ask her what the Shillings intended to do with us, whether we were free to go. Would the party end in bribes or threats? But I could tell by her cockeyed grin that I'd never get a straight answer. I called back as she headed for the bathroom: "Better than sucking sweat socks."

Andrew skulked by the fireplace, a love ballad

strumming from the speakers mounted somewhere over his head. Shilling had eclectic tastes. He looked up and grimaced at me for a moment. His jaw worked at some word, some phrase, impossible to pronounce. I knew he had intended no harm, not even humiliation. Deceiving me had been a form of chivalry in his mind. It was the best I could expect from a fraud.

"Don't bother." I left him drowning in his unspoken words.

I followed Melissa's giggles to a side room. Richard had her in front of some wall-sized painting. He looked like a lecherous art professor with an undergraduate, her back cupping his paunch.

"I'm leaving."

They both looked up. I wasn't sure if I was testing a theory or fulfilling a guest obligation.

Shilling met my eye as though contemplating a challenge. "I'll have a boat readied."

"Thanks. I have one."

"I'm afraid my servants have already left with it."

Was that a threat? Were they destroying evidence? Even an honest cop would rule my disappearance an accident. What idiot goes boating in a storm?

"To return it to the rental shop," he explained. "They're picking up your bags on the way back." He was either very thoughtful or very thorough. He smiled magnanimously. "I'll let you know when they're here."

I retreated to the dining room, feeling for Haboush's card in my pocket. I could have smuggled my phone into the bathroom, but the numbers were too smudged to read.

Andrew only tried to approach me once. His reflection grew in the windows of the French doors and then vanished when I shoved the knob. It slammed with more finality than I had intended.

Shilling's cement-edged heart bubbled before me. Parker looked up from the deep end. Her empty snifter dangled upside down from her fingertips.

"Do you ever root for the bad guy, Ashley?"

I watched a plastic chlorine dispenser drift complacently toward the diving board. It would have been easy to forget the color of congealing blood, the texture of a drowned man's skin. "Do you regret murdering Kevin Anderson?"

She smiled at herself. Wave after perfect wave lapped at her feet. "Not much."

A voice announced my name behind me. I wanted it to be Andy, but a servant, a young anemic-looking man, handed me an envelope. I peered inside at a thin row of twenties. It seemed a paltry bribe.

"What's this?"

"Your boat deposit, ma'am." He gestured through the house. "Your bag is waiting on the dock."

Parker waved good-bye with her empty glass. "Don't be a stranger."

Gebre was waiting in a speedboat, engine humming. I eyed the pistol snapped in his holster. I half expected to be murdered, dumped overboard between islands, but we never slowed until the Lovelund lights widened in the bay. Half the people in the disco stumbled out to gawk at Shilling's speedboat, and Gebre toted my suitcase onto the dock like a porter. It was the grandest entrance of my life. I wasn't sure why, but we shook hands.

My bill had already been paid when I checked out in the morning. I mumbled something when Phoebe asked about McGuffin and handed me a stack of

Lovelund message notes from my irate office. I was halfway to the sidewalk when it occurred to me I would never see her again. Her head tilted toward her screen as the next couple fidgeted with their sunburns.

It could have been worse. Columbus had left the New World for the last time in chains, still believing the Terrestrial Paradise lay just over the horizon. I had slumped in my plane seat, watching the Islands shrink to pebbles before the ocean swallowed them.

Randy jerked awake when the stewardess tapped his shoulder to say they had to sit up for the landing. Most of the passengers looked edgy from hours of turbulence, but Randy and Melissa had slept like newborns. One night of debauchery and they were fearless pros. They didn't even clap when the wheels touched down.

The captain mumbled weather conditions as we wrestled our bags free. Randy and Melissa worked in sync, straps and handles passing flawlessly—a couple's rhythm. I clutched my ruined purse and inched into the aisle as Randy made space for me. I wanted to think that his smile was flip or condescending, but it wasn't. He simply smiled at me.

Melissa got teary-eyed while we watched luggage revolve on the carousel. Mine surfaced last, a cloth tote crushed between two hard-shells. "Oh, Ashley, I just—I just don't know how to thank you." She knocked me off balance with a full-body hug, her breasts crushing mine. "If it weren't for you—"

She turned an adoring gaze at Randy as he finished stacking our suitcases on a baggage cart. When Melissa freed me, he poked my shoulder with a fist. "Hell of a weekend."

We braced for the breeze as people in jackets jogged through the electric doors. I was relieved to find two *Who Wants To Be A Blind Date* limos idling at the curb. I had phoned in our arrival time from the plane while the secretary stammered and cupped his mouthpiece. Most of the messages in my pocket were from him.

Melissa and Randy performed an Oscar-worthy farewell kiss on the sidewalk, wailing and clawing as the drivers dragged them into separate cars. Pedestrians lowered their bags to applaud.

After flagging my own taxi, I sat in forty minutes of exhaust fumes, watching a tow truck spin its strobe light. I would have worked up my resignation speech, but I'd rehearsed it for years. The conference room doors would swing open as I stepped onto the carpeting. Every network peon would "happen" to be strolling past as I humiliated Rollins.

I doubled the driver's tip, giddy with unemployment, and smiled at every stranger in the lobby before catapulting up the skyscraper.

The secretary whitened and looked away as the doors parted in front of his reception desk.

"Afternoon, Percy. Loved that press release."

I marched past him, then turned when I recognized the framed Frida Kahlo print jutting out from the file box on the floor. The Matisse calendar that Donna had given me last Christmas was stuffed in behind it. I stared into my jumbled possessions, realizing that they had already cleaned out my cubicle.

The secretary's hand shook as he slid a sealed envelope to the corner of his desk, and he continued grunting and nodding to the voice on his headset. It was a dial tone for all I knew. His eyes widened when I plucked the knife-shaped letter opener from his pen cup. Mine was buried too deep.

I recognized the legalistic diction, having drafted the boilerplate last year when we had to fire a string of temps. The wheels on the secretary's chair squeaked as he inched further away. His initials were typed at the bottom, under the producer's signature. I was sure he had repeated every incriminating word I'd said to him on the phone last night, plus probably a few more.

I considered smashing the electric pencil sharpener over his head, but Henry, the floor security guard, hovered by the glass doors. It wasn't a coincidence. He was a sweet guy, maybe two hundred and fifty pounds. If he said a word to me, I was going to drop him down the elevator shaft. I tossed the letter opener on the blotter and started walking.

The secretary stood as I pressed the elevator button. He gestured at my file box.

"UPS it to me."

"We can't—"

"You want me to come back for it?"

He frowned as the doors closed.

The subway ride and walk along East 15th seemed longer than usual, the faces unfamiliar. A panhandler caught me at my building door, and I dug out a handful of quarters, her coffee cup thumping like a toy drum. It took me five minutes to break into my apartment. My key always stuck after long weekends, demanding smooth talk, not invectives.

Three of the nine messages on my answering machine were from my mother, not counting the one from my dad after she'd gotten tired. He chattered a whole minute, hoping I wasn't screening him, too. *Who Wants To Be A Blind Date* tied with four, the secretary's voice rising one note with each call. Donna offered the most sincere half-dozen seconds on the tape.

"Ashley, wherever you are, I hope you're okay. They can't page you at Lovelund, and your cell phone must be dead. I hope you know what you're doing."

I braced for the last click, knowing Andrew hadn't called. I could imagine his voice and knew exactly which words I wanted. I could have written them out on a cue card the way I did for bachelors in case of stage fright. Forgiveness dangled before me like a noose. I dragged it to the bathroom and peed.

Who Wants To Be A Blind Date came on at seven. The network always delayed the broadcast a week, so it was episode #71, Melissa's and Randy's debut.

The microwave hummed as I punched up the volume. The host exchanged manly handshakes with each bachelor and read Randy's bio: "A sports enthusiast and amateur pilot, Randy Sanders works as a stock associate on Wall Street. His ambitions include circumnavigating the globe in a custom plane and making a million dollars before the age of thirty." Randy jogged into the cheers with his arms raised, ignorant of the neon Applause signs surrounding the stage.

A lewder undercurrent echoed under the cheers when Melissa strutted out. She beamed and blinked in the right direction, but I could tell she was blinded by the lights, the faintest hint of panic in her breathing. She clutched the host's arms as he helped her into the chair, a literal pedestal.

"Bachelor Number One?" She read a question from

a pink notebook in her lap, the pen absurdly phallic. "If Columbus discovered you naked on the beach, what would he conclude about the New World?" The audience tittered and clapped.

Randy watched his competitor leer at the camera. "Well, I think ole Chris would turn that ship of his around and never come back because he'd know he couldn't measure up." The camera cut to an audience reaction shot, two girls blushing in the front row. The director made sure we got plenty of cleavage.

My doorbell saved me from Randy's scripted retort as I thumbed down the volume and checked the peephole. I half expected Parker's gun barrel or Agent Haboush's badge.

"Who is it?"

Andrew looked up. "It's, ah—it's—" His face warped in the curve of the glass. "Andrew Olmstead."

I closed my eyes and counted to five before jiggling the latch open. Andrew stepped back as the door creaked. He was wearing the same shirt he'd worn at the Lovelund pool Friday night, only more rumpled. It looked gray in the hall light, as his hands dug in and out of his pockets.

"May I—?" He did that cute Hugh Grant hair-tugging thing again, only now it looked rehearsed. "May I come in?"

I opened the door and walked away, the TV applauding as I stomped into the bedroom. My bag lay zippered on the bureau, a destination tag taping the handles together. My nail bent trying to tear it. I knew I would never have made it through an X-ray gate with Andrew's snub nose inside, so I'd crammed it into my toiletry bag with a couple of handfuls of

Lovelund gardening pebbles and stowed the bag at the airport check-in counter.

Andrew had inched his way toward the kitchen counter, a Lean Cuisine steaming by his elbow. I raised the gun at him. "I believe this is yours."

He jolted. He thought I might really shoot. It was the high point of an extraordinarily bad day. I flattened my palm and waited for him to take the gun, but he didn't want to.

"I would like to explain."

I lobbed it to him instead, but my aim was a little low. He juggled it between his hands and hip, neither of us certain whether the safety was on.

"How did you find me so fast?" The correct answer would have revealed not only his devotion but his skills as an investigative reporter, all the more impressive because he had obviously spent the day stuck on an airplane. He hadn't even stopped to change before coming here. I liked that.

"One of Shilling's people got the address for me."

He was lucky I had already tossed him the gun. "Get out."

The words knocked him off balance. The noise from the TV expanded in the silence.

"Bachelor Number Two?" Melissa's voice sounded higher but more confident now as she posed her next question. She'd acclimated to the elevation of the bachelorette chair. "Would you take a bullet for me, and if so, where?"

The crowd laughed. The crowd always laughed.

Randy's voice cut in too quickly as he drew a target around his heart. "Oh baby, I'd take that and a whole lot more." The applause filled the speaker like static.

Andrew rubbed his mouth. “I didn’t plan to mislead you. When you showed up on the yacht like that—I just thought it would be easier to play along.”

“Easier on you.” I glared at Randy. Bachelor #1 was giving him a high five.

“I wasn’t lying about Cosway wanting me dead. He knew that if Shilling got to me first, they’d force his name out of me.”

“So you thought you’d save them the trouble?” I padded to the set and slapped the power button. Randy vanished into a white dot. I wished I had that power over all men. “Are you that loyal to all your contacts?” I had to keep moving, picking up Thursday’s newspaper from the coffee table, arranging the edges for recycling.

“Cosway’s men picked me up behind Bluebeard’s. I was hiding behind a garbage can. I thought I was safe at first. I actually waved them toward me. Then one of the young ones pulled his gun. He didn’t aim, but I knew. I heard shots as I ran. I mean, it was just dumb luck. They should have had me.” The gun rotated absently between his hands. “Ashley, I’ve never been so scared in my life.”

He lifted his face with an urgency and vulnerability I’d never seen before. Something shifted in the air between us as he stepped closer. I felt myself slipping. This was what I wanted, wasn’t it? To be wooed?

“Cosway was as bad as Shilling. He ran the Islands for him. He only gave me information that incriminated their competitors. He was as rotten as the rest of them.”

This should have been enough. I could feel his fingers on the curve of my spine, my bare collarbone. He should have had me. I inhaled slowly, remembering the warmth of his body. I didn't intend to speak, but my voice defied me.

"So why did you work for him? Why didn't you turn your information over to the FBI?"

Andrew's jaw locked, and he looked down as though searching for a dropped cue card. "Cosway gave me good stories."

"The same way Shilling is giving them to you now?"

His arms rose in protest. "I have no choice. He knows me. I lost my cover." His voice was less dignified at higher registers.

"That's not all you lost." I grabbed my microwave dinner from the counter and dumped it into the garbage can. He was still in the corner of my eye as I picked up a sponge and started working at Friday's breakfast dishes.

His voice suddenly roared. "What the hell do you want from me? I'm not your goddamned Prince Charming!" My body stiffened, but I didn't turn to look at him. His voice rose so violently that the wine glass on the counter rattled. "You only liked me because I fit some fantasy of yours—a rake, a special agent, someone dangerous and thrilling. It's not my fault I can't live up to that. I thought the same thing about you at first, and yes, I admit it, it was sexy as hell. But what good is that? You can't live in that fantasy. We're real people, Ashley."

I could hear his agitation as he paced, but when he spoke again his voice had sunk to a rasp. "When are you going to pull your head out of your dreams and really look at me?"

It was true. We were practically strangers. Something still tugged at me, trying to make me turn and face him for the first time. Maybe there were real possibilities between us, a shot at love even, but I didn't move. Even if the fantasy were dead, I still deserved better than a Mafia collaborator.

I twisted the sink spigot on and rinsed a mug of three-day-old coffee down the drain. I couldn't hear his footsteps over the running water, only the front door closing.

31

When I Open the Card You Gave Me for Our Anniversary, What Do I Read Inside?

My producer called the next morning at nine, sounding almost panicky. He wanted to give me my job back, plus a raise—a fact I could only attribute to a whimsical memorandum from Richard Shilling's penthouse. I pictured Parker holding a gun to Rollins' temple. His voice trembled when I turned him down. I got to perform my resignation spiel after all.

I didn't know if Andrew was involved in the phone call or not, and I didn't care. I had already broken into my savings and mailed the Richard H. Shilling Foundation a check for my third night at Lovelund and the first-class plane fare. A clean break, no threats, no strings, nothing. That was how Wakefield had put it.

I stopped the desperate dating, too, no bars, no Personals. When I thought about Andrew I tried to keep it to small servings, with the occasional binge. Last weekend had been bad. When Melissa's and Randy's wedding invitation arrived in the mail, it had included a personal note scribbled in red: "All thanks to you—our gun-toting chaperone!" Melissa still dotted her *i*'s with smiley faces.

Unemployment proved more work than overtime. If my third interview at the Discovery Channel fell through, I was tempted to call that 1-800 number on TV and start a correspondence course for my private detective license. I already knew the logo for my business card: Cupid with a snub nose.

I imagined FBI agents and Mafia thugs trailing me everywhere, but they always turned out to be mail couriers or hot dog vendors. I was standing in a 7-Eleven checkout line, resting my dry cleaning bag over my shoulder, when I startled at the sight of the cashier, those brawny arms, a neck as thick as my thigh. She was a dead ringer for Wakefield, the scanner gun gripped in her fist like a Magnum. When she called the store manager to her register to void a faulty receipt, I braced for Zelda or Parker to appear. Maybe Haboush was crouching behind the refrigerator doors. I still had her card rolled in a ball in the change dish on my dresser, my only physical evidence, every letter illegible.

The scanner beeped as I skimmed the tabloids. The Shillings' reunion still dominated the headlines. According to the *Enquirer*, Nostradamus had listed it among his top ten signs of the Apocalypse. I couldn't help eyeing the porn rack in the top row. If no one had been around, I would have pulled the stack down and read for anonymous articles on Caribbean crime syndicates. I adjusted my dry cleaning over my other arm and read the *Times* headlines instead.

The fold obscured half the words, so I almost missed it. At the bottom, under the Congressional deadlock article, I glimpsed "Richard Shilling Indicted after FBI Probe." The photo looked like a science teacher's headshot in a high school yearbook. The paper rose to my face as I registered the byline. "A. McGuffin."

The Amazon cashier drummed her nails on the counter. "Let's move it, honey."

After paying, I stumbled outside and walked into a parking meter while reading the article, unable to absorb the information fast enough. After a list of the twelve indictments, most beginning with the phrase "conspiracy to," there was a long quote from Special Agent Rachel Haboush, leader of the investigating team. She credited her success to persistence, hard work and an anonymous informant. Prosecutors predicted a minimum of ten to twelve years for Shilling. His foundation had already named a new chairman.

I studied each syllable on the subway. The prose was clean, economical, with a tinge of lyrical whimsy. I'd never read anything so beautiful in my life. Andrew had risked his life for those few hundred words, proving me and Haboush and every thug in Shilling's organization wrong.

The cellophane on my dry cleaning fluttered like wings as I pinballed up the subway steps. My lock clicked with one twist, and I threw my suit over a kitchen chair and dug for the phone book. After boxing in all fourteen of the "Olmstead, A" listings with my orange highlighter, I started calling.

Most were annoyed hang-ups or answering machines with unfamiliar voices, but a woman answered at the last number.

"Hello?" She sounded cute.

"May I speak with Andrew Olmstead?"

"Just a minute." My heart knotted. This was him. Then I realized he was living with another woman, probably married with two kids and an SUV. I could picture the wedding album, the vows, the kiss, the cake frosting on his cheek.

"Hello?"

My chair knocked against the counter. "Why you miserable son of a bitch."

"Excuse me? Who—?"

"I should have shot you in the head when I had—"

"Who is this?!"

I realized that the voice was wrong. "I'm sorry, is this Andrew Olmstead of *Playboy* magazine?"

The slam deafened my ear.

Plan B didn't go much better. I left a voice mail for the personnel director at the *New York Times* but wasn't betting on a return call. If Andy was still using his pseudonym, they weren't going to give his address out to women on the phone, no matter how desperate or horny I sounded. You never knew who might be a Mafia hit man.

The phone went off in my hand as I was sifting though the Os again. I yelped and stared. I knew it was him. I'd never been so sure of anything in my life. My finger quivered as I pressed the talk button.

"Hello?"

"Hiya, girlfriend."

It wasn't Andy. I sighed something, stalling as I tried to place the woman's voice.

"It's Meg."

I didn't register the name at first—I was thinking college reunion coordinator. Then my muscles constricted. Margaret Parker. "What do you want?"

"You read today's paper?" She sounded cheery, like

an overzealous telemarketer. I hoped she wasn't perched on the neighboring roof, eye pressed to a rifle scope. "Our Andy came through for you, huh?"

She snickered in my ear as I found an innermost wall and backed against it. "What do you want?"

"Relax. I just like to show off my handiwork. Check out NBC. I'm on next."

The receiver died, and I stabbed the dial button to make sure the line hadn't been snipped.

Peter Jennings finished chatting up a pair of spin doctors about the Senate filibuster as the TV blinked on. I was hoping Parker hadn't branched into politics when Richard Shilling materialized over his right shoulder, the dates "1953–2002" cross-hatching his chest.

"Millionaire Richard Shilling was found dead this afternoon in his New York penthouse. Forensic experts believe his wounds were self-inflicted. His suicide follows an FBI announcement this morning of his arraignment on several high-profile charges."

The image cut to Zelda Shilling grimacing behind a bouquet of microphones, her favorite pairs of shades and diamond earrings repelling the camera flashes. "I'm just so sorry for Richard—I'm just so sorry he chose this way. My husband was a proud man. He could never have stood the humiliation of a public trial."

The sound faded as she brushed her cheek. It was a good sound bite, but nothing compared to her boathouse performance. Jennings capped it with a reference to the couple's reconciliation and an assurance that Mrs. Shilling was not implicated in the FBI's investigation.

I punched off the power, trying not to picture Parker stripping Shilling's drugged body, rolling it into his tub, and slicing the wrists. I didn't believe the suicide story for a second. Parker had knocked off her own boss rather than risk his blabbing more to the prosecution.

My dry cleaning curled against the table leg as I collapsed into a kitchen chair. Of course Zelda knew the truth, too. I wondered if Parker had warned her before staging her husband's death. As far as I knew, Zelda helped, the old sleeping pill in the wineglass routine.

I scooped my best interview suit off the floor and noticed an envelope safety-pinned on the jacket. My dry cleaner's address filled the flap, but the front was blank. I shook it gingerly, wondering how flatly Parker could construct a letter bomb. I thought of poison-edged paper cuts and deadly airborne viruses, aware that I was alive only because a Mafia assassin thought I was adorable.

The envelope didn't burst into flames when I tore the seal and wiggled out an airplane ticket. I was booked to arrive in San Juan four o'clock Saturday. Zelda Shilling's voice rattled in my head: *He contacted me. He hid messages in my dry cleaning. The last envelope had a plane ticket in it.*

My hands shook as I thumbed open the Lovelund confirmation slip tucked behind the ticket. The reservation was for "Mr. and Mrs. A. McGuffin."

I already knew what I was going to wear to dinner.

Do You Believe in Love at First Sight?

I peed four times on the plane and didn't collide with Andrew once on the way to the toilet. The couple in my aisle frowned suspiciously, certain I had an infectious bladder disease. When we landed in San Juan, I violated a dozen safety regulations elbowing to the exit hatch, then waited at the bottom of the mobile stairs until the field crew shooed me away. No Andrew.

He didn't materialize at the Charlotte Amalie airport either. I kept eyeing distant strangers, willing them into his shape. Any minute he would appear behind me, my legs swinging into the air.

The ride to Lovelund was dustier than I remembered. I inhaled a cloud of asphalt as we swerved around a pothole crew. I kept waiting for the taxi driver to peel his wig and beard off.

Phoebe's eyes bulged as I wheeled my suitcase over the curb. "What are you doing here?" It was a shocked smile, but still a smile. "Donna checked in yesterday with the new—"

"I'm not with the show anymore." I swept my hand through the air as though wiping a slate clean. Innuendoes, smutty chuckles, braggarts' small talk, Donna could have them all.

Phoebe waited for the rest of the explanation.

"I'm on a date."

Her eyebrow rose as she glanced down and adjusted the angle of her computer. "Need a room?"

"Already got one." I pointed at the screen. "Under McGuffin."

I could sense the bubble in her chest. Suddenly everyone thought I was adorable. She placed the key card into my palm. "Your *husband* checked in an hour ago."

My face warmed. Was I actually blushing?

I tipped the bellhop with the first bill I pulled from my wallet. He looked happy as he deposited my suitcase on the bungalow patio and vanished. The doorknob clicked in my fingers. I pictured Mr. McGuffin sprawled across the bedspread in his paisley briefs, a bottle erect in the ice bucket.

The foyer light glowed over my head, but the bed was empty, the bathroom black.

"Andy?"

I slipped my shoes off, figuring it was both sexy and good for detecting blood puddles. I had spent half of the flight worrying how Parker would track and kill us, her last loose ends tied into a convenient bow. The other half I'd spent in mental foreplay.

The bathroom bulbs blinked on, but I found no bodies in the tub, dead or otherwise. Andrew's suitcase grinned on the bureau. I didn't check for the *Playboy* or the snub nose.

My suitcase bounced on the bed, and I wrestled my deodorant from the toiletry bag and stripped to my underwear. If an assassin was poised in the closet, I was dead. I unrolled my white dress and climbed in. The hem didn't quite cover the morning's razor gash on my knee, but I liked the neckline. A stranger could have mistaken my breasts for breasts.

I nearly broke my ankle on the path steps, unaccustomed to the two-inch heels I'd dug out from the back of my closet. An Aterciopelados song wafted up from the pool. The diving board twanged as I rounded the bushes, a splash resounding like a cymbal crash. I scanned the blonde heads and crimsoned shoulders, ignoring the ample protrusion of breasts and bellies. No Andrew, but I wasn't ready to panic yet. I would swallow a few shots before searching for his body along the bay path.

Uche threw me a double take from behind the bar when I waved. It was Saturday, so Donna would have been shepherding her chickadees through town. I slid into an empty table and pretended to read the laminated beer list, my dress glowing orange in the candlelight. Not my best color.

"Hi. Is this seat taken?" I turned, relieved to see Andrew smiling down at me, two umbrella drinks in his hands. "I'm tired of sitting by myself."

I was too busy staring to grasp the cup. Eyes the color of swirled sand, curls that begged fingers to run through them.

"My name's Andrew."

I made my hands release the menu and folded them

in my lap. "Hello." That was the tone I used on cute strangers. I was relieved to hear it again.

He sat and slid a drink toward me, licking spilled daiquiri from his thumb. His chest flickered in and out of the candle glow. A shirt the same shade of olive hung in my closet.

"Don't worry. It's not poisoned."

"Thanks." The glass almost slipped through my grip. We were sipping virgins again.

His face might have looked dangerous—eyebrows dark slashes in the candlelight—if not for the goofy grin. Rollins would never have passed on those crooked teeth. "I hope I'm not interrupting anything. It just seemed dumb for the only single people on the island not to introduce themselves."

"I must look pretty conspicuous."

"No more than me." The table edge dented his stomach as he elbowed closer. I would have preferred him on my lap. "So where do we go from here?"

My toes balled as I watched a string of candle smoke snake between us. Anticipation is Paradise's sweetest fruit. "I'm willing to negotiate." I twined my fingers around the base of his neck and pulled his mouth into mine as my eyes closed. What was all the Garden compared to this?

That was the most you would ever see on *Who Wants To Be A Blind Date*. Usually it was only a hug, maybe a chaste peck, bachelor and bachelorette posing side by side as the host described their Virgin Islands destination. They always held hands as the credits rolled, staring dumbly into the moon-round lights, a crew of handlers awaiting them offstage.

I pulled Andrew out of his seat, his thumb massaging my palm as we walked. My heart bucked in its ribs as I teetered on stilts. The breeze and waves didn't sound anything like applause.

Andrew pawed his pockets for his room key. He couldn't quite get it in the slot. I considered making a joke but restrained myself. He pulled the curtain behind us, his body quivering when my fingers reached around his stomach. He inhaled as I untucked the long tails of his shirt.

Now even I have to cut to commercials.

I didn't remember nodding off but woke to a darkened room and the curl of his body against mine. The strangeness jolted me, as Andrew's arm flopped off my shoulder, limp as a dead man's. Terror wrenched me around as I groped his neck for a pulse, my face hovering over his until I felt the slow churn of his breathing.

I hugged a mumble from him, and he twisted away when my arms unlocked. A crueler woman would have woken him. I could think of ways.

I got up, knowing the double dose of adrenaline would have me up for hours. Andrew's buttoned shirt lay at the foot of the bed, and I pulled it on. My pajamas had never made it out of the bottom of my suitcase.

Moonlight spilled over me as I clicked the curtains back. Azalea petals gleamed on the patio like shards of sea glass. I was thankful not to find Parker reclined in the chaise with a cigarette.

I considered taking a walk but felt too lazy to dress, the scent of Andrew's sleeping body too enticing to leave. I pulled out two chairs from the table and propped up my feet instead. The half moon illuminated a jumble of brochures on the table, Andrew's wallet resting atop a paperback. I'd survived the whole flight without a novel of my own, a first in my life.

A white envelope protruded as a bookmark. I creased the spine, content to start where Andrew had left off, but the thickness of the envelope intrigued me. My fingers coaxed out an airline pamphlet. A ticket and a Lovelund reservation stub were bent inside. My unease was vague until I saw the return address for a dry cleaner's printed on the back flap.

I reached for the light. "Andy?" He was startled when my weight buoyed the mattress. "Is this your dry cleaner?"

He flailed upright and blinked at the envelope I was holding in front of his face. "Yeah. How'd you find out about that anyway?" His other eye cracked into a slit as he groped into a sitting position. "I thought Zelda was setting up another meeting till I saw the bridal suite on the reservation." He grinned, but the blood was draining out of my face.

"She contacted *you?*"

"Yeah, notes in my dry cleaning. She must have told you that, right?"

My voice slipped into business mode. "Tell me again."

"Zelda started sending me information about her husband's organization a few months ago. The notes always came attached to my dry cleaning. I figured she must have liked my articles and had found a way to track me down. After the first few tidbits, she said she wanted to pass major information to me in person about Shilling, real headlines stuff. Her note said it would destroy him. I took my suit back to the cleaner's with a note inside suggesting that we meet here, figuring Cosway would check if it were a trap. I still trusted him. I knew everything was on track when the suit came back with a plane ticket inside and a Lovelund reservation."

I closed my eyes, remembering Zelda's expression when I'd leveled the gun at Wakefield's nose. She'd said *Andrew* had arranged the meeting. She'd said he had sent *her* the ticket. Someone else had initiated the entire rendezvous, convincing both of them that they were dealing exclusively with the other. Someone else had organized the whole plot.

"How did you get the evidence against Shilling? I mean, for Haboush and the article in the *Times?*"

"The way we had originally planned. Zelda fed me documents." His voice trailed down. He hadn't intended to confess that yet. "Look, I know she's no angel, but it was my best shot. I—"

He was missing the point. "When did you contact Haboush?"

"I didn't. She was waiting for me when I got home."

"But she thought you were going to turn up in some Dumpster."

"I guess she heard differently." He gave a defensive shrug, but he knew something was wrong.

I grabbed his shoulder. "Someone told her."

"Who would do that?"

"The same person who sent you and Zelda to Lovelund in the first place. Someone who was getting all the pieces into position to topple Shilling."

He rose and grabbed the envelope out of my hand. "You're saying Zelda didn't send me the first ticket?"

He pulled out the reservation stub as I shook my head no. I was terrified by what he was going to ask next.

"And you didn't send me these either?"

"I have an envelope just like that in my purse. I assumed it was from you."

Andrew looked around the room as though he'd never seen it before. The fact turned everything alien: someone else had set up our date. There was no hint of grogginess in his voice now. "Cosway was the only one who knew about me. He wouldn't have told; it was too risky."

"He didn't have to. If the FBI found you, so could someone else."

"Parker?"

I shook my head. "She used me to find you. Whoever was behind this knew who you were before you stepped foot on the island."

"But why set up a meeting between Zelda and me only to let Parker interrupt it?"

"Maybe that was part of the plan?" Sweat snaked down my ribs. What if Parker had been working for someone else all along, someone who wanted to dismantle Shilling's organization piece by piece? What if Andrew had only made it out of the restaurant alive because Parker had been ordered to gun down Cosway's cops herself? Someone wanted him on the run, desperate enough to betray his informant. It was the best way to trap and expose Cosway.

I stared into the lamp as I spoke. "Destroying Cosway was step one. Someone found out that he had leaked the *Playboy* story to you, but instead of exposing him to Shilling right away, they bided their time, working you into a vulnerable position so you would have to surrender to Shilling. I think he was the real target all along."

Andrew's voice cracked. "But why not let Zelda slip

me the information as we'd planned? Wouldn't that have been easier?"

I lowered my voice, suddenly aware of the walls' thinness. It hadn't occurred to me once while making love. "Then Cosway would still be running the Islands. They needed you to rat him out first so Shilling would order an attack on his house, killing Cosway and everyone loyal to him. And now with Shilling dead, too, the Islands are up for grabs."

Andrew was in sync with me. "That's why Zelda went back to him. Whoever was running the show from the wings convinced her that it was her best shot at revenge. Leaving Richard hadn't worked. He could have kept sending killer after killer to knock off her bodyguards. Zelda needed a permanent solution, and someone provided it for her."

My finger jabbed toward him. "And there you were, the perfect leak. As long as you were an unknown reporter pilfering information from unknown contacts in his empire, Shilling feared you. Your anonymity was a threat. But they turned you into just another of his lackeys. Once you and Zelda were on the inside together, it was just a matter of her slipping you the right evidence. You didn't need covert messages and secret rendezvous anymore. All of the incriminating evidence was at your fingertips, and Shilling suspected nothing because he thought he had Parker safeguarding both of you. Every move was masterminded, beginning to end."

Andrew whispered, "By whom? Who was Parker working for?"

I realized I was standing with my legs apart, muscles tensed, a fight-or-flight pose. But where could I go? I imagined the hum of cameras behind the vents, the wallpaper bamboo blooming into microphones. I would have bolted outside, but the moon was staring between the curtains, a half-lidded eye, lazy but constant. Even if I'd phoned Haboush, I had nothing to tell her that she didn't already know. Someone had put her into position, too, a ready contact for Andrew to relay his evidence to. She'd made a trade with a demon to get her Devil.

Andrew threw the covers back, inching toward me as though I were perched on a window ledge. "Ashley." He was naked but didn't seem to notice. He held his hand out, and I stared, sensing an impossible drop between us. "Ashley."

I looked half at him, half at the box of wilderness surrounding us. "We're pawns. We control nothing."

"We never did. We just know it now."

I fought down a wave of nausea. "You can live with that?"

He was about to speak, then faltered. "I can live with you." My skin tingled where his hands hovered above my elbow. He was careful not to touch me. "I know you hardly know me. We've spent maybe a dozen hours together—half of them with guns pointed at one of us." He frowned and looked down, whispering. "And I know I haven't given you much reason to trust me. You thought I was just a notch up from Parker and the rest of them. But I don't care who got us into this room. We're together." His eyes met mine. "I'd trade the world for this."

I thought of the old world I had known, a place oceans and lifetimes away. A solitary garden where a thousand fantasies thrived and perished daily. There must be more than that. My guardian angel worked for the Mafia, and God just kept snoring. I wanted no ties. I wanted to be innocent. But I wanted this, too.

I took his hand. It was sweaty and shaking, but I thought it could be enough. When he held me, his bare back tingled with electricity. I closed my eyes and rested my head on his shoulder, grateful for the illusion of blindness. Maybe this was as close to heaven as anyone got.

"Ashley, I would do anything—"

My head struck him in the jaw when I opened my eyes and jerked away. A pair of eyes peered at us between the curtains. I braced for a spray of bullets, our mastermind assassin come to finish us off, but the face appeared so girlish. She backed out of sight as Andrew scrambled for his clothes. Then a knock followed, so tentative we could barely hear it. I rolled the door open as he buttoned his pants.

"Ah, hi, I'm really sorry to bother you." A young woman stood on the patio, her face familiar despite its generic beauty. "We're looking for an Ashley Farrell?"

I poked my head out, but other than the square-jawed hunk slouching behind her, the coast was clear. "Yes?" These were not the killers I'd expected.

"Donna told us we could find you here."

Andrew stuck his head over my shoulder. "Donna?" Then I remembered her face from the last pair of headshots I had forwarded to Rollins. These were this week's winning bachelor and bachelorette.

"Yeah, we were supposed to meet her for dinner, but when we got there, there was just a note from her telling us to find you when we got back."

I was surprised Donna even knew I was on the island. Did she think I was going to cover for her even now? If she hadn't canceled her weekend with Melissa and Randy, I would never have gotten into any of this mess to begin with.

"Well, hon, I'm afraid you've got your story wrong. I'm not a chaperone anymore; I don't even work for—" My throat closed as I clutched Andy's wrist. "*Where did you say you ate?*"

The intensity if not the apparent irrelevance of the question rattled her. "At, ah, ah—"

The hunk chimed in. "You know, that place with the tower?"

"It looks like a big chess piece?"

Andrew's voice dropped to a suspicious rumble. "Bluebeard's Castle."

"Yeah!" She snapped her fingers. "But Donna never showed up like she said and we just went back to the room and all her stuff is gone now."

"Gone?"

"It's like she just vanished or something."

My grip tightened as Andrew and I exchanged another glance. "Let me see the note."

The bachelorette dug into her clutch purse, lipstick and key card rattling as she produced a white envelope, the front covered in black ink:

> *Dear Samantha & Chuck,*
>
> *I'm afraid I can't have dinner with you after all. But don't worry, I'm turning you over to capable hands. You'll find Ashley Farrell in room Thirty-one. She doesn't know it yet, but she's the new producer for* Who Wants To Be A Blind Date. *I told the Board to rubber-stamp*

her promotion this morning. I can't wait to see how she overhauls the show for season three!

Sorry for the inconvenience, but I have other matters to attend to now. I just worked myself into a bit of a promotion, too. Give my regards to Mr. McGuffin; I couldn't have done it without him.

XXXOOO,
Donna

The envelope quivered in my hands as I turned it over and saw Andrew's dry cleaner's logo on the back flap. The bachelorette couldn't figure out why we were staring so wide-eyed.

"She's the new Don."

Andy pulled the envelope from my fingers. He understood now. "Shilling made a lot of enemies when he invaded the Islands, recolonizing them in effect. There were other families running things down here until he made Cosway his puppet." He couldn't disguise the admiration in his voice. "Donna must have worked for years infiltrating Shilling's organization, getting ready for this takeover."

I didn't want to admit it, but I shared his respect. She had pulled it off.

The bachelorette was getting antsy on the patio. "So what's going on?"

I smiled, the new producer staring down at my pubescent-looking stars. Oh, there were going to be changes all right.

"Enjoy your last night in Paradise, kids. We check out in the morning."

Acknowledgments

First thanks to my first reader, private editor, and resident soul mate, Lesley Wheeler. I am grateful to my agent, Ruth Cohen, for plucking my letter from the sea of queries inundating her office and sailing me through revisions. More thanks to my editor, Carrie Feron, for taking me on and prodding the novel into its best and final shape. I am grateful to everyone at HarperCollins who contributed to this work, including Gena Pearson, Judith Myers, and Leesa Belt. I thank all my family and friends who served as the earliest readers and supporters of my writing, most especially John Gavaler, who has seen and helped proofread countless drafts; Judy Gavaler; Joan Gavaler; Margaret Gavaler; Pat Wheeler; Claire Kerr; Annabelle Robertson; Jeanine Stewart; Steve Buyske; Ann Jurecic; and my children Madeleine and Cameron, whose afternoon naps made the composition of much of this novel possible.

My apologies to the residents of the Virgin Islands. I honeymooned on St. John in 1993. No one shot at us, and we did not see a single dead body. No doubt the police force is a model of integrity and professionalism. I cannot recommend staying at Lovelund Bay, however, as the resort is my invention. The view from Bluebeard's Castle is wonderful, but like Ashley, we didn't stay for dinner.